RAVES FOR
MONSTER OF THE WEEK

"Lukens' effervescent storytelling navigates with heart and nuance the complications of what we owe to one another and what we owe to ourselves, and is a heartwarming validation of found families and what makes relationships thrive."

dekick

"A light read with all the r

views

RAVES FOR
THE RULES AND REGULATIONS FOR
MEDIATING MYTHS & MAGIC

2019 American Library Association GLBT Rainbow Book List

Gold Winner, 2017 IBPA Benjamin Franklin Awards | Teen Fiction

Gold Winner, 2017 Foreword INDIES Book of the Year Awards | YA Fiction

Finalist, 2017 Cybils Awards | YA Speculative Fiction

"Creatures, comedy, and coming out: check."

—*Kirkus Reviews*

"A humorous fantasy about a bisexual teenager whose day job plunges him into a world of pixies, unicorns and other fantastical beasts."

—*Foreword Reviews*

"F.T. Lukens brings a joyfully charming innocence into this endearing adventure…"

—Tanita Davis, author of *Finding Wonderland*

"It is literally laugh out loud, clap a hand over your mouth and check to see if anyone noticed your outburst levels of funny."

—D.E. Atwood, author of *If We Shadows*

RAVES FOR
THE BROKEN MOON SERIES

"Lukens writes a satisfying balance of action and romance in a science fiction setting that will feel familiar to fans of the genre… Add this title to young adult sci-fi collections, and expect readers to eagerly anticipate the next book in the series."

—*School Library Journal* on *The Star Host*

"I continued my science fiction kick with a YA novel I have been eyeing for quite some time. *The Star Host* by F.T. Lukens hooked me from the blurb. It still hasn't let me go, and I finished reading it hours ago. I want more… like right, the heck now. I need more Asher and Ren in my life. You need more Asher and Ren in your lives."

—*Prism Book Alliance*

"The mythology of the stardust is absolutely gorgeous; the worldbuilding is fantastic, with so many tiny details building a perfectly clear view of a world that is not our own… The short version is that this book is amazing, and I am hard-pressed to be more coherent than ASKLJFDAH and OMGFLAIL."

—D.E Atwood, author, *If We Shadows* on *The Star Host*

"VERDICT A solid purchase for libraries with a sci-fi reader base or those looking to develop LGBTQ genre fiction collections."

—*School Library Journal* on *Ghosts & Ashes*

"FIVE STARS… *Ghosts & Ashes* continues the adventures of *The Star Host*, Ren, as he comes to grips with his power and searches for his place in the cosmos. This is a rollicking adventure that blends elements from westerns, sci-fi, YA, and romance into a cohesive page-flipping thrill ride."

—*Foreword Reviews*

"Fans of queer sci-fi adventure, this is the series for you. Start at *The Star Host* and plow right on through *Ghosts and Ashes* in one go. Told in Lukens' no-nonsense prose, this story will draw you in and not let go."

—*Teen Vogue*

MONSTER OF THE WEEK

F.T. LUKENS

interlude press • new york

ISBN 13: 978-1-945053-82-5 (trade)
ISBN 13: 978-1-945053-83-2 (ebook)
Published by Duet, an imprint of Interlude Press
www.duetbooks.com
Book Design and Cover Illustration by CB Messer
10 9 8 7 6 5 4 3 2 1

interlude 🧩 press • new york

To Lauren, Joshua, Catherine, Bobby, Andie, Emmarose, Kevin, Michael, Elin, Alexander, Ezra, Elijah, Zelda, Jayla, Remy, Sarah, & Leo

May your lives be full of happiness and unicorns

Now I will believe
That there are unicorns

—The Tempest (3.3.24-25)

Some readers may find some of the scenes in this book difficult to read. We have compiled a list of content warnings, which can be found at www.interludepress.com/content-warnings

CHAPTER 1

Unicorn poop.

It was real. It was a thing, one that, unfortunately, Bridger had intimate knowledge of—size, texture, aroma, number of sparkles—and had handled on more than one occasion in an official capacity, though finding and scooping said poop was not something he'd be able to put on future resumes because: one—poop—and two—unicorns.

No one was supposed to know about the unicorn that lived in the woods next to the shopping complex. Well, no one other than his boss, Pavel Chudinov, an intermediary between the world of myth and the human world, and his boss's roommates, who happened to be pixies.

Well, and him. Yes, him. Bridger Whitt, seventeen-year-old, awkward dumpster-fire and graduating senior. That was not his official job title, but it seemed more apt than *assistant*.

He had the dubious privilege of access to unicorn-poop knowledge because hanging out with cryptids was his after-school job. How he'd obtained the job and held down the job while in his first semester of his senior year of high school was a long story, novel length in fact, and it involved Bridger, his boss, his best friend in the whole world, a cute hero masquerading as the guy-next-door, the aforementioned pixies, an angry unicorn, and the Beast of Bray Road. It also featured a lot of running away from things intent on harming him and copious amounts of what-the-fuckery.

Looking back, he was surprised he'd survived it with limbs and wits intact. And he supposed he should be grateful that his current worst worry was to be walking in the forest looking for mounds of sparkly excrement and not, say, getting mauled by the Ozark Howler. For the record, the Ozark Howler was kind of cute and fluffy if you didn't focus on the glowing red eyes or the massive claws and teeth, or the little fact that it was an omen of death.

Anyway, the pixies, Nia and Bran, were the reason for Bridger's current unicorn-poop gathering excursion. He held a plastic sack of the poop; the distinct smell of cotton candy wafted out every time he jostled it while he combed the woods for more because the pixies needed a heap for their side business of making and selling cosmetics. Bridger didn't ask questions. He'd learned the hard way not to ask questions when it came to certain aspects of the magical life. The answers only led to headaches and thinly veiled disgust at exactly what certain cryptid byproducts were used for. Okay, so he had asked about the unicorn poop. Apparently, it was an essential ingredient in a spectacular anti-aging cream. (It was their best seller.)

Hands wrapped in plastic gloves, Bridger scooped up another handful of the glittery stuff and dropped it in the bag. Sweat beaded his hairline in the late afternoon sun. Spring was finally edging out the remnants of the long Michigan winter. Despite the warm weather and the shopping complex teeming with teenagers nearby, in the woods Bridger was alone. Only a few months ago, he would've hated the silence and the feeling of loneliness which clung like a ghost. But now that he had found another family—a weird, loud, family with members who sparkled and other members who growled—he didn't mind the quiet. After a long week of school and work, he quite enjoyed it.

A crunch in the flora and a tinkle of bells made the hair on the back of Bridger's neck stand on end. He spied the magnificence of the unicorn through the trees. The blinding white of its coat was beautiful as freshly fallen snow under a rising sun; the gleam of its horn was sharp and shimmering as a sparkler on the Fourth of July. It whinnied at him, pawed the ground, and tossed its silky mane, a waterfall of strands that prismed rainbows as it moved. The rest of the forest went still, and the far-off sounds of cars and people at the shopping complex dimmed and disappeared. Magic bled into the air, poured onto the forest floor, and the atmosphere went dense with it as the unicorn moved toward him. Its dark, intelligent eyes were framed by long lashes; its silky ears pricked forward.

"Yeah, I see you." Bridger stripped off the gloves and stowed them in the bag. "Don't waste your whole L'Oreal photo shoot act on me. I'm literally picking up your poop."

It nickered in greeting then trotted over to nose at his backpack. Watchful of the sharp point of its horn, Bridger pushed its snout away. His fingertips lingered on the velvet fur, and his soul found peace in the thrum of magic and joy around him before he slid his bag off his shoulder. He pulled out a heavy lump wrapped in tinfoil.

"Is this what you want?"

The unicorn snorted.

"Well, come on then." Bridger walked deeper into the trees, with the unicorn following him, until he came upon a large rock in a clearing. He squirted hand sanitizer onto his palms and rubbed them together, then he peeled back the wrapper to reveal a large bean and cheese burrito with extra guacamole and absolutely no tomatoes. He pulled a paper plate from his bag, plunked the burrito on it, and set it down in the middle of the meadow. Sitting heavily on the rock, he dropped both the bag of poop and his backpack onto a bed of springy grass. "I wish I had known the effect burritos have on you the first time we met."

It rolled his eyes.

"Oh, don't even! We both know you were a dick back then. I mean, we're friends now, but chasing me, *twice* I might add, with the intent to skewer me puts you firmly in the asshole category."

Bending its neck, it nibbled at the burrito, then nudged Bridger's leg playfully. Bridger scratched between the unicorn's ears.

"My birthday is this weekend," he said, relaxing on the rock. "I'll be eighteen in three days. I think my boyfriend, Leo—you haven't met him—I think he might have something special planned. Which is cool, but also a little nerve wracking."

He and Leo had been dating exclusively for the last six months, since the homecoming game when Bridger kissed him in front of the entire school, and the alumni, and the other school's team and fans, and, well, it was about as big a *hey I like you* gesture a high schooler could pull off, short of an elaborate promposal. And as awesome as it was and as comfortable as Bridger was in the relationship, a few things made his anxiety spike. One was explaining to people that, even though he was in a relationship with Leo, the most ridiculously hot guy in school, he still was also attracted to girls. Another was navigating the whole intimacy issue. As it was, he was still very much *unicorn friendly.*

"I mean, it might make me less maidenly, if you get my drift." Bridger rubbed a hand over his forehead, trying to forestall the tension headache he'd get from worrying too much. "Can we still be friends if I'm like fifty percent less virginly? Are there percentage points when it comes to purity? A sliding scale? Because I mean, I am not a hundred percent right now. Definitely down to, like, eighty. And let's be real, the whole purity thing is basically antiquated oppression based on heteronormative thinking. You know?"

The unicorn didn't respond. Instead it happily munched on the flour tortilla and refried beans.

"Okay, so I didn't know all that until recently. I've been educating myself. Anyway, will you try to skewer me again if something does happen between me and Leo? Because I'd miss our little talks. You're crap at conversation but you're a great listener."

The unicorn lifted its head and eyed Bridger in an exasperated-parent way. Bridger knew the look. Then it went back to the burrito. Okay, maybe it wasn't such a great listener—stupid unicorn.

The sound of a million marching-band cymbals rang from the bottom of his backpack and broke the bubble of magic between them. Bridger sighed and fished around until he grasped his compact mirror. Flicking it open, Bridger pushed his blond hair out of his eyes.

"Hello?"

Nia flitted into view, her gossamer wings flapping madly, pink and purple sparks flying off her tiny shuddering body as she pointed at Bridger.

"Where are you?"

Bridger pursed his lips and turned the mirror toward the unicorn. "Gathering ingredients for your wildly successful cosmetic line."

"Well," she said, her voice a demanding squeak, "you're taking too long. I need you to bring the unicorn donation back to the house immediately."

Bridger's burgeoning headache intensified. He pressed two fingers to his temple. "I'm near the Commons. It'll take me at least thirty minutes by bus to get to the house. Can I bring it tomorrow?"

She huffed and crossed her arms. Agitated sparkles billowed around her. "Absolutely not! We'll send the portal."

Bridger's eyebrows shot to his hairline. "The portal? Wait, is this some type of emergency? Are the toasters ringing? What's going on?"

Bran budged into the frame; his shoulder knocked into his sister's. His blue face took up most of the screen. His cheeks flared like a chipmunk's, and he had frosting smeared all over his chin.

"Hi, Bridger!" Little bits of food flew out of his mouth; the words were slurred by whatever he'd shoved in there before bouncing into the conversation. "Don't argue with Nia. She's about to explode. Just listen for the portal. It should be there... now! See you in a few seconds!"

Bridger heard a shrill *Did you eat the cake?* just as the mirror winked out.

He shook his head. He stood and gave the unicorn one last pat on its neck, while it finished the burrito. Then he headed to where the portal hovered and hummed.

Floating a few inches above the ground, the portal was a glassy, swirling, black oval of magic. It was the fastest way to travel between two locations, and it was immensely helpful when trying to find a sasquatch on the Upper Peninsula or when someone needed rescuing from a horrifying hag. But it was usually reserved for emergencies and came with a few rules that Bridger didn't understand. It couldn't be summoned to a location, but it could be sent, and it was calibrated to specific people, but, in a pinch, anyone could use it if they were with a magical person.

If Bridger really thought about it, which he tried not to, it was *absolutely terrifying*. The portal was semi-sentient and completely beyond the realm of understanding. Entering it was like stepping through a warm waterfall, if the waterfall was a rip in the space-time continuum and sounded as if a drain had unclogged and all the water rushed downward in a giant slurp.

"Hi," Bridger said, standing in front of the inky blackness. "Hope you're well. Been a while since we've seen each other."

The portal quivered.

"I'm good, thanks. Take me to Pavel's office please."

Bridger had learned that politeness went a long way in the myth world. Asking nicely was one of the most important tools in his assistant-to-an-intermediary tool box.

He stretched out his hand, and the darkness latched onto his fingers and leeched up his arm. Bridger took a breath and stepped through. Noise filled his head, and heat tingled over his body, and he was squeezed on all sides, and then—Bridger popped out into the second floor of Pavel's home and office and right into a surprise birthday party.

"Surprise!"

"Holy crap!"

Bridger jumped backward at the yells and the blare of party horns, clutched his heart, and dropped the bag of unicorn poop. He would have stumbled right back into the portal if not for the quick reflexes of the Beast of Bray Road, otherwise known as Elena. Elena's sharp fingernails dug into the fabric of his T-shirt, and it tore as she jerked him toward the gathering of people and cryptids.

"The personification of grace as always, Bridger," she said, her pouty lips curving into a smirk. Her luxurious, long brown hair swung behind her, and her amber eyes glinted, clearly amused.

Bridger's traitorous heart double-thumped, and he blushed as she manhandled him to the group and a table laden with cake and food. Elena was super-model gorgeous and a werewolf. She was also kind of a bitch and she'd be the first to admit to it. They tolerated each other for Pavel's sake—she being Pavel's best friend and Bridger being the only assistant of his who had stuck around for longer than a few months.

Pavel held his arms out wide. His orange-and-pink striped shirt clashed horribly with his plaid pants, but Bridger had become so used to Pavel's awful fashion sense that it didn't register beyond the fact that his clothes appeared new and crisp and not his usual thrift-store chic or his rumpled, rolled-out-of-bed-and-rocked-up-to-the-party style. He'd even brushed his black hair, and it fell artfully across his forehead.

"Happy birthday, Bridger!"

Bridger's eyes went wide as he took in the stack of pizza boxes, the hideously large cake with a section of frosting missing, obviously Bran's doing, and a pile of presents. "What is happening?"

"A surprise birthday party is happening!" Astrid yelled, tackle-hugging him out of Elena's grip. "Look, the pixies made cake. Elena decorated."

There were no decorations beyond a few limp streamers and one sad-looking balloon. Elena bared her teeth at him, obviously daring him to say anything. He bit back his comment. Wisdom hadn't always been his strong suit, but he'd grown wiser in the past few months.

"And I got you this." Astrid, his best friend since middle school, jammed a tiara on his head. "Happy eighteenth, you giant nerd!" She released him and held him at arm's length. "Why do you smell like cotton candy?"

Bridger adjusted the plastic tiara so the points weren't digging into his scalp. "That is a question for the pixies. Also, please tell me you don't use their cosmetic line."

Nia flew by in a stream of pink and purple twinkles. "Say nothing!" she screeched as she dive-bombed the plastic sack. She carried it to a bubbling cauldron at the corner of the room before darting back as quickly as Bridger could blink.

"Wow," he said, looking at the beaming faces of Pavel, Nia, Bran, and Astrid and the begrudgingly happy one of Elena. "Just wow. Thank you."

Bridger wasn't one for emotional displays and definitely not in front of other people. The last time he'd cried was when a hag showed him his darkest fears and memories. But in this moment, tears clogged his throat. He'd never had a surprise birthday party. He'd always thought they only happened in family sitcoms. They were setups for things to go horribly wrong for a few laughs, and then the episode would end all tied up in a bow with a heartwarming message about love. They were for people with large groups of friends and a loveable dysfunctional family: things Bridger didn't have and never expected to have.

His last birthday was spent at home alone because his mother had to work, and Astrid was sick, and he had sat on the couch watching Jeopardy and eating out of the ice cream carton, wondering if this was how lonely he'd always be.

Now, he had people who cared about him and he brimmed with unexpected emotion at the thought that this group of oddballs deemed him special enough for a plastic tiara and multi-colored party hats. He knuckled a tear out of his eye.

"Did we do something wrong?" Pavel asked, mouth pulled down in concern. "Is it the pizza? Astrid said you'd like pineapple and ham, but I questioned how anyone could like that combination."

"No," Bridger said, wiping at his cheeks. "No, I do love pineapple and ham. This is awesome. Everything is awesome. Thank you."

Bran flew from his spot on the table near the cake. His blue face was scrunched; icing was smeared over his face and into his hair. "You're crying."

"I am not."

"Oh, my God, are you overwhelmed with happiness?" Astrid asked, smiling. "Are you pulling a Yuri-Katsuki-after-the-Grand-Prix-Final?"

Thankful for Astrid's levity breaking the intensity of the moment, Bridger snorted out a laugh. "Shut up." He punched her on the shoulder. "You're the worst. And it's more of a Ron-Swanson-at-the-Grand-Canyon moment."

"I have no idea what you two are saying," Pavel said, hands on his hips.

"Business as usual then," Bridger said, grinning.

"Yes, but since you're smiling, I'm going to assume you're okay and direct you to the questionable pizza."

Bridger took a plate from the stack. "Pizza it is. Then cake. And are those actually presents for me? You guys are awesome."

Hefting several slices of pizza onto his plate, Bridger plopped into one of the high-backed chairs in Pavel's study. The leather creaked beneath him as he threw his legs over the arm and balanced his plate on his knees. Through the archway into the kitchen, Bridger spied a line of toasters, some old and with rusted parts, others bright and shiny with strange settings. They were cryptid emergency alarms and they were silent for the time being.

Astrid snorted pop out of her nose when Bran cracked a joke. Bridger blew out the candles on his cake on the first try and kept his wish close to his chest. He opened presents: a tub of magic acne cream from the pixies, a gift card from Elena, and new sunglasses with rainbow frames from Astrid. The last one was a blue gift bag with tissue paper hastily shoved on top.

"Happy birthday," Pavel handed it to Bridger; a genuine smile tugged at the corners of his mouth. "I know it's not a car or the right to vote, but I hope you like it."

"I'm sure it will be—" The bag squirmed. Bridger gasped. "Oh, my God, did you get me something alive?"

Pavel's smile turned mischievous. "Open it."

Astrid craned her neck over Bridger's shoulder. She nudged him. "Is it a dragon? Please, let it be a dragon!"

"I don't know how many times I have to tell you, Astrid. Dragons aren't native to Michigan."

"Neither is the Bladenboro Beast, but I have a specific memory of kicking its ass."

Pavel pinched the bridge of his nose. "Those were special circumstances."

"Hey," Bridger said, "can your bickering wait until after I open this?" He frowned as he poked at the bag and the alive-thing inside made a low squeak. With a shaking hand, he reached past the multi-colored tissue paper. Whatever it was, it was furry and soft and tiny, and he lifted it out and—holy shit! Pavel got him a kitten.

A kitten!

Bridger gently extricated the kitten from the gift bag and held it to his chest. It was pure black and so small, with massive ears, and it looked up at him with big yellow eyes and meowed the tiniest meow.

"Oh, my God. Your mom is going to freak out. She is going to hate it and Pavel. But it is the cutest!" Astrid clapped her hands together; her eyes rivaled the size of an anime character's.

"I'm not allowed to have pets." Bridger winced as the words slipped out and the kitten dug its adorable claws into the skin of his chest. "They're too expensive. And I'm leaving for college in a few months to live in a dorm. And it's not that I'm ungrateful, because a kitten, but—" It meowed again and purred and butted its head into his chest. "Never mind, I love it. I will cherish it and name it George and cuddle it the rest of my life."

"Don't worry." Pavel shook his head; his smile now seemed amused. "It's not a kitten. And she already has a name."

Bridger and Astrid shared a glance. "Uh, not a kitten? It is totally a kitten, Pavel. Have you forgotten what regular animals look like after all this time dealing with the weird ones?"

Pavel shook his head and bopped the kitten on the nose with his fingertip. "It may look like a kitten, but it's a familiar. It's magic."

"Your boss gave you a magic pet," Astrid breathed, softly running a finger down the kitten's back. "You are the luckiest person alive."

Pavel huffed. "Her name is Midnight Marvel, and she's not a pet, but she is now your companion. She won't need to be fed, though she will need a dish of water on the windowsill and a designated bed in your room, so she has a safe place. Otherwise, she's there to comfort and protect you as needed."

"Midnight Marvel," Bridger said, holding the kitten up in his hands. She batted at his chin. "May I call you Marv?"

She blinked her eyes slowly then licked his nose with her sandpaper tongue.

Bridger took that as an affirmative. "Hello, Marv. I'm Bridger."

Squirming out of his grip, Marv climbed up Bridger's chest to sit on his shoulder with her tail curved around his neck. Her little claws dug into his skin and she hissed at the others for good measure. Bridger scratched her head.

"Whoa. Maybe not a dragon, but close enough," Astrid said, taking a step back.

Pavel was unfazed. "Oh, good. She likes you already."

"What would have happened if she didn't like me?" Pavel's expression shuttered, and Bridger stopped him. "You know what? It's my birthday. How about we leave that little scenario a mystery."

The party ended when it was time for Bridger to clock out. It was Thursday, and he still had homework to finish.

He bounded down the stairs, Marv perched on his shoulder, and stopped at Mindy's huge, gothic wooden desk. Mindy, Pavel's receptionist and office manager, was almost as bad at fashion as Pavel, and sported a blue-and-purple-plaid business suit with a neon-pink scarf. Hair perfectly coifed into a beehive, she eyed him over the rim of her cat-eye glasses.

"Hey, Mindy. There's pizza and cake upstairs from my birthday party that I'm sure you were invited to but decided to avoid."

Mindy smirked. With a flourish, she smacked his timesheet on the tiny space on her desk not taken up by bobbleheads.

"Write your times."

"Yes, ma'am."

Despite meeting a bunch of different folklore characters over the past few months, Mindy remained the most interesting to Bridger. She knew about everything that went on in the house but had no desire to partake in any of it. She followed instructions and took care of the paperwork but wasn't fazed an iota at the weirdness that permeated the general vicinity of Pavel.

"Happy birthday," she said, her tone flat. She nudged a gift bag that sat on the edge of her desk.

"A gift? For me? Mindy, you've gone soft."

"Take it or leave it. I don't care."

Bridger smiled and fished around in the bag. He pulled out a unicorn bobblehead. He barked out a laugh, which roused Marv from her sleepy drape on his shoulder.

"It's perfect." Bridger bopped the unicorn's head, and it bobbled uncontrollably. "Thank you."

Mindy shrugged and snatched the timesheet. She turned away and dropped the paper in her tray, but Bridger caught the hint of a smile.

"Ready to go?" Pavel asked, coming down the stairs. He twirled his car keys on one long finger.

Despite Bridger's polite refusals, Pavel insisted on driving him home.

"Yep," he said, stomach churning in anticipation. He scratched Marv between the ears. "Let's go."

It wasn't that Bridger wanted to take the bus and then walk, but Pavel's car was less than safe. It backfired upon starting. It rattled when they idled and squealed when Pavel took a turn and was best described as a tin can strapped to a motor and held together by duct tape, glue, and sheer force of will. Bridger couldn't figure out what make and model it was. Even the color was some version of taupe and so awful that Bridger could only liken it to vomit. Bridger hated riding in it with every fiber of his being.

But Pavel had seemed so pleased with how the birthday party had gone and the fun the group had had that when he offered to drive Bridger home, even with Astrid as a viable option, Bridger couldn't turn him down. Pavel may be weird, and they may have had an inauspicious beginning to their mentor and mentee relationship, but they'd grown close, and Bridger suspected that, despite his occasional grumbling, Pavel cherished their found family as much as Bridger did—possibly more so. Pavel was over a hundred years old, and his relatives were all gone. Their group was all he had in the way of family.

They stopped at a four-way intersection near the high school, and Bridger did his best impression of a slug, sliding down in the seat and peering over the lip of the window hoping the area was clear of students and teachers. He was lucky. The parking lot was empty save for Mr. Peterson's car which was normal— his relationship with Ms. Harrison wasn't as hush-hush as they pretended and often one of their cars was left in the parking lot as they went home together—and a large white van. The van had Georgia plates and no windows in the back, and two people ambled about looking into the classroom windows.

It was odd, even creepy, but not the weirdest thing Bridger had seen that day. He had a magic kitten sleeping in his backpack and had fed a burrito to a unicorn.

"Thanks for the party, Pavel," Bridger said as they pulled onto his street. He lived in a picturesque neighborhood with neatly gridded roads and sidewalks in the heart of Midden. "It was awesome. You didn't have to do that for me. I really appreciate it."

Pavel had the grace not to point out that Bridger had almost cried from *feelings* and instead merely shrugged. "You're welcome. I understand that eighteen is a milestone. You're an adult now." The corner of Pavel's mouth raised as if he found that fact hilarious.

Bridger found it petrifying. "I'm an adult in age only. In everything else…" Bridger held out his hands "…I'm pretty much bullshitting my way through."

Pavel stopped the car in front of Bridger's house.

"I'll let you in on a secret," Pavel said, gripping Bridger's shoulder. "None of us really know what we're doing. Seriously," Pavel continued when Bridger made a face, "becoming an adult doesn't come with a handbook. It isn't just about knowing how to balance a bank account or knowing how to change a flat tire, though I do suggest you learn how to do both before you leave for college. Growing up is about gaining experiences so when you encounter a situation a second time, you know what to do. It's about having good judgment because you've made mistakes in the past and you learned from them."

"No one has really explained it that way before."

"No one else you know is over a hundred years old."

"Technically, untrue, but I'll let it slide." Bridger picked up his backpack. "Thanks."

"Have a good weekend. I'll see you Monday."

Bridger slid out of the car and slammed the door, praying it didn't fall off in the street. He waved as Pavel pulled away and he jumped onto the sidewalk then crossed to his yard. He still lived in the same house he grew up in, a small two-bedroom on the corner, with a front lawn about as big as a postage stamp, though with enough grassy area that Bridger had to mow on the weekends. His front door faced the street, and across the asphalt was his boyfriend's house.

"Bridger? Is that you?" his mom called to him from the living room as he entered.

"Yeah, it's me," he yelled back, kicking off his shoes. He never understood why she asked. If it wasn't him, then they would be destined for an episode of *Forensic Files*.

"How was work?"

Bridger placed his backpack on the stairs leading up to his room and unzipped the top. Marv was curled up asleep on the top of his biology textbook. He petted her head, and she blinked lazily at him. He pressed a finger to his lips, and she yawned, then went back to her nap.

Satisfied she wouldn't make any noise, he padded into the other room and dropped on the couch next to his mom, who was watching TV. She wore a T-shirt and pajama bottoms, and her blond hair, streaked with gray, was pulled up in a ponytail. She was curled up next to the arm of the couch with her feet tucked under a throw blanket as old as he was.

"Good. They threw me a surprise birthday party."

She muted the show, and her eyebrows went up. "Really? That's nice. I heard Pavel bring you home. I really wish you wouldn't ride in that death trap of his."

"Easier than taking the bus," Bridger said with a shrug. "And he offered. I didn't want to be rude, especially since he fed me a lot of pizza and cake."

She rested her chin on her knees. "I'm glad you had a good time. I don't really like that you have a job, but it seems you landed a good one, especially with how generous your boss is."

The job had been a point of contention between them. Bridger had needed money to go out of state for school when he was hellbent on moving to Florida in a misguided attempt to be himself. But after he'd realized he didn't need to move to do that, he'd decided to stay in Michigan and go to State. He hadn't quit the job. He enjoyed it, and it paid well, and, despite the overall hazards of magic and myth, it was probably the best job a teenager was going to find. His mom tolerated it, as long as his grades didn't slip and he maintained a social life.

Besides, the extra money would help him avoid loans and maybe even help him afford a car. Then he wouldn't have to rely on rides from Pavel or Astrid or Leo.

"You like my boss, huh? I mean, I didn't know he was your type. He's a little eccentric for you."

His mom rolled her eyes and poked his thigh with her foot. "You're awful, kid. I am not into your boss."

"Wait, why not? He's smart, successful, and not on the bad-looking side." Pavel might even be called unconventionally handsome, if someone was so inclined to remark on his appearance—which

Bridger was not. "Granted, he's not, like, Chris Evans hot, but he's not bad."

"Hemsworth, honey. If you're going to pick a Chris for me, always go with Hemsworth."

"Really?" Bridger narrowed his eyes and made a frame with his fingers, centering his mom in his imaginary photo. "I always pictured you with Evans. Pine as a close second. Then Pratt and then Hemsworth."

She raised a finger. "That's completely wrong. It's like you don't know me at all. I think we need to reevaluate our relationship. We've grown apart. We need an intervention of tacos and Marvel movies."

Bridger dropped his hands and slouched into the couch cushions. "You know, everyone wonders where I get my mouth and penchant for theatrics. They never believe me when I say it's my mom."

She laughed.

"Okay, spill, who'd you pick for me? Which Chris?"

She waved her hand. "No Chris for you. They're all too old. Besides, you've got Leo, and he's pretty darn perfect for my little boy."

Bridger's cheeks heated. "Yeah, he is."

"But if that doesn't work out, I wouldn't mind Tom Holland as a son-in-law." Bridger gasped, scandalized. His mom threw a pillow at him. "Was he at your party?"

"Tom Holland? Um. No. Sorry to say."

She rolled her eyes. "No, smartass. Leo. Was Leo able to make it to your party?"

"No, he had baseball practice. We're going to do something together this weekend."

"Uh huh," she said, eyeing Bridger knowingly. "Do we need to have the safe sex talk?"

"Um, no. No thanks. That talk was mortifying when I was thirteen, and I can only imagine it would be at least ten times worse now."

She pursed her lips. "Well, I've had to update it since the whole…" She waved her hands. "…liking boys thing. I've done research. I've added new content. See, when two young men like each other very much they may want to experiment—"

"Oh no. No no no no no!" Bridger held up a hand and closed his eyes. "Nope. No thank you. I appreciate the effort. Ten out of ten on that front but still, sadly, would not recommend. I'm good. Leo's good. We're good. Thank you."

"Now who's dramatic."

"I just…" He opened his eyes. "I'm good."

"I gathered." She reached over and ruffled his hair. "By the way, your dad called."

He groaned. "Ugh."

"Oh, stop. He just wanted to check in and see how you were doing. He's going to call back on your birthday."

His pending headache threatened a resurgence as he slumped into the cushions. "Yay for the twice-a-year awkward conversation. Just the gift I wanted."

"Bridger," she said, slightly admonishing, "be nice. He's your dad. He just… isn't very good at it."

"Understatement." Bridger turned back to the TV and frowned when the program flashed a picture of Nosferatu and then panned over a cemetery. He waved at the screen. "*What* are you watching?"

"Oh, it's a silly monster show. I always get the myth questions wrong on Jeopardy. I thought I'd bone up."

Bridger grabbed the remote from the coffee table and unmuted the channel.

The reporter, a woman with blond hair and piercing blue eyes, looked straight into the camera. "Whether the creature sighted here was W.W. Pool, a vampire chased out of England in the 1800s, or whether it was an ancient evil unearthed during the construction and subsequent collapse of the Chesapeake and Ohio Railroad's Church Hill Tunnel, we'll never know."

Bridger did know. He'd studied the entry on W.W. Pool in the myth guidebook. Pavel had met him a few years ago while on vacation. Pool was a nice guy, by all accounts, save the bloodsucking.

"But with strong evidence that *something* supernatural is haunting this cemetery and preying on the students of the nearby university, this makes the Richmond Vampire our Monster of the Week." She smiled, all perfect white teeth, but it didn't reach her eyes, and there were absolutely no lines around her mouth. Her tone lacked inflection, and, beneath her television veneer, she seemed almost bored. "Check our schedule to see when we might be stopping in your town. We'll be taking a break for the summer but join us in the fall for our special month-long series about a recent hotbed of supernatural activity—Midden, Michigan. I'm Summer Lore and thanks for watching."

Bridger dropped the remote. "What the fuck?"

CHAPTER 2

"IT'S YOUR DAY OFF," PAVEL said when he answered the mirror. His hair was in more disarray than usual, and he yawned, rubbing a hand over his stubble. "And it's very early."

"Did I wake you up?" Bridger asked, slipping on his shoes. "Some of us have to be up at the crack of dawn because we have school that starts unscientifically early."

"Unscientifically?"

"Studies show teenagers need more sleep than adults, and yet we start school two hours earlier than the standard work day. And then we have extracurriculars and homework and statistically spend more hours working than a nine-to-fiver."

Pavel thumped from his bedroom into the kitchen; the background changed as he moved. "A travesty."

"Tell me about it," Bridger mumbled. He teased his fingers through his hair, trying to tame his bedhead that rivaled Pavel's.

"Is that why you're calling? The unfairness of sleep and expectations?"

"No. Um. No." Bridger fidgeted, tugging at the cuffs of his hoodie. "Have you ever heard of the show *Monster of the Week*?"

Pavel's sleepiness evaporated in a blink. He narrowed his eyes, and the teasing vibe disappeared. "Yes."

"Do you know they're coming to Midden?"

"Midden."

"Yes."

"Huh."

"Yeah. Here. This town. *Our* town. Filming. For their next season."

"Huh."

"Yeah, apparently all the shenanigans from last fall made their radar."

"Huh."

Bridger frowned. "Did I break you? Is that all you can say?"

Pavel's look could only be described as withering and unamused. "You didn't break me."

"Well, what do you mean?" Bridger tapped his foot. "Huh, as in 'that's interesting, Bridger, thank you for the information'? Or huh as in 'panic now'?"

Pavel studied Bridger and was silent for so long Bridger thought the mirror might have dropped the call. Could the mirror drop a call? Was that something that could happen? If he went through a tunnel would he lose magical call service?

"Um, you still there?"

Pavel twitched. "Yes. I'm here. I was just— " Red seeped across the bridge of his nose in an uncharacteristic blush. Bridger's internal warning claxons blared. "Thank you for alerting me. I will look into it."

Bridger shrugged on his backpack. He was going to be late if Pavel didn't at least pretend to worry soon. "And?"

"That's all."

"That's all? Seriously? That's all? It's a television show. A show about cryptids. Literally, about exposing cryptids and researching sightings. And all you've got is you'll look into it?"

Pavel waved away Bridger's growing apprehension. "It's fine. Intermediaries deal with researchers all the time. There are so many of these shows that we have a protocol."

"Does that protocol involve maybe showing a little more concern than you are right now?"

Pavel gave him a flat look. "You're panicking."

"I'm not panicking!"

"Bridger," Pavel pinched the bridge of his nose, "I haven't had enough tea yet to decipher your ramblings. But please don't worry about this. Go to school. I will handle it."

Blowing out a breath, Bridger checked to make sure he had his keys. "Fine. Fine. I'm going to school."

"Have a good weekend and a good birthday. I'll talk to you soon."

"Okay. But call me if you need me. Seriously. I'll be—"

The compact winked out.

"Here."

Bridger sagged. He ran a hand over his face. Maybe he was overreacting, panicking in a way that only he could, overthinking, perseverating on the worst-case scenarios. Pavel could handle this. There was protocol. He knew what he was doing.

Most of the time.

Kind of. A little bit.

Bridger rubbed his temple.

Crap.

BRIDGER SLAMMED HIS LOCKER DOOR shut and leaned against it as Astrid hefted her backpack over her shoulder. Behind her, a big banner congratulating the graduating seniors fluttered against the wall. Next to it hung a poster reminding everyone to purchase their prom tickets. And just across the way was yet another poster about cap and gown fittings. The senior hallway was a perfect storm of constant reminders that he was on the brink of adulthood and his world was changing. Bridger did his best to swallow his insecurities. He wasn't successful.

Astrid clutched her calculus book closer to her chest. "Are you certain the show meant here? As in this Midden?"

Tapping his phone, Bridger pulled up the *Monster of the Week* website where it proclaimed in big, flashing, block letters that its next stop was indeed their home town. He held it out to Astrid. "Yes."

She squinted. "Oh, shit."

"That's what I said! I called Pavel this morning, but he doesn't seem to think it's a big deal. Apparently, intermediaries deal with these pseudo info shows all the time."

"Well, there's your answer. Nothing to worry about."

Bridger shook his head. "Nothing to worry about? Do you not remember last semester?" He dropped his voice. "You beat up an evil old lady with your hockey stick. I was almost drowned by lake mermaids."

"Yeah, but everything was out of whack because of your boyfriend's hero cycle. It's fine now." She brushed her blue hair off her shoulder. "What's not fine is that I have a calculus quiz this afternoon and I'm not doing well in that class. And I've still not been asked to prom."

"Astrid," Bridger rested his head on his locker, "you're not taking this as seriously as I'd hoped. What if this Summer Lore lady comes here and finds the unicorn? Or runs off the bakery ghost? Or reveals Grandma Alice? She could disrupt everything."

Astrid rolled her eyes. "Bridge, I think you should trust Pavel on this one. He's the expert." She patted his shoulder. "And I think you need to focus a little more on graduating and less on myth emergencies that aren't going to happen."

"Trust Pavel? Trust the man who didn't think getting stabbed by a manticore tail was a big deal? That guy? He is the master of understatement. He's the literal embodiment of the 'this is fine' meme. You know, the one with the dog sitting in a room engulfed in flames, with the speech bubble 'this is fine' over his head when it is very much not fine?"

"I know my memes, Bridger," she said, clearly insulted.

"Right, but what I'm saying is that Pavel isn't always a good barometer for when it's time to freak out."

"Like you are now?"

"I'm not freaking out."

"You're on the precipice, my dude."

"I just…" Bridger gritted his teeth. "This is the best my life has been in a long time, Astrid. I don't want someone barging in and ruining this for me." He pushed his hand through his hair. "I'm happy."

She paused, and her expression softened to the one she'd given Marv. "You're a mess. But okay. Fine. Does your mom work tonight?"

"Yeah."

"Your house. After school. We're going to Netflix this bitch and her show. If what they report is close to what is in the cryptid guidebook, then we'll freak out."

"Um." Bridger bit his lip. "I'm supposed to meet Leo when the team gets back from their away game tonight."

"Oh, my God. It was so much easier when your social life only consisted of me." She whined, but Bridger wasn't fooled. She was secretly pleased he had found a few other friends and that he wasn't as lonely as he used to be. She hid that secret under an exterior of snark, but he had noticed the fond looks she shot his way when he talked with Leo or Zeke or Luke—like he was all grown up and saving China.

"No, it's good. He can meet us at the house. If you don't mind."

"Why would I mind? I'm all for you being cute with your boyfriend." She raised an eyebrow, and her piercings glinted in the light. "As long as everything stays unicorn friendly."

Bridger groaned. "I never should have told you about that!"

She cackled. "Sorry. It was too good to pass up. Anyway, after school we'll meet at your house and see if we really need to panic. And you're paying for the takeout."

Bridger puffed his cheeks and slumped. "Thank you, Astrid. You really are the Chidi to my Eleanor."

At the reference, Astrid winked, pleased. She adored *The Good Place*. "You can repay me by helping me study at lunch."

"Are you sure you want my help? I stopped at trig. Math is, uh, not my strong suit."

"Right. I'll ask Janet." She slapped his arm, and he staggered. "Don't worry, Bridger. I'm sure there is nothing to worry about."

Bridger fervently hoped she was right. Things had been relatively quiet for six months; he only needed to hold out a little longer.

BRIDGER'S MORNING WENT SMOOTHLY. HE managed to dodge questions from his teachers about what he wanted to major in because he had no idea. He stayed out of the conversations that buzzed around him about who was planning a major promposal and who was going backpacking through Europe after graduation and who had barely passed their language requirement. When the bell rang, Bridger rocketed out of his seat and wove through the hallway to the lunchroom, ready for a reprieve from his own circling thoughts. When he squeezed into the line, Bridger's stomach growled, and he was ready for a hot and greasy high school lunch.

"Hey, Bridge." A girl behind him leaned over the shoulder of her friend. He vaguely recognized her as the underclassman sister of one of the seniors, certainly not someone who knew him well enough that she should feel comfortable using his nickname.

"Um, yes?"

"We're totally voting for you and Leo as best couple for the senior superlatives. You two are so cute together. Seriously, you are relationship goals."

"Oh," he said, face flushing. "Thanks."

"We ship you guys so hard," her friend said. "Like OTP of my heart." She made a heart with her hands and bumped them against her chest.

Bridger was afraid that he understood what they said. He blamed Astrid—and a few fanfics he'd read over the years. Hey, when canon content failed to deliver, you could always count on the fan authors, and he was certain these two had at least one AO3 account between them.

He cleared his throat. "Wow. That's great."

"You know that Colton came out because of you, right? Like, we all knew he was gay, but he didn't say it until after you and Leo went to homecoming together."

Bridger had no idea who the hell Colton was and he really wanted out of this conversation. It had veered from kind of flattering, run straight through awkward, then barreled into cringeworthy in the span of a few moments.

"I'm sorry; I don't know who he is. But good for him. I hope his friends and family are as supportive as mine are."

"He's a freshman, like us. And we totally told him it was okay to be gay. We don't mind at all."

Bridger furrowed his brow. "That's nice, but you know he doesn't need your permission, right? Even if you weren't comfortable, it would still be okay for him to be gay if that's how he identifies. I mean, it's great you want to be understanding, but maybe phrase it a little better."

They were obviously as surprised as Bridger was at his little lecture because they both looked away. Their faces reddened, and one of them looked about to cry.

"Uh," he said, grimacing, looking around for help as the line inched forward. He needed to flee, quickly and gracefully. "Thanks for your vote? I'll tell Leo."

And they went from dejected underclassmen to effervescent fangirls in one second flat. He swore their eyes sparkled.

"Really?" one of them squeaked, hands over her mouth. "That's so awesome."

"Yeah. What are your names?"

And that's how he left the lunch line with a hastily scribbled note from Laura and Courtney in his pocket. At his usual table,

Bridger put down his tray, then plopped into the seat between Astrid and Zeke.

"You know," Astrid said, popping a cherry tomato in her mouth from her salad. "It's not a good look getting freshman girls' numbers when you're a senior and especially not when you're dating the hottest guy in school."

"Oh, my God." Bridger dropped his face in his hands. "Is that what it looked like?"

"Yes," Astrid said at the same time Zeke said, "Sorry, bro."

"Ugh. No. It was… they were trying to tell me things about their friend who is gay and voting for Leo for a superlative and, really, I don't remember, because I was a little mortified."

Zeke nudged Bridger with his elbow. "Hard to imagine we were that small once."

"Zeke," Bridger said, "I've known you my whole life, and you were never that small."

Zeke shook his head, then turned to the conversation on his right. Bridger turned to Astrid on his left and found her attention already back on the field hockey girls.

He sighed and picked at his fries. Leo didn't have the same lunch period, so Bridger didn't get to see him much during the day. Because baseball practice ran so long after school, Leo woke up early on weekdays and completed his homework before the first bell, which made him unavailable for morning locker talk. Then with Bridger struggling through AP Bio and AP Comparative Government in the morning and Leo in Visual Arts and Psychology on the other side of the school, they didn't even see each other in the hall. Their third blocks were near each other, but Leo took

Journalism and Bridger had snuck into a mythology elective, *because hey, why not.*

For fourth block, Bridger had somehow conned his way onto the yearbook staff, while Leo, with Astrid, labored through Calculus. Bridger had no desire at all to take pictures or write copy, so he used the yearbook class as a study hall whenever he wasn't coerced into typing captions and senior quotes. With the yearbook mostly finished, the staff goofed off a lot, which was a reprieve after months spent confirming with students that they really wanted an excerpt from *Rick & Morty* to be their high school legacy.

With their schedules at odds and Bridger's job and Leo's baseball practices and games, they had very few opportunities to socialize. At lunch, Bridger was left with a conglomeration of Astrid's friends on one side and Leo's on the other. Zeke was always welcoming, especially after they'd resolved the tension between them because of Bridger's early missteps with Leo. And Astrid was Astrid, easily able to navigate between the sports teams and the geeks.

"And then she said that she wanted to interview all of the students at the beach the day that Bridger drowned."

Bridger snapped his head up and zeroed in on Lacey. He'd known her since they were small, but she hadn't paid any attention to him since elementary school, not until he was suddenly thrust back into her orbit through Leo. She was beautiful and apt to be Prom Queen and she volunteered at the local nursing home on weekends because she had loved her nana fiercely.

"What was that?"

Lacey tossed her hair over her shoulder and took a delicate bite of her chicken nugget. "She wants to interview everyone."

"Who does?"

She rolled her eyes. "God, Bridger. Have you been listening at all?"

No. But he knew better than to say that.

"The monster reporter," another kid said. "She's interviewing Luke because of that animal who bit him."

Bridger froze, but his heart skipped a beat. The Beast of Bladenboro had taken a chunk out of Zeke's best friend, Luke, the day before the homecoming football game.

"And she wants to interview everyone about the day the big dog showed up at the sports field."

"I thought we all agreed it was a very lost elk?" Bridger said, throat tight. "Because that's what it sounded like. An elk's bugle."

It sounded like an Ozark Howler because that was what it was, but he couldn't say that because it was a *very big secret.*

"Yeah, but Chelsea said Derek said that Gretchen totally saw a bear with glowing eyes."

Oh, shit.

Leaning over the table, Astrid elbowed her way into the conversation. "Yeah, but doesn't Gretchen wear really thick glasses? Could she really see that far?"

"She was wearing her contacts that day. And not cool, Astrid. You know she's sensitive about her eyesight."

Astrid exchanged a glance with Bridger and backed down. "Yeah, sorry."

Lacey pointed her fork at Bridger. "I'm sure she'll want to talk to you because you were the one who drowned at the lake and all."

Oh, shit.

"Hey, I didn't drown. It was an almost-drowned situation."

She huffed. "Fine. But you got scratched by the same thing I did. There was something in the water."

"Lake weed?" he offered.

She scoffed and didn't deign to respond.

Zeke turned in his seat. "Hey, weren't you at the football field too, Bridge? That was the day Leo drove you home." He raised his eyebrows.

Oh, shit.

"Leo told you about that?"

"Dude, I heard about nothing but that for a while. You held hands."

Bridger blushed to his hairline. "Anyway," he said, "moving on. Did you guys really order a ton of graduation announcements? Because I have to be honest, they were kind of expensive, even for the few I ordered."

"So, if Luke is giving an interview," another girl continued, "does that mean he is going to be on TV? That's so cool."

Bridger wilted.

Lacey's eyes flashed with envy and Bridger could practically see the word "stardom" in neon lights blinking over her head.

"I think I may have underestimated our problem," Astrid said around a mouthful of Bridger's fries.

He cast her a withering glare. "Manticore tail."

BRIDGER SAT IN THE YEARBOOK room for the last class of the day. The editor, a junior named Taylor who looked like they were constantly going to burst a blood vessel, held a meeting with the lead staff while Bridger hid at the very last desk in the corner of the room. He had his mythology and folklore book open and perused the list of suggested topics provided for the final paper. There were a few interesting ones, and he was certain he wouldn't be bereft of sources for any of them. The question would be how he could cite those sources. He'd have to ask Pavel. Or he could have the pixies write the paper. Now that would be fun and interesting. Though he'd probably fail when whole paragraphs were devoted to the wonders of freshly churned butter and double chocolate-chunk cookies and frosted blueberry Pop-Tarts.

An announcement crackled over the speaker releasing the baseball and softball teams early for their away games. A few minutes later, Bridger received a text.

You got freshman girls' phone numbers at lunch?

Bridger hid a smile behind his phone, and his stomach did the whole butterfly thing. He could practically hear the incredulousness-mixed-with-teasing tone of Leo's voice. From experience, Bridger knew his eyebrows would be raised and his mouth tipped into a half-smile.

Bridger held his phone beneath the desk and texted back.

Untruth. But who told you?

Several interested parties. Should I be worried?

They're not #'s but notes for you from your eager fanbase. Should I be worried?

The response was immediate.

I'm in a committed relationship. Also, not my type.

Bridger snorted. A few of the yearbook staff shot him dirty looks, but he ignored them. His cheeks heated.

See you tonight after your game. Just come over. Good luck.

He tacked on the kiss emoji.

Bridger waited for the reply. And waited. He wondered if he'd get one at all. Leo must be on the bus by now, traveling to the game, focusing and entering his sports headspace. Finally, Bridger's phone lit up.

C U 2nite. I'll bring ur bday present. Followed by the eggplant emoji. *Hope ur DTF.*

A high and truly undignified noise escaped before Bridger clapped a hand over his mouth. His classmates whipped their heads around, and their dirty looks became glares. He ducked his head in embarrassment as his pulse thundered.

What the hell?

That wasn't like Leo. At all.

Oh, God. Bridger choked on air. He should've talked with his mom the night before instead of blowing her off. He needed to talk to Astrid. He needed to shower. He needed to figure out how to buy a box of condoms. He needed to ditch his monster-show-viewing party with his best friend and spend the time between the end of school and Leo's arrival trying not to vibrate out of his skin. He needed—

His phone screen lit up.

I am so sorry! Cal stole my phone and texted you that. That was not me.

Bridger's brain came to a screeching halt. He blinked. He breathed. He rebooted. The abrupt bucket of ice on his adrenal glands left him shaky, but at least he hadn't amped himself up to the point of no return before he found out his sex life was someone else's joke. *Not cool, Cal. Seriously not cool.*

Your birthday present is not an eggplant. Or my dick.

Bridger dropped his head to his desk with a thud. He tried not to laugh or cry hysterically; both were options. His fingers hovered over his phone. *How to respond to that?* He wasn't going to lie and say he wasn't disappointed that his night wouldn't involve… an eggplant. But he wasn't going to type that. Not with baseball bros hovering around Leo's phone.

Ugh. How to respond?

Each passing second that he didn't say something made it all the more awkward. *Think, Bridger. Think.* Type something witty you could both laugh about later. A joke about how he hated eggplant. No. Too much room for insinuation or error there. A remark about how Leo probably forgot his birthday and that's all he could think of as a present. Ugh. No. That's even worse. *Is it an aubergine?* Maybe? But that's still dick joke territory.

Quick. Something. Type something.

LOL.

Bridger stared at his hands, betrayed. LOL? Laugh out loud? Seriously? That's all he could come up with? Fuck.

Bridger? You okay?

This wasn't happening. This couldn't be happening. Why was this happening?

I'm good. Tell Cal he sucks, btw. I hope he strikes out.

I'll pass that along. Also, I think we should talk.

Bridger dropped his phone. It clattered on the linoleum, and the only reason the screen didn't shatter was that it clipped his shoe before striking the ground.

I think we should talk?

That was bad. All the knowledge he'd gleaned from romantic comedies told him that "we should talk" was the death sentence of relationships.

He scrambled for his phone; the legs of his chair scraped across the floor while he tried not to fall off. Scooping it up, he shot an apologetic look to Taylor. They scowled back, their expression pinched, murder in their eyes. Taylor scared him. They were one typo away from losing their shit on their staff, and that would include Bridger despite the very little work he did. He wouldn't put it past them to erase him from the whole book if they thought they'd get away with it. Bridger went back to pretending to study. Gulping, head down, he tapped out the most chill reply he could think of.

Sure. Tonight.
Cool. Gotta go. Need to focus on the game.
Ok. Kick ass.

There wasn't a response. No cute follow up emoji or acronym. He didn't expect one. Leo did have to focus on the game. Baseball was his ticket to college, and Bridger wasn't going to interfere with it no matter what. Leo's future career was more important than Bridger's relationship drama. But he did keep his phone in his hand the rest of the class period, just in case.

CHAPTER 3

BRIDGER DIDN'T TELL ASTRID ABOUT his horrible faux pas during the text conversation or the dreaded "we should talk" that came toward the end. He didn't want to ruin their fact-finding mission with his boyfriend crisis. Living in his head and being epically self-centered had almost cost him her friendship last semester, and he didn't want to make that mistake again.

He wasn't going to lie though. He was jittery. But if Bridger was good at anything, it was compartmentalizing. The Leo conversation was a concern for Future Bridger. Present Bridger had other problems—mainly a TV show.

"According to Wikipedia, *Monster of the Week* has been on the air for ten seasons. How did we not know about this before?"

Bridger shrugged. "Uh… cryptids literally weren't on my radar until last semester. Also, new episodes air on a pretty obscure network. It's not even cable. It's like cable's third cousin."

"Huh? And you're worried because?"

Bridger leveled Astrid with a look. "Have you met me?"

Sighing, Astrid scrolled through the information on her phone. "Yeah. Fair point. Anyway, it looks like there was a break of a few years between the sixth and seventh. Wonder what happened."

"Maybe it was cancelled and brought back? That seems to be a trend these days."

Astrid shook her head. "I don't know. I don't see anything about a cancellation. Oh, well, the important thing is that it is still airing, and Midden is going to host the season premiere for season eleven."

"Great. Just what we need: a ratings grab." He picked up the remote. "The first few seasons are streaming on Netflix." Bridger scrolled until he found an episode featuring something he knew about. "Aha. A hominid monster: a hoax by local teenagers, a misidentified bear, or a cousin to my good friend sasquatch? The real answer: all of the above. Okay, *Monster of the Week*, show us what you got." Bridger put his feet up on the coffee table. He balanced a carton of beef and broccoli in his lap and held an eggroll in one hand. With the other, he hit play.

Astrid jammed her chopstick into a piece of sweet and sour chicken and lifted it to her mouth. She'd never mastered the art of eating with chopsticks and preferred to hunt and spear her food, which was fine, but she always refused a fork.

"We'll know if you're wrong," Astrid said to the TV.

Bridger forced a grin. "Please be wrong. I really need you to be very wrong."

The guidebook was open beside Bridger on the couch. Leather bound and ancient, the book was handwritten on parchment, sewn together, and full of information about varying cryptids. By no means a full compendium—that sat on a very sturdy shelf in Pavel's library—the small version Bridger carried was meant as a field guide, vital information for assistants out in the wild cavorting with real live folklore. Notes from previous intermediaries and assistants jotted along the edges added and corrected information; Pavel's cramped script was distinctive.

Marv had curled up on the pages, purring like a machine, absently flicking her tail. Her big yellow eyes followed Bridger's hand each time he lifted a piece of beef to his mouth. He offered her a tiny piece, and she abandoned the guidebook for Bridger's side and licked his fingers with her rough tongue.

The opening credits of the show were cheesy, as expected, full of spooky music and fog-machine effects and altered pictures.

"Fake!" Bridger yelled when they showed a grainy picture of Bigfoot as part of the title sequence. "Looks nothing like the big guy. At all."

"I'm so envious you met a sasquatch."

"It was awesome," Bridger said around a piece of broccoli. "But terrifying and freezing. And I cried that day, so, kind of a win?"

"God, you're a mess. I worry for your college experience."

"You and me both, friend. But at least I'll have you."

"And Leo," she said, spooning rice into her mouth.

The knife in Bridger's gut twisted as he smiled. "Yep."

The episode opened on a picturesque shot of a small town; the camera panned over a welcome sign declaring the town as Fouke, Arkansas. Then it focused on the host, Summer Lore, standing in the middle of the street and staring into the distance with a pensive look on her face. She turned to the camera and walked toward it down the centerline of the main street; the wind blew her blond hair behind her. She wore a skirt suit with heeled boots, not suitable attire for tromping after cryptids.

"This is Fouke, Arkansas," she said, her tone professional but tinged with excitement, her movements animated as she gestured at the scene behind her. "A sleepy town with a population of less than a thousand. A safe community, built on faith, family, and friends. A haven in an otherwise bustling world. The residents, mostly born and bred, didn't have anything to fear in this quiet part of the state. That is, until the night of May second, 1971, when two residents were brutally attacked by an ape-like creature. Described as having long hair, three toes, and a horrible smell, it had no business being in Arkansas much less trying to break into a family's home. Today's Monster of the Week is the Fouke Monster. Hi, I'm Summer Lore, and over the next hour, we'll investigate the numerous sightings of this terrifying creature and separate the facts from the fiction. Is the Fouke Monster real? Or a product of the town's imagination? Join us as we investigate."

The show launched into a dramatic narrative and reenactment of the cryptid trying to break into a house and then cut to interviews with various residents.

"This is really cheesy," Astrid said.

"This is the first season. Production values are going to be lower. But look how hard she is selling it. Like she believes the people she's interviewing."

"So?"

"So this is way different from the tenth-season episode I watched with my mom." He pointed at the screen. "This Summer Lore is an investigative journalist tasked with finding the truth. The Summer Lore from season ten is a mannequin brought to life for an hour to woodenly recite tidbits from the Internet."

"But what about the information? Is it correct? Is there a monster wandering around the creeks of Fouke, Arkansas?"

Bridger grabbed the book and knocked into Marv with his hip, earning a kitten glare. He flipped through until he found the appropriate entry. "Well, they're not wrong. A cryptid does indeed live near there." He angled the page to allow Astrid to see the hand-drawn depiction. "Also known as the Beast of Boggy Creek, it's a combination of Bigfoot and Swamp Thing. It's not as tall as they're making out on the show and it doesn't eat people. It's a vegetarian. Oh, and look." He pointed to a scribble in the margin made by another intermediary. "It has a family."

"I'm sensing we'll have to watch another episode. This one seems too straightforward for our purposes." She popped open the tab on her can of pop. "I can't believe this is how we're spending our Friday night."

Bridger bit his eggroll. "I can. We're too awesome for all the weekend parties."

"You keep telling yourself that."

"I will. It helps me sleep at night."

"At least you have a boyfriend." She sighed. "I don't even have a prom date. No one has asked me." She fiddled with the end of her sleeve. "I don't think anyone is going to."

Prom. Bridger hadn't totally forgotten about it, but it wasn't on the forefront of his radar. It was at the end of the month followed quickly by graduation.

"You still have time." A sentiment meant for him as well.

"Yeah," she said. "Maybe I'll ask Carrie from the field hockey team, and we can go together as friends. And we can double with you and Leo, and be the two cutest couples at the dance."

"That would be adorable. I say go for it." He didn't mention that he hadn't asked Leo to prom yet or that maybe he'd blown it and would be staying home alone that night because he didn't know how to respond to a dick joke. *Ugh.* He was a teenage boy; he should be able to handle an aubergine. "Okay, how do you feel about ghost lights?"

By episode five, Marv had disappeared to whatever it was she did when she wasn't visible. Bridger had long finished his dinner and opted to sprawl on the couch with a bowl of popcorn within reach. Astrid held her chin in her hand with her elbow propped on the arm of the sofa.

Overall, the show was a mixed bag. The information on ghost lights was way off but the description of the Pope Lick Goatman was too close for comfort according to the guidebook. After that episode, Astrid and Bridger called Pavel via mirror to ensure that Kentucky was out of their jurisdiction because no way in hell could they sleep at night knowing otherwise. Pavel chuckled and assured them that there were no interactions with the Goatman in their future, but also never to walk on train trestles, especially if compelled by a song.

In the episode they were now watching, Summer tromped through a wooded area on the lookout for a Witch of the Woods in Missouri. There was information about witches in general in the guidebook, but nothing about one who lived in Missouri and definitely not one who mimicked the Blair Witch. Bridger lost focus sometime after the intro to the episode and, concerned that he hadn't heard from Leo yet, checked his phone. The game had to be over. Had they won? Lost? Was Leo feeling as weird as Bridger over the dick conversation?

Throughout the baseball season, Bridger had attended most of Leo's home games, but away games were trickier, especially if they had far to travel. Also, Bridger did his very best not to be a distraction. Baseball was important. Baseball was Leo's ticket to college. Bridger would hate to interfere, no matter how much he enjoyed watching his boyfriend play.

Bridger glanced at the TV just as a figure in a gray tattered outfit appeared from behind a tree and screamed in Summer's face.

"Holy crap!" Bridger jerked backward, fell and thumped on the floor, wedged between couch cushions and the coffee table.

Astrid jumped and clapped her hands over her mouth to muffle her own curse. Her pop hit the edge of the table and erupted, sending a zero-calorie volcanic spray over the living room.

"What the hell is that?" Astrid yelled.

Breathing hard, Bridger propped himself up on his elbows. "I don't know!" On the screen, the figure flashed again, a blurred face with dark sockets for eyes, and emitted a wail that curled Bridger's toes and etched into his bones. "Is that the wood witch?"

"I don't know!"

A cackle was followed by a shriek, then hard breaths and snapping twigs and crunching leaves. Bridger climbed back onto the sofa and perched on the edge with his gaze fixed on the screen and his heart beating as if he was sprinting.

Summer ran, followed by a screeching figure in gray. The camera shook and fell, landing on its side. Leaves stuck to the lens obscured most of the picture, but still visible was a horizontal shot of Summer's boots. The sound bled in and out of panicked shouts and horrible screaming. The feed cut out.

Bridger's phone rang. He launched it across the room with a throw that would've impressed his gym teacher. It smacked the wall and left a dent before clattering to the hardwood floor.

Astrid shook. She grabbed the remote and jabbed the pause button. Face pale, she turned to Bridger. "What the hell was that?"

"I don't know!" He wiped a hand over his sweaty brow, then pressed his hand to his chest. His heart raced beneath his palm. "Oh, my God. It's living the football game all over again." He took an unsteady breath. "Why was that so scary?"

"Because it was! It was a jump-scare in the middle of a stupid forest romp. Oh, my God."

Bridger nodded. "And we definitely know what it's like to be chased by a supernatural creature." He shook out his clenched fists. "I can't believe I'm freaking out. It must be a sympathetic response."

Astrid cast him a withering glare. "Seriously? You can't handle the mildest horror movie without me holding your hand. And that…" She flailed toward the TV. "…scared *me*."

Bridger lifted his chin. "That was before-the-job Bridger. Or don't you remember how I confronted a hag."

"That I fended off with my hockey stick."

"My hero," Bridger said, with a roll of his eyes. Astrid poked him in retaliation. "Was that the end?"

"No, there's like ten minutes left."

Bridger ran a hand through his hair. "What even?"

"It's the season six finale. It has to be fake. No way."

"Yeah," Bridger nodded. "Fake," he agreed, not at all convinced. He cleared his throat. "I hope I didn't break my phone—"

The front door opened, and Astrid and Bridger startled so badly the last of the popcorn went flying. Bridger let out a yell, and Astrid jumped into his lap. Marv appeared out of nowhere, back arched and hissing, balanced on the back of the sofa, her body fuzzed out.

Leo walked in, eyebrows raised. "Did I interrupt something?"

Bridger slumped into the cushions. Astrid laughed sheepishly and as gracefully as possible, which wasn't graceful at all, extricated herself from Bridger's lap. She straightened her shirt and picked up the wayward bowl. Sensing Leo wasn't a threat, Marv ceased her impression of a Halloween decoration and disappeared up the stairs to Bridger's room.

"I mean, first girls' phone numbers and then I walk in on you two in a compromising position." His lips quirked in a teasing smile, and Bridger melted at the sight. Leo. It was only Leo. Not a hag or a witch. No, wait. It was *Leo*. "We need to talk" Leo. Pushing Astrid's leg, Bridger stood.

"Hey," he said. Popcorn kernels and fortune cookie crumbs tumbled from the creases in his shirt. Attractive. "We were just watching a TV show. A scary one."

Leo scrunched his nose. "Really? Bridger, you know how you do with horror movies."

"Ha!" Astrid said, scooping up the popcorn from the couch.

Bridger shot her a quick glare. "So how was the game?" He turned back to Leo, whose hair was damp and unstyled, missing the usual swoop and spikes. The silver chain around his neck glinted. He wore jeans and a T-shirt, and when Bridger hugged him, he smelled like body wash. Leo's arms wound tight around Bridger's shoulders, and Bridger tried not to melt into the comfort of the embrace with Astrid standing right there, though she'd seen probably more PDA than she'd wanted from the two of them over the months. Still, Bridger couldn't help but sag into Leo's arms, rest his forehead on Leo's shoulder, and twine his fingers into the beltloops on Leo's jeans. Their relationship might be over in the space of a conversation tonight anyway, so Bridger was going to be greedy when he could.

"We won. I hit a home run and turned a double play."

"Hero."

Leo chuckled; his breath skirted the shell of Bridger's ear. "Sometimes," he admitted.

Reluctantly, Bridger pulled away. "Want some cold Chinese food?"

"Yeah. Sounds great."

Leo ate while Bridger vacuumed the popcorn and Astrid wiped up the droplets of pop. When Bridger finished, he plopped next to Leo and squirmed into his side. "Hey," he said.

Leo set the carton on the table, then rubbed the back of his neck sheepishly. "Hey."

Somehow, the ease of their earlier interaction dissipated despite their physical closeness. The conversation to come hung over them like a dark cloud and sucked the air from the room. Bridger straightened from his affectionate sprawl, and Leo didn't stop him.

Sensing the tension, Astrid's gaze darted to each of the two boys. She yawned. It was a fake; Bridger could tell, but he appreciated the effort. "Look at the time on this wild Friday night," she said. "I should head home."

"Really?" Leo gave her a grin. "It's only nine-thirty."

"Yeah, but, I have… things tomorrow." She slapped Bridger on the back. "Happy birthday, Bridge. Have fun tomorrow with your mom."

"Thanks. I will."

"Text me later." She waved at the TV. "We'll have to talk about that."

Bridger sighed. "Yeah. I will."

She grabbed her things and ruffled Leo's hair as she walked out. "Bye, Romeo."

"Later, Mercutio."

The front door opened, then closed, leaving Bridger and Leo alone.

"It amuses me that you have Shakespearean pet names for each other," Bridger said, waving his hand toward the door. "Though I don't know if Romeo and Mercutio are really appropriate. Doesn't Mercutio die?"

Leo shrugged. "They're BFFs."

"For the first act. And then Mercutio curses both houses as he dies in Romeo's arms. And does that make me Juliet in this scenario?"

Leo shook his head then poked Bridger's cheek. "Are you going to be on this tangent for a while or do you want your birthday present?"

Bridger froze, then cleared his throat. "Sure. As long as it's not an eggplant."

"No, it's not." Leo reached into the pocket of his jeans and pulled out a necklace. He looped the chain over Bridger's neck. Bridger lifted the medallion in his palm. It was an oval, like the one Leo wore, but instead of Saint Christopher, it showed a woman.

"Who is it?"

"Saint Dymphna. The patron saint of stress and anxiety."

Bridger let out a breathless laugh. "Seriously?"

"Yep. It's to help you. During all the changes that are coming."

Bridger's mouth went dry. Changes. Of course. "It's perfect." He ran his thumb over the ridged picture. "I love it." Bridger slipped it under the collar of his shirt. It sat on his breastbone; the metal felt warm on his skin.

Leo smiled softly. "Awesome."

"So," Bridger said, voice shaky. He rubbed his hands up and down his thighs, the worn fabric of his jeans felt soft on his palms. "We should talk?"

Leo drooped and smacked his forehead. "That was an awful thing to send in a text, wasn't it?"

"A little."

"Yeah, sorry about that. It's nothing bad. I mean, it shouldn't be. I don't know." Leo raised his head. "I hope you haven't been worrying this whole time."

"Me?" Bridger asked, pointing to his chest where his heart threatened to break. "Worry? It's like you don't know me at all."

Leo chuckled. He tapped the medallion beneath Bridger's shirt, then took his hand and laced their fingers. "I know you too well."

His skin was warm against Bridger's. His large brown eyes were soft, and he looked at Bridger as if he was the most special thing in the world. Bridger's middle fluttered. He couldn't help it. He was smitten beyond coherence, and he never wanted to lose the feeling he had right then: as if he could take on the world if only Leo would smile at him, affectionately and a little crooked, for the rest of his life.

"Okay, maybe I worried a little." Bridger's throat tightened. "But I didn't help things with the LOL."

"Actually, I knew what you meant. That was Bridger for 'I don't know how to respond.' You panicked."

"Ugh," Bridger said, collapsing back on the cushions. "You do know me too well."

"It's like I'm your boyfriend or something."

"You're still my boyfriend?"

A shadow flickered over Leo's expression, and Bridger held his breath. "Yeah. But I just, um, we should talk."

"So you've said."

Leo bit his lip. "I really like you," he blurted, then grimaced. He ran a hand through his dark hair. It was starting to dry after his shower and it fluffed up in adorably weird places. "I mean, I really like you, Bridger."

Don't tempt fate. Don't tempt fate. Don't tempt fate. "But?" Ugh. Why did he ask?

"But I'm not ready for sex."

Bridger blinked. "Wait, what?"

"I know that there is this perception that teenage boys should be ready and willing all the time, but I'm... not. When Matt texted you that, it really embarrassed me. I didn't want you to think that I was ready for things that involve eggplants."

"Eggplants as in the literal sense or the figurative?"

"Figurative." He made a face. "Why do I have to explain figurative?"

"I lead a weird life, Leo. I need to make sure."

Leo laughed. "I really like how funny you are."

"Thanks."

"And I really like you." His palm smoothed the wrinkles in Bridger's shirt. "I want things to be natural and easy between us and not because we feel pressured into it."

That's all? This was the "we have to talk" talk? A sex talk? Bridger's relief was palpable.

Bridger swallowed. "Okay. That's good to know. I respect that. Have you felt pressured by me? About eggplant stuff?"

Leo winced. "Not really? It's been in my head to talk to you about it, and with your birthday and prom coming up, I didn't want there to be any miscommunication. I hear the other guys talking about hotel rooms after prom and expectations they have. They all know your mom works nights and they think that… we take advantage of that." Leo cleared his throat. "You're not going to break up with me, are you?"

"What?" Bridger's voice did not screech. It merely cracked. "No. No. No way. Oh, my God. Are you kidding? You're stuck with me. Sorry, those are the rules. No substitutions or trade-ins allowed."

Leo knocked his shoulder into Bridger's, then melted into Bridger's side and threw his arm over Bridger's shoulders. "Good."

"I'm glad we're talking about this. Because it has been on my mind. And I don't want you to do anything you're not comfortable with and if I do something wrong, please tell me. I'll stop."

Leo's smile was blinding, like sun on lake water. "Thank you. I don't know why I was nervous to talk to you. I knew you would understand."

"I do. And for the record," Bridger said, "I really like you too." Leo beamed.

"Also, for the record, I was freaking out since school. I thought *you* were breaking up with *me*."

"Why?" Leo made a face. "Why would I want to do that?"

"Really? You're asking. Do you need reasons? First, I'm kind of a geek, if you didn't notice. I'm also kind of anxious trash." He ticked them off on his fingers. "I am awkward in every situation. Like, there's literally no situation that I can get through gracefully. I have no idea what I want to do with my life. I have little-to-no athletic ability unless it's running from things and—"

Leo cut him off with a kiss. Bridger's brain screeched to a halt; words died in his mouth. His lips tingled even after Leo pulled away.

"Oh, hey, that worked. I'm filing that away for later."

"You… I can't…."

Leo's eyes crinkled in clear amusement. "Wow. Do you need a system reboot?"

Narrowing his eyes, Bridger shook his head. "Oh, it's on now."

Intent on tickling him into an apology, Bridger jumped on Leo, but Leo was an athlete and stronger, and Bridger's offense quickly turned into defense and peals of laughter. Wrestling on the cushions, Bridger's anxiety ebbed with the heat of Leo's body next to his and Leo's laughter ringing in his ears and gave way to happiness and gratitude for someone as understanding and perfect as Leo.

Leo pinned Bridger. Hands on Bridger's shoulders, stretched along the length of Bridger's body, he grinned like a Cheshire cat.

The position wasn't lost on either of them, and Bridger raised an eyebrow. "We can still make out, right?" Bridger angled his elbow to nudge Leo's side.

Leo smiled brightly. "I thought you'd never ask."

Bridger surged up as Leo bent. A few months ago, they would've knocked heads or teeth, but this was familiar and comfortable. They kissed. Leo's mouth was hot, and his breath smelled like fried rice, and he kissed Bridger with the focus of an athlete trying to win. Kissing Leo was thrilling and soothing at the same time, and, while Bridger didn't have much kiss experience, he could say that Leo's were by far his favorite, soft and sweet and intent. Leo rolled so he was wedged between Bridger and the back of the couch, and Bridger cupped Leo's cheeks. His stubble felt scratchy under Bridger's hands, and, yeah, he'd gone from thinking Leo was going to break up with him to having a really good talk about peer pressure and consent, and Bridger was on cloud nine. Judging by the way Leo's hands grasped Bridger's shirt, he was up there as well.

Bridger's phone rang. For the second time that night, Bridger fell off the couch.

"Why is your phone all the way over there?" Leo asked, amused, propped up on one arm. "And why is it so loud?"

"I threw it in a fit of terror. The volume must have screwed up when it hit the wall or the floor."

Bridger crossed the room and scooped it up. It was probably his mom. No one else would call him at this time of night, except Astrid and Leo.

He answered it. "Hey. Yes, I've eaten. Yes, I'm home. No, I'm not out partying and no, I'm not going to stay up too late."

The voice on the other end cleared their throat. "That's great, Bud. Good to hear my son is keeping to the straight and narrow. Even on a Friday night."

"Dad?" Well, this night was one full of surprises.

"Hey, Bridger. Yeah, it's Dad."

Bridger plugged his other ear with his finger and walked into the kitchen. "What…"

"Happy birthday, kiddo. How's eighteen treating you?"

"It's tomorrow."

"Yeah, I know. That's why I'm calling. I'm actually in Grand Rapids settling your grandma's estate and wanted to drop by and see you tomorrow."

Bridger paced, blindsided. "Really?"

"Yeah. It's been a while."

No shit. Try about five years since Bridger had last seen his dad. And five years before that when he left—a decade of distance between them.

"It has." Bridger clenched his jaw. His brow furrowed, and he rubbed his finger between his eyes to smooth out the stress wrinkles forming there. "Um, tomorrow? I usually do something with mom and—"

"That's okay. I'll ask her if I can tag along. She won't mind. She knows I'm close to town."

"Oh," Bridger swallowed the lump in his throat. "Okay then."

"Great. I'll see you tomorrow, kiddo. Anything in particular you want for your birthday?"

No. He'd already gotten a magic cat, an anxiety-reducing necklace, and a tiara. What else could he want?

"Not really. I'm good."

"Cash it is then." He laughed, his voice rich and warm.

The sound lanced through Bridger's body. A confusing ache of loss overwhelmed him, and he rubbed tears out of his eyes.

"See you tomorrow, Bud. And for the record, I do hope you're out partying right now."

"No, no parties for me. I'm spending a night in with—" He cut himself off. Boyfriend was on the tip of his tongue, but he bit it back. "With my best friend."

Lie.

Bridger had spent most of the fall lying—to everyone and himself—and while he didn't feel great about it, it didn't distress him. Not like this. This one hurt. It hurt a lot.

"All right. Maybe tomorrow night."

If Bridger knew anything about his dad, he might guess he'd wink now, or maybe shoot finger guns, or pat Bridger on the back. There'd be some action, but Bridger couldn't envision it, and that strange sense of sadness cut through him again.

"Night, kiddo."

"Yeah, goodnight."

Bridger hung up. Dazed, he wandered into the living room to see Leo's concerned expression. He dropped to the couch, then slumped into Leo's embrace. He buried his head in Leo's chest and groaned. Leo tightened his arms.

"Want to talk about it?"

"No. Not at all."

"Okay." Bridger lifted his head into Leo's fingers, which were running through his hair. "We'll watch TV. What had you and Astrid completely freaked out when I walked in?"

Bridger closed his eyes and mumbled into Leo's shirt. "That monster show I told you about." With his face buried in Leo's collarbone, he didn't see when Leo unpaused the show. But he heard Summer Lore's shaky voice as she wrapped up the episode, and he felt the shaking when Leo laughed.

"Why is Grandma Alice on your TV?"

"What?" Swirling thoughts and emotions about his dad forgotten, Bridger turned his head. "What are you talking about?"

Leo jerked his chin toward the screen. "Grandma Alice. Right there. Wait, is she the Monster of the Week?"

Bridger sat up so fast he made himself dizzy.

The camera had captured blurry footage of the *thing* that had jumped from behind the tree. Hands raised like claws, mouth open in a scream, eyes wide and feral, white hair blown back from a wrinkled face full of fury, the picture was a dead ringer for Grandma Alice—local uncanny apothecary and supplier of weird ingredients and trinkets to intermediary Pavel Chudinov.

"Oh, *shit.*"

CHAPTER 4

BRIDGER TUGGED AT THE COLLAR of his shirt. He'd chosen a button-up for his birthday dinner, though it was only tacos at his and his mom's favorite Mexican restaurant. He didn't know why he was wearing it, except that his dad, a man Bridger hadn't seen in five years, would be there. And why Bridger felt the need to impress him, God only knew.

The texts between him and Astrid and Leo had flown fast and furious all day. The whole Grandma Alice situation was a hot topic as were his birthday and his dad and the fact that he and Leo fell asleep, tangled up on the couch together and sharing a pillow, to be found when his mom came home from work that morning. They were also shirtless, and the chains of their necklaces had twisted together in the night, which was fine. What was not great was trying to get unstuck with his mom watching and laughing until she cried.

Luckily, Leo hadn't been grounded for staying out all night, since his parents knew he was only across the street.

"Nervous?" his mom asked, coming up behind him and fixing the collar he'd pulled askew.

Bridger would never readily pass up an opportunity to be a smart-ass. On any other occasion, Bridger would've flown into a rant about being "cool as a cucumber" or would have scoffed at her assertion and talked in depth about how he was the pinnacle of calm and collected. This wasn't any other occasion.

"Yeah, actually."

Lips pursed, his mom paused. "You know what? We're calling it off. It's your birthday, you shouldn't look like you've seen a ghost on your birthday."

Oh, the irony. It burned.

"No, it's okay. Just… could we invite Leo? Or Astrid? As a buffer?"

She rubbed her temples. "Honey, your dad, well, he had a traditional upbringing. He wouldn't… I don't know if he could play nice with either of them. He might say something to offend them. Unintentional of course, but…"

"Okay. So my gay boyfriend and my pierced and dyed best friend would upset his cultural sensitivities. Got it. Great. Happy birthday to me."

"We're cancelling."

"We're not cancelling. It's okay, Mom. It's one day. One day in a decade. I'll be fine."

She slung her purse over her shoulder, then placed both of her hands on his shoulders. "I love you. I love you. I love you."

"I love you too."

"Good." She hesitated. "Are you going to tell him?"

Bridger knew what she was referring to, but he pretended he didn't. He pretended it wasn't a big deal to everyone else. He'd come to terms with himself months ago and finally felt comfortable in his skin for the first time in a long time. He hated that anyone could ruin that for him.

"Tell him what?"

"Bridge."

"No, okay. I'm not going to say anything about being bisexual or being in a relationship with the cutest guy in school. It's a can of worms he doesn't need to know about. Happy?"

"No." She cupped his face in her hands. "My baby is eighteen, which means I'm old. And he's so special and so great, and everyone who knows him sees it, which makes me happy. I hate that you feel you have to hide any part of yourself."

"It's fine," he said with his cheeks smooshed together. "Can we go eat tacos now?"

Standing on her toes, she planted a kiss on his forehead. "Okay, now we can."

Bridger bounced his knee through the entire ride. He chewed his fingernails. He tapped messages to Leo and Astrid. He patted the compact mirror in his pocket and both hoped and dreaded a myth emergency.

At the restaurant, they found a table and ordered their drinks. Bridger sat across from his mom, leaving the third seat at the end open. Bridger stared at it as he drummed his fingers on the tabletop. His phone pinged. He sneaked it out of his pocket and glanced to his lap. It was from Astrid.

Drop your napkin and look to your left.

Bridger pushed his roll of silverware off the table with his wrist. It thumped on the floor, and he bent to pick it up while glancing to his left.

Astrid and Leo waved to him from a booth. They shot him thumbs up and mouthed "good luck" while smiling at him with large cheesy grins. Leo made his hands into a heart.

Warmth suffused him, and he returned their smiles with a large toothy one of his own. He suppressed the laughter that threatened to bubble out of his throat. He sat up and knocked his head on the side of the table.

"Bridge?" His mom grabbed her water to keep it from sloshing. "You okay, kid?"

"Fine." He nodded with his palm on the crown of his head. "I'm good."

Another text lit up his phone. This one from Leo.

Let us know if you need us. I play baseball, I know hand signals.

Bridger didn't hold back his laugh. His mom propped her chin on her hands. "Something funny you want to share with the class?"

"No. Just Leo being cute."

"Ah. Good. I'm glad he's being cute."

Bridger blushed and shoved his phone back into his pocket and focused on his mom. Dad or not, this was his birthday. Next year, he'd be at college, and he wouldn't have this moment with her.

"So," he said with a sly smile, "want to tell me who you were giggling about with your co-workers the other day?"

It was her turn to blush. "HIPPA laws prevent me from sharing that information, young man. Unless you want both of us to go to jail?"

"No way. I'm eighteen now. I'd be tried as an adult."

Bridger took comfort in their banter, and his nervousness eased. With his mom smiling at him and his moral support at his back, he'd be okay. But thirty minutes later, his dad hadn't shown. They went ahead and ordered because Bridger's stomach growled. Fifty-eight minutes after their arrival, Bridger pushed his half-eaten enchilada around on his plate. His appetite was non-existent, and his attention flitted between his mom's frowning face and the front door.

"I don't think he's coming, Mom."

"I'm so sorry, honey." She reached across the table and grabbed his hand. "We should've just cancelled. I know you try to be brave all the time, and face things head on—"

Bridger snorted. Far from the truth. He was a definite skirter of issues. Though he had been better recently.

"But your dad…"

"It's okay. I get it. Mom, he hasn't shown up in ten years. I don't know what I expected."

"Do you want me to tell them it's your birthday? Do you want to wear the sombrero and eat fried ice-cream?"

Nothing sounded less appealing. "No thanks. I think we should just go."

She gave him a soft, sad look that made his insides squirm with embarrassment and unease. "Okay. We can do that."

He sighed and dropped his fork on his plate. He pulled his phone from his pocket and sent Leo and Astrid a text—they were still hanging out in the booth. Bridger could feel their stares on the back of his neck and he flushed with a mix of mortification and inexplicable anger.

Leaving.

As his mom dropped cash on the table, the front door opened and a tall man with blond hair swooped in. He made a beeline for their table, and Bridger straightened from his slouch.

Braxton Whitt had broad shoulders and an athletic build and tanned skin. He wore a goatee and an easy smile and distressed jeans and a T-shirt. In his presence, Bridger felt small, gangly and unsure, as if he was eight years old instead of eighteen. He absently tugged on his collar.

His dad pulled out the chair and dropped into it. "Sorry I'm late. Traffic." He flashed a grin to Bridger and reached over and ruffled his hair. "Wow, you're huge. Happy birthday, Bud."

"Thanks," Bridger mumbled, patting down his hair.

His mom rolled her eyes. "Braxton, you're over an hour late."

He waved her off. "I said I was stuck in traffic, Susan. It's an hour drive. What? You couldn't wait for me?"

"Couldn't you have called?"

"No. I don't use the phone while driving. It's unsafe."

"Well then, no. We couldn't wait. We were hungry and now we're leaving."

His dad held out his hands. "I just got here! And it's Bud's birthday. You're being unreasonable, Susan."

This was starting well. While his parents argued, Bridger rubbed his eyes and squeezed them shut. This would be a great time for a cryptid emergency or a fire. He'd take either. His head began to ache at the temples, and he had to consciously unclench his jaw.

"Bridger? You okay?"

He looked to his mom. "Yeah, just a headache.".

"Eighteen, huh?" his dad said, steamrolling over the awkwardness. "How does it feel?"

"Exhausting," Bridger said, smile still firmly in place.

His dad laughed. "Yeah, being an adult is exhausting. And it only goes downhill from here." He grabbed Bridger's shoulder and shook. "You look good though. All grown up. Maybe room for a little more muscle," he said, playfully jabbing Bridger in the ribs with a fist.

Bridger flinched. "I'll get on that. Thanks."

"Here." His dad fished his wallet from his pocket. He pulled out a crisp hundred and slapped it on the table by Bridger's plate. "For you."

Bridger stared at the money. The casual way his dad thumbed through a wallet full of cash made Bridger's gut churn, and his enchilada gurgled into his throat. Where was all that when Bridger was contemplating fleeing to Florida but couldn't due to money concerns? Where was it when his mother worked every night in a week because the mortgage was due?

Bridger swallowed, hoping the acid and indignation would ease. "Thanks."

"Buy yourself something you want. Not something you need. And please don't spend it on a girl. Okay? That's just for you." He finally released Bridger's shoulder and tented his fingers.

Bridger felt sick.

"Now, who do we have to yell at to bring you a dessert?"

"No thanks," Bridger said, folding the bill and putting it in his pocket. "I actually would just like to—"

"Then we'll go somewhere else for dessert. This place probably only has fried ice cream, right? Not the greatest."

"Braxton."

"Oh, what now?"

His mom fiddled with her napkin. "How've you been?"

His dad blinked. "Oh, fine. Well, mom died. Your grandma," he said, turning to Bridger. "Do you remember her?"

"Um, vaguely?" Bridger had a few hazy memories of visits to her house, and a phone call once or twice, but nothing concrete.

"Yeah, you only met her a few times. She wasn't a big fan of…" he trailed off and cut his eyes to Bridger's mom. He cleared his throat. "Anyway, she passed a few weeks ago and now I'm stuck settling the estate because my two younger brothers are too busy with their own lives."

Wow. That was… a lot of information. Information that Bridger could've done without.

"I'm sorry to hear about your mom."

"Why? You never liked her."

"Braxton."

"What? It's the truth."

Bridger couldn't do this. Not here. Not on his birthday. Not in his favorite restaurant. Not with Leo and Astrid within earshot. He needed to go. He needed *out*. His pulse quickened. His chest tightened. Bridger dropped one hand next to his hip and waved it while he pressed the other to the medal under his shirt.

Luckily for him, Astrid knew hand signals too. "Bridger? Hey!" she said, coming to stand by his chair. Leo was right behind her. "How are you? Isn't it your birthday today?"

His mom shot Astrid a thoroughly unimpressed look. But his dad lit up at seeing the two teenagers hovering over the table.

Bridger went for nonchalant. "Oh, hey, Astrid. Hey, Leo."

"Are you going to the party?" Leo asked. He made a show of checking his phone. "It started like thirty minutes ago. We can give you a ride if you want?"

"A party?" his dad asked, eyebrows shooting up in rapid succession. "Oh, that's why you're acting so weird. You've should've just said, Bud. What eighteen-year-old wouldn't blow off his parents for a party?"

"Well, I mean, I hadn't seen you in so long."

His dad waved the statement away. "Go with your friends. I actually have great news. Your grandmother's estate is going to take me a couple of months to get through. I'm going to live in her house in Grand Rapids for a while. I'll be around and I'm going to be able to come to your graduation. Isn't that great?"

Bridger paled. "Awesome."

"Go with your friends," he said with a smile. His gaze roved over Astrid and Leo. "Just be home before the morning."

"Um…" Bridger shot a look at his mom. Her frown was deep, and her forehead wrinkled.

"Midnight curfew and only if you're with Astrid and Leo the whole time."

"Midnight? He's an adult now. And it's a Saturday."

Bridger winced at the death glare his mom sent his dad. "Um, midnight should be fine," Bridger said and nodded.

"Don't worry, Mrs. Whitt," Leo said, with a charming smile. "We'll take care of him."

"Go then," she said with a weary sigh.

"Have fun, Bud," his dad said. He handed Bridger another twenty. "At least get a little birthday dessert somewhere. It'll soak up all the alcohol."

"Braxton! He's eighteen, not twenty-one."

His dad merely winked.

Bridger shoved the twenty into his pocket. "Thanks, Dad."

"See you later, kid. Have fun."

Leo and Astrid pulled Bridger out of the restaurant, and he all but collapsed between them once they were in the parking lot.

"Shit, that was tense," Astrid said. "You okay? I thought you were going to pass out."

"I was close," Bridger admitted, throwing his arm over Leo's shoulders and leaning into his warmth. "Come on. I don't want to be here any longer."

They walked to Astrid's car; Leo and Astrid talked over Bridger's head.

Above them, a bird squawked, crying several times from atop the restaurant, over the door. Bridger looked back and saw a large black bird—a raven—flapping its wings and ruffling its feathers. It took off and landed on a tree branch on the side of the parking lot near Astrid's car. Its yellow eyes followed them until Bridger settled in the back seat. Clicking his seat belt, Bridger looked out of the window, and the bird flew off.

Weird.

"Is there really a party?" Bridger asked. "Because I'm not in the mood."

"No. That was a lie," Leo said, ducking his head. "You mentioned last night that your dad wanted you to party. It was the first thing I thought of."

"You're a genius, and I adore you." Bridger leaned across the seat and kissed him, a quick peck on the lips.

"Okay, so what are we doing?" Astrid asked, starting the car. "My parents are home so, unless we want to hang out in my room all night, we can't go there."

"Let's go to the lake," Leo said. "For a while. Then we can head to mine."

Bridger leaned his head on the back of his seat. "Wherever is good with me."

"Got it," Astrid said, starting the car. "Ice cream first though. We definitely need ice cream."

Bridger grabbed the crumpled money from his pocket and slapped it on the console by Astrid's elbow. "I'm paying."

"Sweet," she said. "That'll get us at least a massive sundae."

"And milkshakes," Leo said. "And maybe a giant cookie."

"I like the way you think, Romeo."

Astrid pulled out of the parking spot, and Bridger relaxed into their banter and the sound of Astrid's playlist and closed his eyes.

* * *

Groaning, Bridger woke with sunlight pouring through his window, right into his eyes, and with a warm weight on his chest. Marv purred as she rubbed her face along the edge of his jaw and meowed; her tiny claws kneaded his shirt.

"Morning, Marv," he said, scratching between her ears. She arched into his hand, and Bridger smiled.

He stretched under his sheets, which dislodged her from her perch, then checked his phone. He had a message from Leo.

Roped into spring cleaning with mom after Mass. Will probably never see you again. Mourn me.

Bridger chuckled.

Okay, so hanging with Leo was out for the day. And Astrid had family obligations as well, since her parents had imposed Sunday family time when they realized that their youngest kid was about to leave for college.

Bridger rubbed his eyes and yawned widely. He considered going back to sleep, but it was already late morning. His mom didn't work that night, and, with the clarity that comes with being an adult for an entire day, Bridger decided he should be a good son and spend the day with her—especially after the awkwardness that was dinner last night.

Marv batted his nose from her spot on his pillow, and Bridger squinted at her. "What?"

She jumped to his nightstand and pushed his magic compact off the surface with her paw. Eyebrows raised, Bridger leaned over, balanced precariously on the edge of the bed, and scooped the mirror off the floor.

Oh, yeah. He'd almost forgotten. The awkwardness of his birthday dinner had actually managed to block out the fact that a shrieking Grandma Alice had chased a reporter through the woods. He needed to talk to Pavel.

Flipping open the mirror, he squirmed into a more upright position, resting against his headboard. His reflection showed his bedhead, the crease on his cheek from his pillow, and the small crust of dried drool at the corner of his mouth. *Gross.* He scrubbed his sleeve over his lips.

"Call Pavel, please."

His reflection wavered, and the glass glowed.

Bran appeared, blue face pressed close to the mirror, cheeks puffed out. "This better be good," he said around a mouthful. "It's Pop-Tart time."

Bridger rolled his eyes. "I need to speak to Pavel."

"Boss!" Bran called. "It's Bridger."

"What have I said about answering my mirror?" Pavel said, plucking Bran up by the back of his shirt.

Dangling between Pavel's thumb and forefinger, the pixie grinned; crumbs and frosting oozed from behind his pointy teeth. "That's it's very helpful?"

"Close," Pavel said. "Only I said don't."

Bran's wings fluttered. Pavel released him, and Bran flew away in a cloud of sparkles.

"Bridger," Pavel said, the side of his mouth lifted in a grin, "what can I help you with?"

"Grandma Alice was on the monster show screaming and chasing the reporter lady through the woods." The sentence spilled out in a rush, and, wow, releasing that felt amazing. He hadn't realized he'd carried around that much pressure.

"Oh." Pavel blinked. "I'm aware."

"You're aware?"

"Yes. Of course, I am." At Bridger's expression, Pavel shook his head. "I know you don't think I'm taking things seriously, but I am. Summer Lore has been on the intermediary radar for years. She's mostly harmless."

"Mostly harmless?" What the hell? Spiders were mostly harmless, but his mom still screamed every time she saw one, and they weren't welcome inside the house. He wouldn't want a spider to interview him and his friends about drowning in the lake. "How can you say that? Granted, this last season she was fairly lifeless on screen but—"

"Lifeless?" Pavel interrupted. "I wouldn't say that. She was unenthused about the subject matter yes, but lifeless? She's bored, not a zombie."

That brought Bridger up short. He sat up in his bed, shoulders tense. "You've watched it? I thought you said it wasn't a big deal."

"It's not a big deal." Pavel cleared his throat and ducked his head. He swept his dark hair off his forehead, and Bridger was horrified to see a blush spread across his cheekbones. "I merely did a few hours of research on the latest season."

"Oh, no," Bridger said. He jabbed his finger at the mirror. "Pavel! You can't!"

"Can't what?"

"You can't have a crush!"

"I don't have a crush."

"Then what's up with that?" Bridger said, waving a hand at his own face. "You look like I look when I talk about Leo. You like her. You're attracted to her. You have a crush!"

Pavel shrugged. "Call it professional interest."

"No, I will not. This is dangerous. One wrong move, and everything weird that happened last semester goes from a series of random coincidences to 'oh, hey, there are concealed mythical beings living in Midden!' And now I have to worry that if she bats her eyelashes, you'll hand over the big book of Rules and Regulations."

Pavel narrowed his eyes. "I would *not*." He said it in such an affronted tone that Bridger believed him. "Bridger, I'm only going to say this once: do not interfere. Just let this run its course. They'll film a few episodes and leave. I've already alerted the local myth community, and everyone is aware. They've all promised to lay low."

"The unicorn is aware?"

"Yes," Pavel said. "The unicorn. The Nain Rouge. The mermaids. Ginny at the bakery. Grandma Alice. Et cetera and so on. Bran and Nia made a few rounds. And Elena is going to talk with the Dogman."

Okay. Pavel sounded proactive. Maybe he'd learned when he almost died from a skewering by a manticore tail.

"But she wants to interview my friends. What should I do about that?"

"Nothing."

"But!"

"Bridger! Do not meddle. I'm on it. Trust me."

Bridger sagged. Trust Pavel. Trust his mentor, who has not only shown him kindness and understanding but has acted more like a dad than his actual dad. He did trust him, but Pavel admitted that he was young and inexperienced compared to other intermediaries. And the learning curve was devastatingly steep.

"Okay, but can you trust me? I'm really worried."

"I do trust you," Pavel said, brow furrowed; the closest thing to hurt Bridger had seen flickered across his features. "And I trust that you'll listen to me about this. Don't engage. I'll take care of it. You have other things to worry about, I'm sure."

Bridger sighed. Pavel was not wrong. "Okay, I guess. I'll stay out of it."

"Thank you. I'll let you know if I need any additional help. But until then, perform your regular duties and graduate from high school."

"Yeah," Bridger said. "Graduation."

"Do you need time off before the summer to finish the school year? If you do, just ask."

"No." No way. Time off was the last thing he needed. He didn't need more free time to spiral. Keeping busy would keep his brain focused on everything but his future. Work was a welcome respite from the crushing anxiety of life after high school. "I'm good."

"If you say so." Pavel sighed, shoulders dropping. "Now, I have somehow become Nia's assistant in her cosmetic enterprise and must pack shipping boxes."

"Have fun with that."

"Of course. Have a good Sunday, Bridger. Don't worry too much."

Pavel's image wavered, then winked out.

Bridger clasped his medallion in his hand. *Right.* Don't worry. He could totally do that.

CHAPTER 5

BRIDGER GRITTED HIS TEETH, DETERMINED to enjoy the rest of his weekend. His mom wouldn't stop apologizing about his birthday and even went as far as to buy him a cake. They had a candle-blowing-out ceremony while watching game-show fails on YouTube. But it was obvious they were both forcing the fun. The atmosphere in his house was awkward and tense.

He contemplated talking with Pavel again about *Monster of the Week* but resisted the urge to meddle. At least Bridger had Marv. The kitten stayed near him all day while he caught up on homework and slept on his chest again that night. Marv purred so loudly Bridger didn't know if he'd be able to fall asleep, but, once his head hit the pillow, he was out.

On Monday, classes were hectic. His mythology teacher prodded him to pick a topic for his end of semester paper. He needed it to pass and graduate, but he couldn't focus on it. The yearbook editor reminded him through clenched teeth that he would be required to hand out yearbooks during fourth block for the foreseeable future. At lunch, everyone left him alone while he chased his popcorn chicken with a plastic fork and accidentally shot a piece at a sophomore when the fork bent. He didn't die of complete mortification, but it was close.

· At least he could see Leo at baseball practice after school. He'd hang out for a while, before running his usual errands for Pavel. The thought buoyed him and kept him motivated until the final bell rang.

Bridger grabbed his bag and headed for the back doors to the field. The sun was high, and the air was crisp with a lingering chill, and the green grass swayed in the breeze. Tugging his hoodie closer and spirits lifting with each step toward Leo, he made a beeline to the baseball field.

He turned the corner at the equipment shack, then walked quickly past the vacant football field and across the field hockey field to the baseball diamond. The bleachers sagged with fatigue and age; the paint was cracked and peeling and faded by the sun. Spectators had to be wary of splinters. Today, Bridger tossed his backpack on the third base side stands and stopped short.

In the closest parking lot, he spied the van he'd seen a few days ago. And crowded around it were members of the baseball team plus Lacey, Zeke, and Luke. Abandoning his bag, and all his joy, Bridger jogged to the parking lot.

Summer Lore was shorter in person than on TV, or maybe it just seemed that way because she stood on the asphalt and the people who surrounded her stood on the curb. But her hair was the same, blonde and straight, and her smile was the one she had in the tenth season, plastic and strained. Impeccably dressed in a billowy blouse and a pair of tailored trousers, she held a microphone in one hand while she prepped the crowd. Her cameraman, a beleaguered-looking, college-age guy, readied the equipment.

Bridger shouldered his way through the group, earning glares, as he moved to the front next to Zeke and Lacey.

"What's going on?" he asked, voice low, as Summer man-handled Luke away from the group. She positioned him in front of the high school, on the side where the banner for their sports teams hung limply proclaiming in purple and gold that Midden High Monarchs Rule, which, while admittedly catchy, was not what Bridger would consider spooky enough for a cryptid show backdrop.

Lacey's eyes were bright. "She's going to interview Luke about the creature that bit him." She clasped her hands in front of her. "Isn't it awesome?"

No. Decidedly not awesome.

But Pavel had told him not to intervene. He shouldn't intervene. He was going to stay out of it. He was a bystander. A simple bystander. But Astrid didn't have to be a bystander. And neither did Leo. Pavel didn't tell them not to intervene. Bridger looked around, but, not seeing them in the crowd, he realized he was on his own.

Okay. Welp. Guess this was happening. He was allowing this to happen.

Bridger shoved his hands in his pockets and rocked back on his heels. He'd be just an innocent witness to Luke's potential humiliation and the outing of the entire myth world. *Yep.* He could stay silent. He could watch his new world go up in flames. He was unbothered. He channeled his inner Pavel and went for nonchalant and aloof, all-knowing but unconcerned.

Summer tipped Luke's head to the side. "If you feel like crying, go ahead. Tears make for great television."

Okay. Nope. He couldn't allow this to happen.

Squeezing past Zeke, Bridger strode to where Summer and the cameraman were lining up the shot.

"Sorry." Bridger grasped Luke by the elbow. "We need to have an aside."

"Bridger?" Luke asked.

They didn't know each other well. Luke was Zeke's best friend. He rode the bench on the football team and was in choir and drama club and played the piano for the talent show every year. He ate lunch with them, but his seat was at the far end of the table. He was shorter than Bridger and had short brown hair, brown skin, and a sharp nose. He had thin scars which raked across his cheek and down his chin. There was also a bite mark on his shoulder, one on his collarbone, and another on his upper arm. Bridger knew about them from the pictures Zeke had taken when it happened. Bridger pushed down his guilt about the circumstances surrounding the mauling because he didn't need to sprint down that road again. He'd done enough of that over the winter break.

"Yep. That's me. We need to talk."

"Oh, no, you don't." Summer stepped closer, eyes piercing. "You're not stealing my interview. I have exclusive rights to Luke's story, which means your little school newspaper project will have to be about the cafeteria pizza this month."

Bridger huffed. "First," he said, raising a finger, "our cafeteria pizza is actually pretty edible."

Luke nodded in agreement.

"And two, I'm not with the school newspaper. I just need to talk to my good buddy Luke before you get your claws into him." Oh, bad choice of words. Smooth. He cleared his throat.

"Sorry, Luke. That was insensitive. What I meant was, I need to talk before you talk. Okay? Thanks."

Bridger yanked Luke onto the grass.

Summer followed, undeterred. Her high heels sunk into the soft ground of the Michigan spring, and she cursed.

Bridger took the opportunity to drag Luke farther. "Hey, sorry, but are you sure you want to do this?" Bridger asked, genuinely concerned, not just for his life, but for Luke as well. "This lady is a harpy, and, believe me, I don't say that lightly."

"Bridger, they're paying me money. Enough to be able to afford a tux and a limo for prom. And maybe the girl I want to ask will say yes if she knows that."

Bridger's eyebrows climbed into his hairline. "You're doing this for money? Luke, I'll give you money *not* to do it. Seriously, have you watched the show?"

Luke pried Bridger's fingers from his arm. "Yeah, I watched the first season on Netflix. It wasn't bad."

"The first season is fine, but have you seen the recent one? The format changes over the years. And the lovely host morphs from interested investigative reporter to snide zombie who pokes fun at the people she meets in towns like ours."

"I take offense to that," Summer interjected. She'd managed to unstick herself and wobble over. "That's libel."

"No, it's not," Bridger shot back.

"Yeah, technically it's slander," Luke said.

"Not helpful." Bridger rubbed the headache blossoming at his temple. "But what he said. What kind of reporter are you if you don't know the difference?"

She flicked her silky hair over her shoulder. "Come on, Luke. Let's get this done before we lose the light."

"Oh no. That sounds serious. Like it could wreck the shot. It would be disastrous. Maybe Luke should think this over a little bit more and talk to you tomorrow when you're not in danger of losing the light and destroying the whole show."

Summer was unimpressed.

"Bridger," Luke said, nose wrinkled, brow furrowed. "Why do you even care? It's not like we're friends."

"Yes," Summer said, interjecting. "Why do you care? Bridger, was it?"

Bridger glared at her. "I just don't want to see anyone hurt or embarrassed. That's all."

"Is it because of the beach incident?" Luke asked, frowning. "Are you, like, embarrassed you drowned? Is this a Leo thing? I wouldn't worry about it. He talks about you all the time, it's kind of annoying."

Bridger internally groaned and resisted the urge to bury his face in his hands.

"Wait," Summer said, smile growing sharp, eyes narrowing. "You're that kid? The beach kid?"

Bridger faced Summer. He put his hands on his hips, stuck out his chin, and glared back. Lying wasn't really an option since Luke had given him away, and, whatever, who cared what this woman would think. His friends had all witnessed what happened. He'd puked on Leo's sandals, and Leo still wanted to date him. "Yeah, I'm *that* kid."

"Bridger, huh. Interesting name."

"Thanks."

"You were the kid who was pulled under? Anything else you want to tell me?"

"No."

She smirked and cocked her head; blonde hair swished flawlessly. "Hey, Luke, why don't you head over to my camera guy, Matt, and let me talk to your friend here."

Luke shrugged. "Okay."

"No, wait, hold on. Luke!" Bridger tried, but Luke walked away, and he was left with Summer. The way she looked at him made him feel like a bug under a magnifying glass. He crossed his arms and lifted his chin, desperate to exude confidence, but inwardly he squirmed.

"Look, kid." She twirled the microphone chord. "I've interviewed a ton of teenagers over the past decade, and they all pretty much fall into two categories: the fame seekers and the yokels. I don't care which one you are or which one your friend is. I don't care if you got a cramp while you were swimming with your friends and nearly drowned and instead of admitting you were a dumbass, you thought you'd save face by coming up with a story. Maybe this is a fame-grab for your friend. He thinks being on television will make him popular with the girls. Whatever the reason, let me be clear. I don't care. Okay?"

Bridger bristled. "I bet you're a delight at parties."

"Oh," she said, adjusting the straps on her blouse. "You're mouthy. A know-it-all, huh?"

Bridger crossed his arms over his chest. "I'm just looking out for my friends. I've watched your show. I see how you treat the people you interview, especially in your later seasons. And I don't want you humiliating my friends, my *town*, over some weird shit that happened in the fall. Yeah, there probably aren't a bunch of cryptids running around Midden." Just call him Liar Mcliarface. "But people experienced something they couldn't explain, and it scared them or hurt them. And if they want to believe in a phenomenon or a piece of folklore to comfort themselves, as a coping mechanism, then that is okay for them. It's not for you to judge and it's not for you to make fun of and it certainly isn't for you to decide what's real and what's not."

Her perfectly arched eyebrows shot up. "Oh. You're the third kind—a believer."

Clenching his jaw, Bridger shook with anger, then with shock. "Wait. What?"

"You really think there was something that pulled you down." She perked up; her blue eyes were alight. "What did you see when you went under?"

Uh oh. He'd said too much. *Danger. Danger!*

"I saw nothing."

"Uh huh." She pressed a finger to his chest so her pink manicured nail dimpled the fabric of his T-shirt. "You're interesting. I think I'm going to keep my eye on you."

Oops. "I'm really not." *Back pedal!* "You're right. I'm in it for the fame." *Harder!* "Totally for the fame. Or, what was that other option? Yokel? Just ask my friends. I am not smart. I'm also the literal definition of strange. Really, really odd. And off-putting. Seriously awkward." Okay, maybe that was a little too hard.

"Uh huh."

"Hey!" Leo showed up, winded, dressed for baseball, bag over one shoulder, and glove in his hand. He stopped next to Bridger; his shoulder banged into Bridger's arm. "Hands off."

She shook her head. "You teenagers are so cute. Teeming with hormones and impulsivity. So ready to be offended and rush in when you're not needed."

"Hey, Summer! We need to get a move on if we're going to make it to the haunted bakery tonight."

"In a minute," she called back.

"Anything else you two have to say?"

Bridger clenched his jaw. He grasped Leo's hand. "No."

"Great."

"I do, actually." In a cloud of perfume, Lacey appeared, holding her phone, and with her pouty lips pulled into an uncharacteristic frown.

Startled, Bridger looked over Summer's shoulder and saw the whole group standing there listening, and he wondered just how long they'd been there.

"I heard what Bridger said," Lacey continued, defiant and calm. She turned her phone screen to where Summer could see it. "And he's right. Unless you're going to take us seriously, we don't want you here."

Whoa. No. "That's not what I said!" Bridger waved his hands. "That's the opposite of what I said. The literal opposite! And since when do you listen to me?"

Lacey's expression was set on serious, one that Bridger didn't often see on her. The picture she showed was from the beach incident. It was of Bridger, passed out on the sand with blood running down his leg from the gashes. Dripping, Pavel stood over him next to Leo. She swiped the screen, and there was a photo of her own scratch from the mermaids. Then another swipe and she showed Bridger on his side, gagging, while Pavel, Leo, and

Astrid hovered. *Awesome.* As if that moment couldn't get more humiliating.

Summer tapped the screen. "Interesting."

Zeke brandished his phone as well. And on the screen was a picture of Luke in the hospital, wrapped in bandages, bruised, bloodied, and swollen. Then there was another kid, whose phone showed the damage to the cars after the football game, and the sparkles the unicorn's hooves had left on the crunched metal.

And suddenly, the whole group had stories: about running from the ball fields the day the Ozark Howler showed up, about going to a club and someone making out with a strange guy and feeling weak for days afterward, about the traffic problems at the bridge and the acid burns on the concrete roadbed.

Bridger gasped, stepping backward as the crowd surged forward to yell at Summer, and he rubbed his sternum with his fist.

The lesson Pavel had given him about belief and human perception slammed into his consciousness. People dismissed the strange when there was no validation. They chalked up shimmering unicorn tracks and troll traffic jams to tricks of the light or other mundane reasons, rejecting the fantastical when a real-world solution was presented, especially if they were the only witness or if someone with them denied experiencing the same thing.

But now, Bridger had just given his friends corroboration. With one ill-timed speech, he'd turned them from slightly interested parties into true believers. He had meddled.

"What have I done?" he whispered.

Summer raised her hands. "All right," she yelled, smirk still firmly in place. She turned to Matt. "We'll postpone the bakery until tomorrow afternoon. This is much more interesting." She addressed the crowd. "I want to talk with each of you." She winked at Bridger. "Especially you."

"The answer is no. Thanks."

"Now, Bridger." She tilted her microphone toward him. "You can't create chaos and then run. That doesn't seem fair."

His heart quickened. His breath stuttered. He rubbed his chest harder. Beads of sweat broke out on his forehead.

A large, black beetle buzzed into the group and landed on Lacey's shoulder. It crawled along the strap of her tank top then pulled a strand of her hair.

She shrieked.

The bug took off, only to bump right into Summer's forehead, before careening toward Zeke. He ducked and swatted uselessly, nailing another kid in the cheek. And suddenly, everyone was yelling about bugs and allergies. They ran for cover.

Bridger took a step back, yanking Leo with him, but the bug didn't come near them. The mutant beetle bounced from screeching student to screeching student, then, after a few minutes of terrorizing the crowd, it zoomed away.

"That was weird," Bridger said.

"Coming from you, that means something," Leo said.

Once the coast was clear, the cameraman, Matt, crept forward from where he had ducked behind the van. "Summer," he said. She peeked around the open back door.

"Yes?"

"We lost the light."

She muttered a curse and stomped her foot. "Fine. Round up the kids. We'll get everyone's names and numbers and we can collect information tomorrow."

That was Bridger's cue to flee. He tugged Leo, and together they walked briskly away and back to the baseball field.

"What are you going to do?" Leo's glove was tucked under his arm, and his ball cap sat askew on his head.

Bridger's headache returned in full force. "I don't know." Pavel said not to worry, but he'd also said not to meddle. "I think I screwed up." He gulped. "I need to talk to Pavel."

"Rivera! Get on the field! Or are you not planning to play on Friday?"

Leo winced. "Gotta go. I'll call you tonight." He pecked Bridger on the cheek and then bolted to the dugout and out to shortstop. "Sorry, coach!"

Bridger brushed his fingers over the spot on his cheek. His body tingled from his scalp to the tips of his toes and he grinned.

Then he remembered *everything else*, and his stomach dropped to his knees.

CHAPTER 6

"I THOUGHT I WAS EXPLICIT in telling you not to interact with Summer Lore."

Bridger winced as Pavel paced around his living room.

"I didn't mean to, if it's any consolation. I really tried to walk away. It was just... I got caught up. She's, um, you weren't wrong. She's magnetic. I see why you have a crush."

Pavel cast him a withering glare. Rubbing the bridge of his nose, he turned on his heel and stalked to the toasters. He used his sleeve to wipe off a fingerprint.

"The toasters have been quiet. No emergencies from her presence. Yet."

Bridger hunched his shoulders. What he wouldn't give for handful of pixie dust so he could disappear into the cushions of one of Pavel's chairs. Bridger had seen Pavel angry—it had been terrifying, and Bridger hoped never to see it directed at him again. This was more along the lines of I-know-you-broke-the-lamp-when-I-told-you-not-to-play-basketball-in-the-house disappointment than I-am-magic-and-pissed-off anger. Still, upsetting Pavel was the worst.

"I'm sorry."

Pavel waved away the apology. He crossed to the window and put his hands on his hips. The afternoon sun threw him into sharp profile: the curve of his nose, the cut of his cheekbones, the bird-like quality of his frame. His tan trench coat hung off his shoulders as if they were a wire coat hanger, and the hem ruffled around the knees of his pinstripe trousers.

"I need to talk to my mentor." His accent thickened, and he clipped his words, which made the consonants sound harsher. "I should check protocol again for interacting with the media. Not that I am strict with protocol." He shrugged. "But Aurelius may have some wisdom."

Bridger knotted his fingers. "What should I do?"

Looking over his shoulder, Pavel knit his brows. "Stay away from her."

Bridger hung his head. "Yeah, I know that part." He scratched the back of his head. "But this week I'm scheduled to see Ginny and pick up an order for the pixies. But—"

"That's fine. Go."

Bridger knew a dismissal when he heard one, but he couldn't resist pressing on a bruise. "I want to help with this. Is there anything I can do?"

"Oh, I think you've done enough."

Bridger slumped.

Pavel sighed. He leaned on the wall, facing Bridger, and crossed his arms. "Sorry. That was… I know you only have good intentions, Bridger. I'm not doubting that. Your judgment isn't stellar. But again, you're young and impulsive. We all make mistakes. And I'm sure this will work out with a little intervention. But let me handle it. You have enough on your plate."

"Okay. Okay. I really am sorry."

"I know. I'm not going to lie and say it's okay, especially since you went directly against what I asked, but I will say that I'm positive it will be fine."

"Thanks for that."

"You're welcome. Now, move along. You don't want to be out too late. Get a good night's rest so you can look at things clearly in the morning."

"Did you, did you just parent me?" The edges of Bridger's mouth ticked up despite the mood.

Pavel lifted his finger. "No, I did not. I merely offered advice."

"Ha!" Bridger said. He stood and grabbed his bag. "You totally did!"

"I would be a lackluster parent."

No. No, he wouldn't. Bridger had experience with a lackluster parent and Pavel would be anything but lackluster. Odd, maybe. Full of dad jokes, most likely. Distant on occasion. But all parents had flaws. Anyway, he'd be awesome, but Bridger was not about to tell him that. It'd be weird.

"Anyway, time to go. Chop, chop. I know you have homework."

"You did it again!" Bridger crowed, as he rounded the banister. Pavel's irritated sputter followed him down the stairs. Bridger snickered as he thumped his way to the first floor. He hopped over the last few steps and hit the floor with a thud. Mindy's bobbleheads wobbled.

"Hey, Mindy," Bridger said with a wave. She had a large pink flower tucked into her sculpted mound of blond hair. Bridger didn't know if it was there on purpose or if she'd walked under one of the flowering trees on Pavel's front lawn and one had stuck.

She wore a burnt-orange jacket over a pink blouse and a matching pink skirt. "How are you today?"

She played a game on her phone and ignored him.

"I'm great, thanks. Pavel yelled at me a little, but otherwise I'm doing well. How's your bobble-head family? Good?" Bridger teased, but stopped short when he noticed that the usual army of bobbleheads had thinned. One, a dog dressed as a mail carrier, had been painted with crossed eyes. Bridger didn't like it, and had tried not to look at it, but it had sat in a prominent space on Mindy's desk and been difficult to avoid. Now it wasn't there.

"Hey, what happened to cross-eyed Postman Rover?"

Mindy sighed. "Do you need something?"

"Obviously not," Bridger replied, hefting his backpack higher on his shoulders. "I'm only talking to annoy you."

Her expression soured, and she went back to her phone.

Huh. Strange. Well, not really. Bridger never had a good read on Mindy.

"Okay, I'm leaving. See you tomorrow."

Casting one last look over his shoulder at Mindy, Bridger left the house, and made his way to the bus stop.

*   *   *

THE NEXT DAY AFTER SCHOOL, Bridger grabbed the bus to downtown to visit Ginny at the bakery. His phone vibrated in his pocket. He pulled it out and scrunched his nose at a text from an unfamiliar number.

Is this Bridger?

He typed back **Yes.**

The phone rang. He swiped his thumb over the screen to accept the call.

"Hello?"

"Bridger, it's Luke. I got your number from Leo. I hope that's okay."

Bridger shot straight up from his uncrowded-bus sprawl. "Yeah. It's fine. Is everything okay? Is it the interview? Did Summer say something weird? Ask you to do anything weird? Was there weirdness?"

There was a pause. "Um, no. That's not why I'm calling."

"Oh." Relief was a palpable thing, like a cold bucket of water over his nervous system. "Um, why are you calling then?"

"I want to ask Astrid to prom."

"Oh," Bridger said, taken aback. And then giddiness spread through him. "I mean, awesome. That's awesome."

"Do you think she'll say yes?"

Bridger had no fucking clue whether or not she'd say yes. Astrid had never given an opinion one way or another about Luke. She hadn't given much information on her crush levels since Bridger's Leo-awakening. She held her cards close to her chest in that area. Or maybe Astrid didn't have a crush-interest now. She always said teenage boys were pretty gross and she wasn't wrong. She also hadn't given any indication of being into other genders, other than the occasional comment on how beautiful certain people were. Natalie Dormer was their most recent topic of conversation, and who didn't have a crush on Natalie Dormer?

"Luke, I have no idea. But I think she'd appreciate being asked."

There was another pause. "That's not helpful, Bridger."

"Yeah. Sorry. Look, she lamented to me that no one had asked her yet. And I know she wants to go. That's all I got."

"Okay. Well. Do you think, I mean, I kind of have an idea for a promposal. Would she like that? I mean, does she like attention? Or do you think I should ask privately?"

And that, that was a question Bridger could answer without a doubt. "Luke, make it as big and obnoxious as you want. She'll love it."

"Really?"

"Oh, yeah. Trust me. And if you ask the field hockey team, I know they'd help."

"Awesome. Thanks, Bridger. I'll do it."

Bridger's mom always warned him that if he made faces that his muscles might stick that way, but he wouldn't mind his face forever pulled into the biggest grin ever.

BRIDGER BOUNDED UP THE STEPS to *Gimme Some Sugar, Baby*, the bakery on Fifth Street in downtown Midden. It was an old building, made of brick, with the front stoop directly on Main Street. Bridger hopped off the city bus a few blocks down. He liked the short walk along the sidewalk, where old trees grew from fenced off squares of soil. The thick branches offered dappled shade and whispered above him in the breeze, and the large roots curled, cracking the sidewalk. Bridger always jumped over them--funny how superstitious he'd become.

Downtown Midden seemed like another world, so different from the perfectly planned and manicured Commons. It was organic in a way that the rest of the city wasn't, as if the little shops and odd-angled streets popped up from the ground, much as flowers did in the cracks in the concrete in the spring. Bridger rarely visited downtown, because finding a parking spot was a nightmare, and Astrid wasn't great at parallel parking. And a lot of the area was boarded up or had for-rent signs in the window, so there wasn't much to do, other than walk around, see a movie at the weird-smell, sticky-floor theater, or eat. Since Ginny had moved into the bakery, Bridger had a reason to visit and amble.

The owners of *Gimme Some Sugar, Baby* were middle-aged hipsters, a couple named Peter and Meadow, who had an affinity for Bruce Campbell movies, baking, and flannel. They lived above the store in a studio apartment. They were also surprisingly chill about the fact that their bakery was haunted, and that Bridger regularly visited to talk with their ghost.

When he pushed open the door, the bell above him jangled, and Bridger waved. Rock music played at a low volume overhead, and the air was heavy with the smell of chocolate chip cookies.

Peter held up a brown paper bag. "Ginger cakes, lemon bars, and frosted brownies." He set the bounty next to the register. "Tell Mr. Chudinov we say hello and thank his friends for their timely payment."

"Thanks, Peter. I will." Bridger grabbed the bag and rounded the counter. He let himself into their storage room and hopped up on a bar stool at a table.

As soon as he was settled, a bag of flour fell, spilling its contents all over the floor. Bridger stared intently as letters appeared in the mess.

Hi, Bridger! It said in curly script. *Happy birthday!*

"Hi, Ginny," he said, shoving his hand in the bag and grabbing a lemon bar. The pixies could deal with one missing treat. "And thank you. I had a great day."

Groovy.

Ginny was one of the side effects of Leo's hero cycle. When Leo moved to Midden, he had, unknowingly, been in the midst of an epic hero's journey which consisted of a series of stages he needed to complete to reach a transformation. Except, Leo had met Bridger—his temptation—and promptly became stuck. Since all myths and cryptids are creatures of habit and routine, Leo's inability to progress in the cycle affected other paranormal entities, like Ginny. She had been drawn to the town and popped up in the middle of a crowded mall scaring the daylights out of a few unwitting townsfolk.

It all worked out in the end. Leo's epic hero's journey turned out to be not-so-epic, and his metaphorical death and transformation consisted of leaving behind the mantle of naturally-gifted-athletic football player and donning the one of naturally-gifted-athletic-hardworking-focused baseball player. Bridger moved from being a temptation to a helper which meant he went from bisexual-disaster-crush to bisexual-disaster-boyfriend. *Awesome.* And Ginny moved into the bakery downtown.

Before Leo's abrupt halt in the hero journey and the subsequent disruption of Ginny's life, she had haunted a bed and breakfast in Pennsylvania for fifty years. According to her, after haunting the same place for half a century, things got boring. And the owners of the bed and breakfast were constantly trying to exorcise her.

Ginny had died as a teenager in the 1960s from the measles and took up haunting instead of crossing over into the "swirling cinnamon roll of light." Those were her words, not his. He couldn't grasp the idea of the bright vortex of death appearing as something as innocuous as a cinnamon roll, but Ginny was a glass-half-full kind of girl. Bridger had questions, so many questions, but Pavel warned him that it was impolite to interrogate the dead. And there was a communication barrier.

Sometimes when Bridger visited, Ginny would fully manifest in a translucent image of a beautiful girl in a skirt and sweater with bright-red lipstick and long hair pulled into a high ponytail and styled in a large curl. On those days, talking was difficult, because Ginny poured all her energy into her appearance and not her voice. On other days, she communicated through whispers and cold touches and moving ingredients around. Today, she was writing messages in flour.

"How are you doing?"

The flour shifted, as if an invisible hand swiped over the letters, erasing them. Then words appeared one letter at a time.

Ok. Bored.

"Yeah, same. I guess you heard from Pavel to lay low. Right?"

There was a sigh followed by a puff of flour skittering over the floor.

Yes.

"Okay. There is this reporter lady in town that has made my life ten times more interesting than I need it to be. So just be aware."

Do you want me to haunt her?

"No. Thanks for the offer though."

"I'd do it, Bridger, for you." Her voice whispered across the shell of Bridger's ear. He shivered. "Pull her hair. Push her into the oven."

The hair on Bridger's arms stood on end. Sometimes he forgot that Ginny was a ghost. She acted like a teenager most of the time, but, every once in a while, she reminded him in funny ways that she didn't hold life in quite the same regard as the living did.

"Um, again, thanks for the offer, but I'm good."

She was here.

Bridger froze. "She was?"

A few days ago.

"And what happened?"

Another sigh. *Nothing.* Followed by a frowny face. Bridger had taught her emojis thinking it might be useful in communicating. It hadn't been.

Bridger rolled his neck, noticed the tension setting in along his spine, and consciously unclenched his jaw. "But everything else good? How are Peter and Meadow treating you?"

Good. Still here. Still dead.

Bridger snorted as more flour spilled from the bag.

How's Leo?

"Amazing."

Ginny giggled. The breath was cold on Bridger's neck; goosebumps bloomed.

"I'll bring him next time," Bridger said, shoving the rest of the lemon bar into his mouth. He chewed loudly, and more letters appeared in the flour. "If he's not busy."

Please. I miss cute boys.

"Hey! I resent that."

She giggled again.

"But I get it. He is cute." Bridger pulled his phone from his pocket and flipped through his pictures. He found a selfie they'd taken together where they both were looking at the camera and neither was making a weird face. He held it up.

She cooed in his ear.

Bridger sat for a while longer and talked with Ginny. Despite the massive differences in their upbringings, she was easy to talk to, for a ghost, and loved to learn about the modern world. But the time grew late, and Bridger had homework.

He hopped down from the stool. "I'll be back in a few weeks. If you need Pavel, use a mirror, or, you know, knock stuff over until one of the toasters goes off."

"Thank you, Bridger."

He shuddered and grasped the straps of his backpack a little tighter. "You're welcome, Ginny. See ya."

Bridger left the storage room, waved at Meadow as she frosted a batch of cupcakes, and bounced to the door. Swinging it open, he walked right into Summer.

Stumbling back, Bridger was saved from falling on his ass by a handy display of insulated travel mugs. He grabbed the plastic-covered metal display rack. His fingers caught in the grid. The cups went flying, rolling along the floor like multicolored barrels in a personal game of Donkey Kong.

"Hello, Bridger," Summer said, with a mean smirk. "What are you up to?"

Nope. Nope. Nope. Nope. He needed to make like an octopus and escape.

"Leaving," he said, attempting to shoulder past her in the doorway and keeping his eyes on the floor to dodge the debris. Her cameraman, Matt, was on her heels. He made his way into the shop, stepped around them, and went to the register.

"Ah, it's your modus operandi then." She gestured at the scattered merchandise. A travel mug with a picture of Ash from the *Evil Dead* franchise and the store's name in bright glittery letters stared up at Bridger. "You cause a disturbance, then leave before the cleanup."

Don't respond. Don't respond. Don't respond. "I guess we have that in common then." *Fuck.*

She cocked her head. "Really? That's what you think?"

He'd said too much. Pavel was going to murder him. But in for the penny, might as well go for the pound. "Well, yeah. You stir up a frenzy with a lot of hearsay and wrong information, get a good feature for your show, then ghost before the town knows you used its legends and traditions for ratings and a laugh."

She blinked. "Wow. You really don't like me. What did I do to piss you off, huh?" She swept her hair off her shoulder, then tented her pink-tipped fingers. "It's a fun show about monsters, and you are treating it like a documentary."

"Whatever." Bridger backed away from her, knocking into the display again. He gathered and carefully restacked the mugs, while keeping his gaze averted.

"You're interesting, Bridger." Summer handed him a mug.

"I'm really not."

"I'll be the judge of that."

Bridger finished picking up the mess. He gave a sheepish look to Meadow, who merely laughed and told him not to worry about it.

Matt returned, carrying equipment. His cheeks were pale, and his eyes were wide. "Summer," he said, holding up a tape recorder. "You have to hear this."

Bridger straightened. "What's that?"

"EVP recorder," Summer said. At Bridger's blank look she rolled her eyes. "Electronic Voice Phenomenon recorder. I thought you were a fan of the show, Bridger? It's a staple in ghost investigations. It picks up voices of the spirits that haunt the locale. Peter and Meadow allowed us to set it up when we first visited."

Blood drained from Bridger's face, and he was sure he matched Matt.

"Listen," Matt said, eagerly. "This is so creepy." He rewound a few seconds, then pressed play.

Ginny's voice came over the speaker, not the fast, light sound Bridger heard when she used her energy to speak, but slow and deep and *creepy*.

"Thank you, *Bridger*."

Oh, no.

Eyes wide, pink lips parted, Summer whipped her head around to stare at him.

"That's your name."

"No, it's not."

"That voice said your name."

"No, it didn't. I didn't hear anything."

Incredulous, she pointed at the device. "That's *your* name. Plain as day. How do you explain that?"

Okay. Denial was not working. He needed a new move. Thoughts whirling, Bridger responded. "That clearly picked up a conversation I had with Meadow earlier."

She crossed her arms. "How come I don't buy that either?"

Crap. Bridger stepped back and did the only thing he could think of.

He fled.

The bell above the front door clanged, and he dashed onto the sidewalk. Summer followed, hobbling after him in her high heels, calling his name as he ran. Dodging pedestrians, Bridger sprinted while Summer yelled. He'd thought he'd finished with running, but no. Last semester he ran away from monsters. This semester he ran away from gorgeous women who wanted to ruin his life. What was his *life*?

He snuck a peak over his shoulder, and, yep, she was still behind him. A little farther back, but on his trail. *Shit.* She'd follow him right to the bus stop, and there was no way the bus would be waiting for him and he could pull a cool, action-movie stunt and jump in just as the doors closed in her face.

His luck didn't work that way. Stumbling over a crack in the sidewalk, Bridger fell to his knees, breaking skin and tearing his jeans. His palms bled from scraping along the concrete. He pushed to a crouch and then froze.

Barking and snarling, a massive black dog barreled toward him with its lips curled back over its fangs and saliva dripping from his jowls. Bridger's brain conjured visions of a dog-like cryptid eating his face. He froze in terror but, at the last second, he rolled out of its way, and, miracle of miracles, it ran right past him.

Huh.

Summer wasn't as lucky. The dog skidded to a halt in front of her and growled. Shooing it away with her purse, she attempted to walk around it, to no avail. It snapped at her and prevented her from moving forward. In fact, it aggressively corralled her back toward the bakery.

Not one to look a gift dog in the mouth, Bridger jumped to his feet. He ran to the bus stop, just as the bus rolled in. He didn't look back as he vaulted through the open doors and, chest heaving, cheeks flushed, slammed into a seat.

Glancing out of the smudged window as the bus pulled away, Bridger saw Summer, disheveled and shrieking, in the middle of the sidewalk.

There was no sign of the dog.

CHAPTER 7

On Friday, Bridger kept his head down and his hood pulled up as he ran up the front steps of the school. He looked over his shoulder a few thousand times. His usual twitchiness was dialed up to eleven, and he wasn't certain he could make it through school without spraining something. His neck already hurt from checking behind him every few steps because he was paranoid Summer would jump out from behind a tree and shove a microphone in his face.

"Bridge?"

He jumped, clutched his chest, and stumbled backward. The squeak that emanated from his open mouth was loud enough that several students turned to look at him. His shoulders slammed into the lockers.

"Holy wow, Astrid. Don't sneak up on me."

She shook her head and frowned. "I literally didn't. I stood at your locker like I do every morning and waited for your dumb ass to show up. What is wrong with you?"

Bridger's heart thundered.

"Nothing."

Raising an eyebrow, Astrid bent toward him. "Is it myth stuff? Hey, whatever happened with Grandma Alice?"

"Nothing. Pavel told me to stay out of it, so I am staying out of it." Bridger tugged on his lock and sighed when it didn't give. Hands shaking, he spun the dial and tried again. "This is me staying out of it."

"It doesn't look like you're staying out of it."

"Well, I'm trying to keep a low profile. I don't need any undue attention. Okay?"

"I really don't know how you deal with all of it. I only made it a month working for Pavel, and that was over winter break. I had to step away because the weird became too weird, even for me."

"Well, he did say not many assistants last. Apparently, I'm the longest to hold on, which is kind of sad, if you think about it. I have no idea how long Mindy has been there, but she pays bills and ignores the rest of it." Bridger tried the lock again. It held fast. "Damn it!" He hit his fist on the locker, then realized that he was drawing attention to himself. He ducked his head.

"You're really doing great with that low profile. Banging on your locker. Screaming in the middle of the hallway. Keeping all that tension on the down-low." Bridger glared. "I mean, I hear ya." She rifled through her bag and pulled out a copy of the school newspaper. "You have to stay totally under the radar. Like this."

Bridger abandoned his lock. He snatched the paper. The front-page headline declared "A Hot Race for Prom Court." Below it was a picture of him and Leo snuggling in the hallway by the gym. Bridger had his arm around Leo's shoulders, and Leo, baseball hat on, was tucked into his side. They were laughing about something, Leo's eyes were crinkled as he stared up at Bridger's jaw, and Bridger wore the dopiest grin in the history of dopey grins. It was obvious by their twin besotted expressions that they were a couple. There was no way to interpret it otherwise. And it was the cutest picture *ever* and it was on *the front page of the school newspaper.* They weren't the only couple featured. Zeke and Lacey were on there, as were a few others from the senior and junior classes, but Bridger and Leo were front and center with their names neatly printed under the photo.

"I always knew I'd be a headline someday," he muttered.

"Cute."

"This is awful."

"Yes, so sad. Alexa, play 'Despacito.'"

"You're not funny."

"I'm hilarious. And this is great, by the way. You're breaking barriers. Did you know that you and Leo are the first same-sex couple to ever be considered for prom court?"

"That's also awful. We shouldn't be the first."

"No one ever accused this high school of being the forefront of progressive thinking. But hey! It's happening now. And it's great!" Astrid punched him on the shoulder. "And you thought you'd have to move halfway across the country to come out."

Bridger rubbed his temple. "I can't deal with this right now." He handed the paper back to her.

"Why? Because of the whole monster-show thing? I thought you were staying out of it?"

"I am! I mean…" He rubbed the back of his neck. "…I was! But there was an incident at the baseball field and then another at the bakery. And now, I really need to focus on school and hiding. Summer chased me yesterday, and it wasn't great."

"Okay," she said, drawing out the last vowel. "I can see it is stressing you out so I'm not going to ask. But you can focus on school and on graduating so we can be besties at State next year. I know you can."

Bridger nodded, quickly. He tried his lock again and failed. "Could you?"

Rolling her eyes, Astrid successfully put in the combination. "What would you do without me?"

"Shrivel up and die. Seriously."

She nudged him with her shoulder. "Seriously."

"Hey, how's your calculus grade? Did the quiz go okay?"

Astrid crossed her hands over her heart. "Oh, you remembered. You really are my best friend."

"Yeah. Yeah. I was a jerk last semester. We've established that. No need to bring it up every time."

He slammed his locker shut, and they walked down the hall.

"I did great on the quiz. My grade is holding steady. I just have to do a little better on the homework and I'll be fine."

"Great. Let me know if I can help."

"You suck at math."

"Yes. I do. But I am a great shoulder to cry on. And I'm kind of good at random facts. I win Jeopardy at least four times a week."

"God, you're a nerd." She slid her arm through his and tugged him close to her side. "I don't know how you ended up dating the prom king."

"Pfft. If you figure it out, let me know."

BRIDGER MADE IT TO LUNCH without doing anything more than mildly embarrassing, which he counted as a win.

Lacey was not happy with him for whatever reason. It may have been about the dive-bombing bug. It also may have been that she was in a tight race with him—of all people—for best prom couple, which was *ridiculous.*

He plopped down next to Astrid with his tray of unappetizing school lunch and, after eyeing it for a long minute, pushed it away.

Astrid poked him. "I am so tempted to quote the Captain America PSA about a hot lunch, but I don't think I can get through it without giggling."

Bridger snorted. Trust Astrid to bring up not only their mutual love of comic book movies, but their fictional BFF counterparts. She was the Bucky to his Cap. "I don't think I could get through it either. I'd probably end up with milk coming out of my nose."

"Attractive."

"Very."

"Hey, so any idea where the girls are?" Astrid said, gesturing at the empty seats on her left. "Or why there is a piano set up at the front of the room?"

Bridger's eyes widened. *Oh. Oh!* He sat up straight.

"Hey," he said, giving her a wide grin. "Remember that you love me and just roll with it."

She paled. "Bridge? What's going on?"

The cafeteria went quiet when several of Astrid's teammates strode in from the side door to the front of the room, holding signs. Luke followed them and sat at the piano. He cracked his knuckles, then began to play. The familiar strains of *Can't Help Falling In Love* filled the room.

"Bridger," Astrid said, voice a breath, eyes fixed on her teammates swaying with the music. "What the hell is happening?"

And wow. Luke was brave. He was so brave. Bridger could never. Of course, Bridger couldn't carry a tune in a bucket; neither could Leo, but that didn't keep him from singing along to the radio every chance he had. Luke, however, was awesome.

Once Luke hit a certain word, the girl at the head of the line flipped her poster. Astrid sucked in a breath at the sight of her name splashed across the sign. Everyone in the room turned to stare at her. Cheeks burning red, she laughed, delighted and stunned, hand over her mouth, as Luke continued to sing. On another cue, the other three girls flipped their signs to spell out *Will You Go To Prom With Me?*

Bridger's smile was so big his face was going to break. For three minutes, Bridger was thrilled, filled to bursting with joy for his best friend, and proud of a guy he only knew because he'd happened to be in the wrong place at the wrong time a few months ago.

Astrid stood when the song finished and met Luke in the middle of the cafeteria. He handed her a bouquet of red roses. Hands in his pockets, Luke shrugged. "Astrid, will you go to prom with me?"

Astrid nodded. "Yeah. Yes. Definitely. You're awesome. This was awesome."

The cafeteria burst into applause and catcalls. When Luke and Astrid hugged, Bridger, taking on the role of annoying helicopter parent, stood and took pictures on his phone. Astrid would kill him if he didn't get at least one good shot.

"They're so cute."

Bridger startled, took an awkward step, and wobbled dangerously. He would've fallen if not for someone grabbing his arm.

"Leo?" Bridger asked, disentangling himself from his backpack and his chair.

Leo twirled a hall pass. "I had to witness it. Luke has been nervous all morning. I thought he was going to puke in first block."

Bridger didn't know why he did it. Maybe it was because he hadn't seen Leo since the baseball field, or maybe he was overcome with happiness for Astrid and Luke, or maybe he really needed Leo's warmth. Whatever the reason, he grabbed Leo in a desperate crushing hug and held on.

Leo hugged him back. "Hey. You okay?"

"I don't know," Bridger said. "I'm overwhelmed."

"Was it the picture in the newspaper? Or the Elvis song? I can see how both could do it."

Bridger laughed into Leo's shoulder. "Both, maybe?"

"How about I come over after baseball practice? We can do homework together."

"My mom is home tonight."

"That's cool. I like your mom."

"She likes you too. You are officially mom approved."

"Oh, don't say that too loud. You'll ruin my rep."

"Your rep?" Bridger pulled away, eyebrows raised. "Do you have a secret rep I don't know about?"

Leo placed his hands on either side of Bridger's face and squeezed, mushing Bridger's lips together. He smacked a kiss to Bridger's fish face.

"None whatsoever."

Bridger squirmed out of Leo's grip. "Fine. A homework date. With my mother. Sounds awesome." It did sound better than Bridger's original plans to do homework and worry about the mess he'd made at his job.

"Good. I'll see you tonight. Now, I have to get back to class before Mr. Stewart starts to wonder where I went."

Leo took time for another quick embrace, then jogged away, waving at a group of people who called his name.

Bridger went back to his seat to find Lacey staring at him with a wrinkled nose and a frown. She threw down her carrot. "Ugh. I'm totally going to lose prom couple to you. And I can't even be mad about it because you and Leo are too adorable."

Flushing, Bridger went back to his abandoned lunch. He was without worry, just happy down to his toes. His best friend had a date for prom. He had a cute and thoughtful boyfriend. And he was going to graduate in a month.

Everything was perfect.

UNTIL IT WASN'T.

Bridger jogged down the front steps of the school with Astrid at his side chatting away about limos and dresses and corsages and everything else prom. Bridger mostly paid attention, but there was only so much room in his awareness and most of it was focused on the homework he had for the night and on Leo. He had yet to pick a topic for his folklore paper, and his teacher was on his case because he had yet to turn in any research. He didn't have space in his brain for sequins and flowers.

Hood up and hands in his pockets, he turned the corner toward the parking lot and completely missed the warning from Astrid. Suddenly, a microphone was shoved into his face.

"How did the bakery poltergeist know your name?" Summer blindsided him.

Bridger jerked to a stop or he would've eaten the mic. As it was, it smacked his cheek.

"Hey! What the—"

"And does it only speak to you or will it speak to others? Why does it use flour to communicate and why did it pick the bakery? Does it have something to do with Meadow's affinity for horror movies?" Summer assaulted him with rapid-fire questions. She was so close her perfume made him lightheaded, and the scratchy fabric of her suit dress brushed over his skin.

Expression expectant, lips bright red, makeup flawless, she angled the microphone toward him.

Bridger managed an eloquent response. "What?"

"You almost drowned at Lighthouse Beach in front of a dozen witnesses and when you emerged you were covered in bloody scratches. What pulled you under? What gave you those gashes? Did it have claws or teeth or both?"

She waved the mic in his face. Crowding forward, Summer forced Bridger to take unsteady steps back. Astrid grabbed his arm to keep him from falling, but Summer pushed forward, politely aggressive. This was a side of her Bridger hadn't seen in the episodes he'd watched, not even in the first season when she was interested in the topics. This was a step in a new and terrifying direction.

"I don't—"

"Is it true you were at the football practice when the large animal appeared and terrorized your classmates? Did you see it as well? Did you have a hand in calling it to that location?"

Matt aimed the camera at Bridger; the lens was uncomfortably close.

"Ever heard of a zoom?" Astrid shoved the camera aside and yanked on Bridger's arm, spurring him into a walk. He stumbled and attempted to sidle around Summer.

Matt swung the camera around, trained it on Bridger's pale face, and somehow matched his stride despite walking backward. Summer also kept up pace. "Can you talk to other beasts and cryptids? Are you responsible for the events that occurred in the fall of last year?"

Bridger ducked his head. Pulse racing, he broke into a jog. Astrid grabbed his hand and squeezed. She met his plaintive gaze, and with a nod of her head, they ran.

Summer followed as best as she could in her heels, yelling questions at Bridger's back, while Matt dogged their steps, camera trained on their retreat.

"This is Bridger Whitt," Summer said into the camera. "Local supernatural magnet. Is he just a kid caught up in the strangeness that has affected Midden, Michigan, since autumn or is he part of the problem? Viewers, I promise an answer to that question and more when we investigate this town. And if Bridger won't talk to us, maybe his best friend or his boyfriend will be willing to give us the scoop."

Bridger skidded to a stop at the door of Astrid's car. Fear and fury lanced through him. He turned on his heel and, despite being a second away from the safety of Astrid's car, he abandoned it and stalked forward. He pointed a finger in Summer's direction.

"Don't you *dare*. You stay away from them."

She smirked. "Hit a nerve, did I?" She crossed her arms; her manicured nails drummed against her biceps. "I promise to leave them alone if you tell me everything you know."

Swallowing the lump in his throat, Bridger dropped his hand and grasped the Saint Dymphna medal hidden beneath his shirt. "There is nothing to tell."

"Bullshit." She cocked her head. "Did you think I wouldn't put it together? I studied journalism. I can investigate. Come on, Bridger. Spill your secrets."

"Bridger, get in the car!"

Bridger balled his hands into fists. He didn't know what to do or what to say. But Astrid and Leo were off limits, and he wasn't going to allow Summer to screw up Astrid's senior year or Leo's baseball scholarship.

Formulating a response in his head, he bit his lip, but didn't get a chance to come up with a retort. A massive, black owl descended from a nearby tree and landed on the hood of Astrid's car. Squawking, it spread its wings and fluffed its feathers. Its claws scraping along the metal sounded like fingernails on a chalkboard, then it screeched like a fisher cat. Bridger's hair stood on end and he clapped his palms over his ears while Summer scrambled away.

Not one to ever make a graceful exit, Bridger threw himself into the car. Astrid revved the engine. With another cry, the owl took flight to land on a branch of a tree near Matt's van.

Slamming the car into reverse, Astrid sped through the parking lot. When they passed Summer, Bridger clenched his jaw and flicked her off.

"Mature," Astrid said. "But not unwarranted."

It said something about Bridger's life that they were not freaking out about the giant owl that interrupted his conversation with the intrusive reporter. Bridger checked the mirrors, until he was certain they weren't being followed.

"I'm sorry," he said, tapping his foot on the floor. His leg shook. "I'm really sorry."

"For what? For her? Screw her." She took a turn at an ill-advised speed. "I had a cute boy ask me to prom by singing to me. Singing! And he gave me flowers! And enlisted my friends! That is way more important than a nosy, typecast, investigative-reporter wannabe."

Bridger sank into the seat. "You are absolutely right."

Astrid flicked her gaze to Bridger. "What?"

"Your awesome promposal is what we should be focusing on. And how we're doing prom. We're obviously going to dinner together and riding in the same limo. Should we color-coordinate?"

Astrid's smile was blinding. "Definitely. Would Leo be into it?"

"Oh, yeah. Haven't you noticed his wardrobe? He's loves fashion. His jeans cost more than my entire outfit including shoes."

Astrid's laugh was giddy and breathless, a release of adrenaline. Bridger echoed it, though he kept his arms wrapped around his middle because his nerves were raw and on edge.

"This weekend, you and me, dress shopping and tux fitting. And fun. We're going to have fun, damn it." She gripped the steering wheel. "We'll invite Leo and Luke for lunch and plan dinner and limo rides and all that. It'll be awesome." She glanced at Bridger. "It will be awesome."

Sure. Awesome. Maybe if she said it enough times it would come true.

"I won't let any of this ruin your prom," Bridger said, seriously. "I promise."

Astrid reached across the gear shift and took his hand. "I know. And I won't let any of this ruin the rest of your senior year."

Bridger's mouth went dry. He was unsure that Astrid had the power to change the trajectory of this semester, but he appreciated the sentiment.

CHAPTER 8

ASTRID DROPPED BRIDGER OFF A few houses down from Pavel's, not that it would help. Anyone who saw Pavel's house immediately knew it was used for eerie purposes. It towered over the other houses on the street and was a masterpiece of various architectural styles pieced together in a frankly odd conglomeration. When Bridger had first seen it several months ago, he'd considered peacing out before even trying to find the blue door. Luckily, he'd mustered a semblance of resolve and climbed a lattice and a drainpipe to get inside. It was simultaneously the bravest and dumbest thing he'd done. His life has ratcheted up since then. And his repertoire of brave and questionable actions has expanded more than he could have imagined.

But he'd met a sasquatch so, it all came out in the wash.

The house had a magic security system. Once someone was admitted over the threshold and then exited through the front door, they could come and go as they pleased. Bridger had entered through the blue door, strategically placed at the highest point on the back of the house. This was the rule. Only if they were a myth or magic themselves could they omit the daring feats of acrobatics. The front door's magic could detect their supernatural aura and would open for them, allowing them access to Pavel and the safety of his magic and of the building. That was how Leo had bounded through the door like an over-eager puppy much to Bridger's and Pavel's surprise.

As Bridger approached, the front door opened, and he walked across the threshold. The familiar tingle of the house's magic buzzed over his skin. His anxiety about being followed sloughed off. There was no way Summer and Matt could shadow him here. It was a haven, and he breathed unhindered for the first time since he'd heard his name on the EVP recorder.

"Hey, Mindy." Bridger waved as he headed up the stairs to the second floor. She didn't respond, and he didn't have the wherewithal to snipe with her. He also didn't count the dwindling number of bobbleheads, though another of the standouts, a dolphin with a sign that read "thanks for all the fish," was missing.

He climbed the stairs at the speed of a sloth. The adrenaline that had kept him buoyed receded with each step, so that all that remained was a headache pounding in his temples and a body that felt like a collection of haphazardly assembled bone and muscle. He oozed into Pavel's study and collapsed into his favorite leather chair.

Pavel popped his head around the trim of the kitchen doorway. "Bridger? Are you all right?"

"No," he answered, petulant. "Far from it."

"I'll make tea."

Tea was Pavel's standard response to all emergencies. Sick? Have some tea. Existential crisis? How about tea. Drowned by mermaids? Tea with honey.

Bridger squeezed his eyes shut and didn't open them again until minutes later when he heard the rattle of a cup on a saucer.

"What's happened?"

Bridger took a sip of his scalding tea. "Where are the pixies?"

"Out. What's wrong, Bridger? Your assigned toaster rang yesterday, then stopped abruptly. It rang again today, and before I could run for the portal, it ceased again."

"You've assigned a toaster to me?"

"Of course. I spelled it after the mess in the fall. You're my assistant. I want to ensure your safety. That's one of the reasons I gave Midnight Marvel to you."

"She's great, by the way. She sleeps with me every night. Honestly, the best kitten."

"She's not merely a kitten."

"I know."

Pavel rubbed his chin. "Do you?"

"Well, I mean, you told me she's not really a kitten. Is there something I'm missing?"

"Anyway, what's happened?" Pavel deflected. Bridger was familiar with the move. But he didn't press him on it then, because, well, there were bigger issues.

He took a breath, opened his mouth, and it all spilled out, punctuated with flails of his arms and a few tears. He told Pavel *everything*: his dad showing up for his birthday, Ginny threatening to push someone in the oven, Summer hearing his name on the EVP, Summer showing up at his school, the dog, the owl, graduation, Leo, Astrid, his guilt about Luke and his scars, and his inability to pick a topic for his mythology paper. He spoke in a torrent of words, a gush of anxiety and fear and, funnily enough, elation that Astrid was asked to prom, and that Leo was still his boyfriend despite how needy and fragile Bridger felt.

Pavel took it all in, sipping his tea, and didn't interrupt but allowed Bridger to fill the space with his insecurities and worries and stress and small joys. When Bridger, chest heaving, face wet with tears, ran out of words and collapsed in the chair, Pavel put his teacup on the table between them.

"What would you like from me, Bridger? How can I help you?"

Reason seventy-five why Pavel was the best: he didn't offer advice; he didn't have the need to hear himself talk. He asked first, and Bridger appreciated Pavel's patience and understanding. Maybe it came from living for over a century or maybe it was Pavel's quiet nature. Whichever, Bridger could've hugged him.

He scrubbed the sleeve of his hoodie over his face. "I don't know."

"We'll start small. Talk to me about this paper you're avoiding."

Bridger pulled his feet into the chair, his knees bent, his arms wrapped around his shins. "It should be easy, but I guess I'm putting it off because it's one more step toward graduation. If I don't do it, then I fail and don't graduate, and I guess that doesn't sound so bad right now. Also, I don't want to accidentally put in information that I shouldn't, if you get my drift. I've already screwed up enough in that arena."

"I understand. And you need the paper to graduate?"

"Yes."

"Then it warrants effort, Bridger. Sometimes, as adults, we have to decide if a task is worth our full effort or if it's something we need to complete but doesn't have to be our best. This paper is good practice at making those decisions. Also, I have books you can borrow. You know this. You organized the library last year."

Bridger shifted, and the leather creaked. "I mean, I just have to get it done. I have a great grade in the class right now, and one slightly not-awesome paper isn't going to kill me." Pavel nodded. "As for your books, I have to cite my sources."

Pavel tented his fingers. "Ah, well, yes. Unfortunately, you cannot use the intermediary parchments or resources, but I'm sure we can find something. Does that help?"

Bridger offered a feeble smile. "Yeah. It does."

"Okay, which next?" Pavel rubbed his hands together.

"I guess the next easiest would be prom."

Nodding, Pavel clutched his knees and leaned forward. "I have no idea what that is, but I'm sure you'll tell me, and then we'll talk through a solution."

Bridger laughed. Of course, Pavel didn't know what prom was. He probably didn't have it in the tiny Eastern European village he grew up in and he was notorious for being decades behind on popular culture.

"It's an important school dance. An adolescent rite of passage."

"Ah, well, um—"

The slam of the front door made Bridger jump. Pavel paused and frowned.

"Pasha!" Elena yelled, stomping up the stairs. "You better be here! And you better not try and hide!"

Pavel's face drained of what little color it had, and his gaze darted around the room as if he contemplated finding a hiding space. But it was too late. Elena, a vision in tight jeans, heeled boots, and a wave of luxurious brown hair, stormed into the room.

Pavel shot to his feet. "Elena. How wonderful to see you."

"Cut the crap. I am not pleased. Not at all." Hands on her hips, eyes flashing amber, she stomped her foot. "Remind me again why I had to waste an entire day driving to Wexford to speak to that *animal*. You couldn't send Nia or Bran?"

Clearing his throat, Pavel fidgeted with the buttons on his cuffs. "You know why."

Elena glared as she prowled Pavel's sitting room. She had several gashes in her shirt and bits of grass in her hair, and her jeans were ripped at the knees. Her expression was set in a hard frown, and every line of her body screamed "irritated predator." Bridger wasn't on her shit list currently, but that didn't stop him from wanting to fight, flee, or freeze. As it was, he gripped the chair arms and ducked behind his knees, trying to make himself as small as possible.

"Larry is a *dick*!" she yelled, picking the blades of grass from her hair. "I have a date with Christine tonight, and he ruined my favorite shirt!"

The corner of Pavel's mouth ticked up. "I thought you were on good terms."

"He's unpredictable. He's an alpha male asshole." She wiggled her fingers into the holes of her blouse, a spaghetti-strap red number that showed off her collarbone and shoulders, and Bridger should not be thinking about Elena's shoulders. "And he owes me new clothes."

Bridger furrowed his brow and, despite every instinct telling him otherwise, he asked a question. "Who is Larry?"

Elena whirled on him. She pointed a clawed finger at him, and he gulped. "The Michigan Dogman. And I went to talk to him about laying low because of the TV show that came here because of your boyfriend!"

"Hey! That's not my fault. Okay, maybe indirectly it's my fault, but I am not personally responsible for the dirt smudges on your face."

She fumed. "I have dirt on my face?" She reached into her pocket and yanked out her compact mirror. She flipped it open. "Why didn't you tell me I had *dirt* on my *face*, Pavel?"

"I didn't notice."

If glares melted things, Pavel was a bubbling puddle. Elena rummaged in her purse until she found a makeup wipe and viciously scrubbed at the mark on her jawline. "I have had it with Larry! I swear, the next time he pulls his scare-the-tourists shit, I am not going to bail his fuzzy ass out. I'm done!"

Bridger shook his head. "I'm so confused."

"Larry is the Michigan Dogman. But he's not a werewolf, like Elena. He can't..." Pavel waved his hand.

"Shift," Elena supplied. "He's literally half-dog and half-man. He's not quite a werewolf but not quite a beast. He's on the wrong side of feral by a smidge. And he has a shit sense of humor."

"And he's one of the most documented among the active Michigan myths. There's no doubt that Summer will travel the short distance to Wexford County to film the area."

"And what? You got into a fight? He refused to go into hiding?" Bridger rested his chin on his knees.

Elena made a frustrated noise that turned into a growl. "Where is Nia? I need to borrow concealer."

Bridger grimaced. "I wouldn't. Do you know what's in those cosmetics?" Elena whirled, eyes flashing amber, and Bridger threw up his hands and pressed back into the cushions. "Never mind. Forget I said anything."

Running a hand through her hair, Elena calmed. "Sorry, Bridger. You didn't deserve that. Usually you do, but not this time. I'm frustrated. Larry is… Larry concerns me. I might have played around on Bray Road when I was younger and had a good laugh chasing cars, but I never hurt anyone. Larry doesn't have that boundary. He's dangerous."

Brow furrowed, Pavel tapped his lips. "I shouldn't have sent you."

Elena huffed. "And what? You'd go yourself? Or send junior here?" She gestured to Bridger, who was still curled up in the leather chair. "He'd have eaten both of you alive."

"I have magic."

"He has abs of steel."

"I'm sorry, Elena," Pavel said, deflating. He sank into the other chair. "I'm sorry." He pinched the bridge of his nose.

"Hey, Pasha. It's fine. I'm blowing off steam. Yeah, we fought, and I kicked his ass. He turned tail and ran into the cornfield, so you know, no harm done." She rested her hand on his head, smoothing his chaotic hair.

"Between Larry and Summer Lore assaulting Bridger, I didn't think things would escalate as quickly as they have."

Elena shoulders tensed, and her eyes narrowed. "Summer Lore did what?" Her voice went deep, and a shiver shot up Bridger's spine. "She assaulted you?"

"Uh." And there was that hyperarousal again, in more ways than one. "She, uh, came to my school and shoved a microphone in my face. It wasn't, it wasn't that bad." *Great.* Way to sound one hundred percent unconvincing.

Fur rippled over Elena's bare arms, and her expression went flat. "I'll kill her."

"No!" Pavel shouted at the same time Bridger said, "Seriously?"

"What?" Elena put her hands on her hips. "He's an annoying little shit of a human but he's a good human and a member of our family. If she so much as puts a hand on him, I swear to the moon—"

Pavel stood. "Elena, don't worry. I'm going to handle it."

"What are you going to do? Blush and stammer? We all know about the crush, Pasha."

Pavel was on the verge of anger. Two bright spots of color glowed on his cheeks. His eyes glinted in the low-slung sunlight seeping through the window. His visage wavered; the young, congenial Pavel melted into someone older, harder, world-weary, but powerful all the same.

"Don't question my loyalty to my duty and my family again, Elena." His accent was harsh and odd syllables were stressed, which made him sound alien.

Elena bit her lip and rocked back. "Sorry, Pasha. That was out of line. You'll take care of it." Effectively cowed, she pushed her hair behind her ear and dropped her gaze. "Put the magic away. You'll scare the kid."

Ah, so Elena was not a fan of magic angry Pavel either. Good to know.

Pavel rolled his shoulders, and the sizzle of tension in the air dissipated. He sighed. "I'll talk with Nia and Bran and see what we can come up with to lead Summer in a different direction. Until then, stay out of her way, Bridger. And Elena," he said, smiling softly, "I'm glad things are going well with Christine."

"She has a sister and a brother. I'd be willing to hook you up with either one."

Pavel shook his head. "Not right now. I have bigger problems. Such as helping Bridger with a paper topic and prom."

Elena smiled, feral and beautiful, and Bridger's heart lurched. *Traitor.* "Ah, high school. Such woes," she said.

"Can it, Scooby."

"You could write your paper on Elena. She *is* the Beast of Bray Road."

Bridger shook his head while Elena gave Pavel a betrayed look with hand resting delicately at her throat.

"I am *not* a research topic, Pasha. My complexity is thesis-level work, to be sure."

"Fine. I'm sure Elena can tell you all about Larry. Does that work?"

Bridger blinked. The Michigan Dogman. Pavel did say he was one of the more well-documented local cryptids. There would be plenty of sources. And Elena had firsthand experience. It could work, if Elena would agree. They weren't the best of friends, though Elena did say she considered him family. Time to weaponize the puppy eyes.

"Oh, don't do the wobbly lip, big-eyed thing," Elena said, covering her face with her hands. "Put those away. I'll do it. Just stop. You're not cute."

Bridger pumped his fist. "Yes!"

"I have an hour until I pick up Christine. I'll drive you home, and you can pick my brain on the way. Deal?"

"Yes. That's perfect."

Elena kissed Pavel on the cheek before she whisked out of the room. Bridger scrambled to follow, grabbing his backpack and jumping from the comfort of the chair.

"Thanks, Pavel."

"You're welcome, though we didn't address everything on your list."

"It's okay. Like you said, one crisis at a time."

Pavel's expression went soft and fond. He patted Bridger hard on the back as he left. "Just remember, I'm on your side. And together we'll handle whatever is thrown at us."

His throat tight with gratitude, Bridger gave Pavel a sharp nod, then followed Elena down the stairs.

ELENA DROVE A SPEEDY RED car and barely paid attention to traffic laws. Her reflexes were incredibly fast, so he wasn't too worried about wrecking, and he bet she could get out of any ticket by either batting her eyes or growling. As she whipped around turns, she told Bridger all about Larry, and he scribbled down notes and focused on his notebook and not the fact that they ran yet another stop sign.

"Piece of advice," Elena said, "make sure to write in half-truths."

"Half-truths?" Bridger asked. "Like bullshit it?"

"Sort of," Elena said with a shrug. "Like I know that Larry hates lights in his eyes because it fucks with his perception. First thought, that would be a great way to scare off the Michigan Dogman if you're ever in his presence, right? Except, it just makes him blind with rage. Really pisses him off. So shining headlights or a flashlight on him is a bad move."

"Huh. Good to know."

"And loud noises. Most dogs hate loud noises. Thunder and fireworks. But again, just pisses Larry off. Don't honk your horn unless you want your tires slashed and your engine ripped out."

Bridger gulped then wrote it down.

"Oh, and Larry positively hates Thursdays. Don't ask me why; I have no idea. It's just a thing of his. It's, like, the best day to catch him out and about because he has to bleed off the restless energy, but also the worst, because he's an irritable fuckwit."

"Well, some people can't get the hang of Thursdays."

She shot him a glare. "Don't make excuses for him. He ripped my shirt, and I'm angry."

Bridger raised his hands in surrender. "By the way, this information is awesome. Thanks so much."

"You're welcome. Remember, Larry is not discreet. His sightings are all online. Most folklorists liken him to a werewolf, but he's not. He's a dick."

Bridger snickered. "So you said. Um, so half-truth. He's a werewolf cousin but more like the black dog lore."

Elena tapped her nose. "Now you got it."

"Hey, so, what should I do if I ever meet Larry?"

"Hmmm. Well, do what Pavel says. But run."

"I'm not going to outrun the Dogman."

"You might." She shrugged. "He's bipedal, so at least you'd have a chance. You might be able to talk to him, but if there's thunder and he's been blinded and it's Thursday, just run and pray to whatever deity you hold dear that Pavel is nearby." She slammed on her brakes in front of Bridger's house, and his seatbelt snapped tight across his chest. "Now, skedaddle, human. I don't have time for you."

Bridger rolled his eyes. He opened the door. "You know, I get why you and Pavel are best friends. And I'm glad you're there for him."

Her expression softened infinitesimally. "He's a mess, but I love him. You're a mess. Now get out! Before your teen-boy hormones stink up my car." She jerked her chin toward Leo's house, then sniffed and made a face. "It's impossible to get out of the upholstery."

"Harder than wet dog?"

She growled, and Bridger scrambled out, only getting tangled in the seatbelt for a second. He congratulated himself for not tripping and landing on the curb.

"Later, Rin Tin Tin."

"Hey, Bridge," she said, rolling down her window and easing from the curb. "Find new jokes." She left in a squeal of tires and a plume of smoke.

Bridger cracked a smile, then crossed his tiny lawn to the door. He dug into his bag for his keys and let himself inside, kicking off his shoes as he went.

"Mom?"

"In the living room."

Bridger entered the room and stood behind the couch where his mom was stretched out, with her head pillowed on the sofa arm and an ancient, crocheted blanket draped over her legs.

"Leo is coming over to do homework in a few minutes."

She yawned. "Okay. I'd prefer you two work in the kitchen. If you go to your room, the door stays open."

"Yes, Mom." He shuffled his feet. "Are you okay?"

"Yeah, just tired. Do you think you can handle making your own dinner? I have become one with the couch and am afraid it will take a complicated surgery to separate us."

Bridger chuckled. "Yeah. I'm good. I'll figure something out." In the kitchen, Bridger dropped his bag by the chair, then popped frozen waffles into the toaster. He dug out his field guide to myths and dropped it on the table with his notebook so he could draft an outline for the paper. He ate his waffles while compiling Internet sources on his phone.

Thirty minutes later, a knock on the door interrupted Bridger's progress on his paper. His mom was asleep on the couch, so, holding his breath, he crept past and peeked through the window. He hoped it wasn't Summer. He wouldn't put it past her to find his address.

It wasn't, thank whatever deity was listening, and he swung open the door. Leo stood on the front steps, holding a single rose. He blushed and ducked his head; his eyelashes swept across his cheeks. "Hey," he said, voice low and rough.

"Hey." Bridger leaned against the door frame, trying to act cool, but failing. His palms slicked with sweat, and his pulse thundered, because Leo looked flushed and adorable. "What's going on?"

Leo cleared his throat and thrust the flower at Bridger. "I know it's not an epic promposal. You know I can't sing. And I know you are not a fan of attention. But I wanted to do something at least a little special." He shuffled his feet on the doormat. "Will you go to prom with me?"

Taking the rose, Bridger was going to combust from affection. "Yes. Yes of course, you romantic nerd." Leo wilted at Bridger's answer until he was slumped in the doorway. "What? Did you think I was going to say no?"

Leo shrugged. "No? Maybe? I don't know. You're not the only one who gets nervous."

"Come here," Bridger grabbed a handful of Leo's shirt and tugged him close. "You have no reason to be nervous. I'm ready for prom. I'm ready for you to be prom king and for me to be the guy that gets to dance with the prom king and kiss the prom king and probably spill food on the prom king's shirt. I'm totally here for matching tuxes and riding in a limo and holding hands while we eat dinner. We'll dance and drink punch and make out and take pictures with Astrid and Luke. It'll be awesome."

"Now who's the romantic," Leo knocked his nose against Bridger's. "That was probably the sweetest thing you've said to me yet."

"Really? I suck."

Leo laughed and closed the scant distance between them. They kissed on Bridger's front porch, in sight of the whole neighborhood, in the fading spring sunlight, with Bridger clutching a rose in one hand and the other cupping the back of Leo's neck. He wouldn't have dreamed of kissing his boyfriend in public six months ago. How far he'd come.

Leo, always the bastion of self-control between the two of them, was the first to break away. He pressed a chaste kiss to Bridger's cheek, then stepped around him to enter the house. "I've got a ton of homework."

Bridger let the back of his head thump on the doorframe. He took a steadying breath. "Yeah, me too."

"Also, was that Elena earlier?" Leo asked, shoulder knocking into Bridger's as he spread his books on the kitchen table. "Not that I was watching from our window or anything." He tugged out a copy of the school paper and tossed it on the pile. Their picture smiled up at Bridger, and his cheeks flushed.

"Yeah. She helped me with my mythology paper."

"That was uncharacteristically kind of her."

"Right? I'd say she's warming up to me, but it was mostly Pavel's doing. Though she did threaten to kill someone for me, so step in right direction?"

"Your life is weird."

"Tell me about it."

They settled in and worked, Bridger's foot snug against Leo's under the table. Leo's kiss lingered on Bridger's lips. Bridger shot Leo a besotted smile and touched the skin-warmed medal under his shirt. The knot of anxiety in his gut unraveled with every scratch of Leo's pencil on his paper. This tumultuous week of highs and lows at least ended on an upswing.

.

CHAPTER 9

Bridger had seen his share of teen movies. If asked, he'd blame Astrid and her love of romcoms, but, if pressed, like when Astrid pinned his arm behind his back and made him admit it, he actually liked romantic comedies. There was just something about a happily-ever-after that got to him. He'd much rather watch one than, say, a horror film. His life was a horror movie, and he didn't need to be reminded of all the ways in which it could go wrong—like death, and maiming, or accidentally ending up as the killer Chuck Wendig and Sam Sykes-style.

Anyway, he knew that if his life was a teen romantic comedy, then the last few hours would be splashed on screen in an epic music montage and would take, maybe, ninety seconds. Unfortunately, that was not how real life worked, and Bridger spent his Saturday morning being dragged from one store to the next helping Astrid try on prom dresses.

If it was hell for him, he could only imagine what Astrid felt. Astrid was not the cookie-cutter girl on teen magazines. She had muscles and mass and was tall. Finding a dress was certainly close to violating the Geneva Convention on torture, and Bridger hated every minute of it for her. He only had to look through the racks and give his opinion and then sit in a plush chair while she struggled in the dressing room. Well, not true, he snuck in a few times and helped with buttons and clasps and ran back and forth to the racks to exchange sizes.

After several stores, a few tears, and one broken zipper, which Bridger pinky-swore never to talk about again, Astrid emerged from the dressing room, and Bridger jumped to his feet.

"That's it!" He threw up his hands. "Oh, my God, that's it, Astrid! It's perfect."

The dress was blue, floor length, and it sparkled. Astrid beamed as she twirled. "You think?"

"Yes!"

"Listen to your boyfriend, sweetie," an older woman looking through the rack with her daughter said. "He's right."

"He's not my boyfriend," Astrid said, looking in the mirror and smoothing her hands down the sides of the dress. "He's my best friend."

"Damn right," Bridger said, puffed up and warm. "BFFs. Cap and Bucky, right here."

"'Til the end of the line."

They high-fived, and Bridger's hand stung because Astrid was way stronger than him. Bridger took out his phone and snapped pictures as Astrid posed and made faces. They took a selfie together and sent it to Leo who responded with a string of heart emojis.

"Okay. I'm going to get out of this, and it'll be tux time!"

Tux time wasn't as awful as dress shopping, and Astrid totally humored him despite the number of times he pretended to be James Bond. His British accent needed work if the store employee's snort of laughter was any indication.

They met Leo and Luke for lunch at the restaurant attached to the mall and talked about plans and the limo and dinner. Bridger held Leo's hand under the table and they playfully teased each other the entire time.

Sitting with his friends, talking about school drama, and baseball, and prom, and graduation was nice. It was relaxing to be a normal teenager, to not worry about myth emergencies or his dad or what his future was supposed to look like.

"Hey, so, Astrid. Do you want to go to a movie?" Luke blushed and he took a sip of his pop to hide the shaking of his hands.

Leo kicked Bridger under the table. Bridger elbowed him back, and they watched the scene unfold.

"Huh?" Astrid swiped a fry through ketchup. "Oh. Yeah. Sure. Today?"

"Yeah. There's a showing of a that new Anne Hathaway movie in a few minutes."

"Anne Hathaway?" Astrid said, looking up, meeting Luke's nervous gaze. "I love Anne Hathaway."

"I know." His face was red. "I asked your teammates."

"You didn't ask Bridge?"

"Nah," Luke said, grin wry. "He's kind of a mess."

Bridger spat water on the table. "Hey!"

"No lie," Leo said, laughing. He wrapped his arm around Bridger's shoulders. "But I wouldn't have him any other way."

"I take offense to all of this, by the way."

Astrid ignored him. "But, yeah, I'd love to go to a movie, Luke."

"Awesome."

"Do you guys want to go?" Astrid asked. "Leo, has Bridger divulged his love of the romcom to you yet?"

Bridger buried his face in crossed arms. Leo rubbed his back.

"Yes. He has. I know all about his movie preferences. And while I don't begrudge anyone their joy or their choices in life, I cannot in good conscience join you for an Anne Hathaway movie."

"Bridge, your boyfriend has besmirched the Princess of Genovia. How dare he."

Bridger lifted his head so his chin dug into his forearm. "I know. He's not perfect. But I like him anyway."

Luke shifted in his seat. "Wait, you like Anne Hathaway?"

"Who doesn't? I mean, other than my dear, sweet, boyfriend. She's gorgeous and funny."

"Uh." Luke tapped the table. "I thought… I mean…" His gaze darted between Bridger and Leo, and he shrugged.

Oh. *Oh.*

"Oh, um," Bridger picked at a crumb on the tablecloth. "I like guys, of course. But I still like girls too. And I like folks who might not fit in a binary." He cleared his throat. He hadn't really said this to anyone other than Astrid, Leo, Pavel, and his mom. But practice makes things less awkward. Right? "I'm an all-of-the-above kind of person."

"Oh," Luke said. "That makes so much sense now."

Bridger's eyebrows shot up. "Excuse me?"

"Well, you dated Sally Goforth last year, and for a long time everyone thought you and Astrid were dating."

"We never dated," Astrid interrupted quickly. "Never. We kissed once. It was a bad idea."

"Extremely bad," Bridger agreed. "Epic fail."

Luke wasn't reassured, if his continued table drumming was an indication. "Okay. Anyway, I was kind of confused when you and

Leo got together. Zeke wasn't. But he never explained it to me, and I was embarrassed to ask. I hope I didn't commit a horrible social faux pas right now by asking."

"No, you're cool. We're, uh, we're friends. I just, uh, wouldn't ask strangers or anything."

Luke's shoulders fell from their hunch. "Cool. Got it." He looked to Astrid. "So, movie?"

They paid their bill; Bridger splurged with his leftover birthday money to buy Leo's. The group parted ways at the exit. Astrid's dress was in a bag over her shoulder, another bag held her prom shoes. She winked at Bridger.

"I'll text you later."

"Enjoy your Anne Hathaway," Bridger called as they walked away.

Leo looped his arm through Bridger's "Come on, Juliet. I'll drive you home." He tucked his hand in Bridger's pocket. "So Astrid can go on her date."

"Oh, God, pick another nickname, please."

Leo snorted, and, bless him, even that was attractive.

Wrapped up in each other, oblivious to everyone but them, they meandered through the mall to the exit near where Leo had parked his car. Once outside, they turned a corner at the back of the building, because Leo had a thing about where he parked his mother's car. She'd never let him drive again if he brought it home scratched, and so, he always found the most obscure and vacant spots. It didn't do much for Bridger's constant dread because low-lit, empty parking lots were not the safest, but at least they were in broad daylight on a Saturday afternoon.

"I'm so tired of these God-forsaken Podunk towns!"

The screech brought Bridger out of his Leo-induced daze. He knew that voice. He knew it well. He stopped and threw out his arm to halt Leo.

"You can't get a decent meal or a decent hotel. And don't get me started on this cameraman they sent with me. It's his first season, and he has no eye for good shots. It's amateur hour. Oh, and these idiots they sent to me to interview. High school students. I have to coach them through the whole conversation."

Bridger craned his neck around the corner of the building. By the dumpsters stood Summer, cell phone to her ear, vape pen in her hand. He ducked back before she could see him.

"It's Summer," he said to Leo in a low voice. "She's on the phone."

Leo's brown eyes were wide. He jerked his thumb over his shoulder to indicate they should go around the other way to his car. But Bridger was curious. Curiosity killed the cat, but Bridger wasn't a cat. And even the cat he owned wasn't quite a cat. He should be in the clear.

He peeked around the corner again and saw Summer pacing; a wreath of vapor curled from between her fingers.

"Is there any word on that pilot?" She paused. "What do you mean they went with someone else? Oh, oh, I'm too old. They wanted younger. Of course." Cursing, she paced and kicked a small trashcan, denting it with the point of her expensive shoe. "There has to be something else then. I can't continue to do this. I can't continue to live traveling from town to town interviewing hicks and hoping for a monster to jump out and chase me to up the ratings."

Yeah, Bridger agreed. He could live without that too.

She made a disgusted noise at the back of her throat. "Well, find something! You're my agent, aren't you?" She tugged on a strand of her hair. "Yeah, well, I don't care if you can't make something appear. I make stories out of nothing every week. You can at least find me a script to read."

She pushed her hand through her hair. "This is all your fault, you know. Take the job, you said. You won't be typecast. It's a good jumpstart. Well, here I am ten seasons later doing the same damn thing." She paused and huffed. "No, no, at least it is somewhat interesting. There's this kid here that... I don't know... He's peculiar. Obviously knows more than what he's letting on. I just have to find a way to get him to crack."

Scowling, Bridger took a step to confront her, because *uncool*. Leo yanked him back and shook his head. Bridger allowed Leo to drag him away, but Bridger didn't put up much of a fight. They circled around the whole mall to Leo's car, and Bridger brooded the entire drive home.

"You're not going to do anything impulsive are you?" Leo asked, forehead wrinkled, lips turned down at the corners.

"Of course not. I'm staying out of it. I promised Pavel."

"Okay. Good." He flashed Bridger a smile. "Because I like you a lot and I want you to be safe."

"I like you too. A lot." He squeezed Leo's hand. "And I will be safe as possible. Cross my heart."

Bridger had made a resolution to cut down on lying, especially to the people most important to him. He'd done a great job since the fall and he really wasn't trying to lie, but the untruth of his statement churned in his stomach, right alongside the burger he'd had for lunch and the feeling that no matter how he'd try to stay away from this mess, it was inevitable that he'd be sucked in anyway.

*   *   *

THE REST OF BRIDGER'S WEEKEND was spent writing his paper and teasing Astrid about her date with Luke. Between texts, he plugged away researching the sightings of the Dogman and how it related to local folklore and folkloric themes in general. He followed Elena's advice and kept some facts purposefully vague. He had a solid outline by Sunday night, with a partial draft. It wasn't due until the last week of classes, but since prom was next weekend, he wanted to have a good start.

With Summer's words echoing in his head and her general disregard for boundaries, Bridger took extra precautions. After school on Monday, Astrid drove her car to the front of the school while Bridger hid in the locker room. It wasn't his best moment, to be sure, but he wasn't about to risk running into Summer, not after his last meeting with Pavel, not when she threatened both Astrid and Leo, not with Elena pissed off and with her claws out, not with Pavel's magic crackling at his fingertips until the air was thick with it. *No.* Bridger was not about to be responsible for another myth incident. So he hid and waited for Astrid to text him the all clear.

The text came quickly, but it wasn't from Astrid. It was his dad.

Dinner, tomorrow?

Ugh. In the chaos of *everything*, Bridger had shoved the fact that his dad was around to the back of his mind. The dad situation was like having a pebble in his shoe while facing down a rampaging wildebeest—annoying, but not what needed his attention. He'd deal with the pebble after climbing a tree, or whatever was the best way to avoid being trampled by a wildebeest. Bridger had missed a Jeopardy question about wildebeest recently, and now, after doing a bit of research—reading Wikipedia articles—his brain was stuck in a loop of wildebeest hell. He was aware that researching wildebeest was a waste of time, because when would he ever need knowledge of wildebeest? Also, how many times could he think the word wildebeest before it lost meaning? Wildebeest.

He swiped the text away. Another followed. This one from Astrid.

All clear. Out front.

Head down, hood up, hands in pockets, Bridger walked briskly down the front steps of the school and got into Astrid's car.

"You okay?" she asked, pulling away.

"Great," he muttered.

She slapped his knee. "Cheer up, emu. I'm taking you to visit with your favorite lady."

Relaxing into the seat, he fiddled with the dials of Astrid's radio. "True."

It was a Grandma Alice day. Bridger loved Grandma Alice.

The first time they'd met, she'd scared Bridger down to his marrow. She'd seen through him in a way no one had and she'd yanked out his faults, examined them, and called him on each one. It had been terrifying. It didn't help that she was also the oldest person Bridger had ever seen. She had paper-thin skin, stringy white hair, and wrinkles so deep they could hide secrets and raisins. She slid down to the precipice of the uncanny valley, danced along the edge, and tipped her toe in just for giggles.

Despite the creepy appearance and her frightening perceptive abilities, she was the nicest apothecary Bridger had ever met. Well, okay, she was the only apothecary he'd ever met, but that didn't change the fact that Grandma Alice was a kind human being, if she was human. Bridger wasn't sure. He was less sure after seeing her chasing Summer Lore through the woods.

Since their first meeting, Grandma Alice had doted on Bridger. She smiled at him. She made him cookies. She knitted him mittens out of something that wasn't yarn but was incredibly warm and soft. Again, Bridger had learned not to ask questions.

Astrid screeched into the tiny parking lot. "Text me when you're done, and I'll swing back around and pick you up."

"You sure you don't want to come in?"

"Ha!" Astrid tapped her steering wheel. "No thanks. She's my hard limit. You live it up with the lizard eyes and toad jelly. I'll be at the comic book store."

"You're missing out, but if she gives me cookies, I'll save you one."

"Nope. Who knows what she puts in those? There could be, like, cockroach jelly."

"You're stuck on jelly today."

Astrid shoved his arm. "Get out. I'll see you in a bit."

He shot her a cocky grin and hopped out of her car. Bridger's spirits were high when he entered the shop. He was grateful that his duties for Pavel meant a visit to Grandma Alice every other week. Usually it was to obtain ingredients for Nia and Bran for their potions and whatnot, and occasionally things that Pavel needed for intermediary purposes. However, all orders had to be called in by Pavel, because Grandma Alice despised the pixies. She adored

Pavel, however, and found him handsome and charming. If there was one thing Bridger had learned in the months since he'd been Pavel's assistant—other than that being polite in the myth world was of paramount importance to not being disemboweled—was that weirdness clumped together. Strange liked stranger and so on and so forth. He wondered what that said about him.

"Grandma Alice," Bridger called as he stepped inside the small shop. Sandwiched between two industrial buildings, the apothecary was so old, seemingly the town had sprung up around it. The inside was entirely made of wood, and the floor and the counter were smooth from wear. The natural fibers had absorbed the pungent smell of herbs and dried plants and a myriad of other things Grandma Alice sold, so the store had a scent all its own, comparable to nothing Bridger had experienced, except maybe the dried flowers pressed into old books he'd found in Pavel's library.

Shuffling into view, Grandma Alice's bent form appeared behind the counter. She carried a crate filled to the brim with glass bottles that Bridger dared not look at too closely.

"Hello, dear," she said, her voice a scrape. "How are you today?" If Pavel was old, Grandma Alice was ancient. She was primordial in appearance: her skin spotted with age, her violet eyes clouded with memories and time, her waist-length white hair stringy and thin. But she was power. Magic bled off her in waves and tingled over Bridger's skin in a terrifying mix of light and shadow that brought him peace and petrified him in equal measure.

"I'm good."

Her thin lips lifted into a grin. "Liar."

"Always," he said. "How are you doing today, Grandma Alice?"

"Old."

"You? Never."

She laughed, a grating painful sound. "Liar," she said again.

With strength that belied her twig-like arms, she hefted the crate onto the counter, then mounted her step stool.

"Now, you tell those nasty little pixies that I need at least a month to scrounge up more black blister beetles. I don't know what they are using them for and I don't care. But they better ration this jar."

Bridger shivered. "Yes, Grandma Alice. I'll let them know."

"And they need to return the empty jars, or I'll start sending them in iron pots."

"Forest pixies," Bridger said, shaking his head. "Iron will hurt them. I'll get them to return the empties next time."

"You've been studying. Good boy." She squinted, violet eyes sharp and assessing. She took his hand; her rough calluses scuffed over his skin. "Your aura is sour. What's the matter?"

Bridger shrugged. "I'm having a couple of bad days. Nothing to worry about."

She hmphed. "When will you learn you can't lie to me." She patted his hand. "I have a tea that will help and a honey I harvested when I went on vacation last year. You'll take both."

Bridger's eyebrows went into his hairline. "You went on vacation?"

She bustled around the counter and shuffled down the rows of shelves while Bridger followed, careful not to tread on the trail of her red dress. "Of course. I can't work all the time."

"No, I guess not."

She grabbed a jar and held it close to her face. Nodding, she plunked it into his hand and scanned the shelf once more. She snatched a bag and pushed it into his chest.

"Have Intermediary Chudinov brew the tea and add the honey. Don't do it yourself. I want you to come back, not scorch the earth. Understand?"

Bridger gulped. "Yes, Grandma Alice."

"Good boy. Smart boy. Loved boy."

She stepped around him and went back to her step stool behind the counter.

"Loved boy?"

She sniffed. "Of course. Seeped into your marrow."

"Grandma Alice, are you looking deeper than you should?" Bridger shook his head, remembering how she'd peered into his being, weighed his heart, measured his character, saw his beginning and end, drew out his self and shoved it back in within the space of a blink. She hadn't done that since, not on subsequent visits, because Bridger had politely asked her not to. "We talked about that."

"No." She gave him a crooked grin and took his hand, cradled it palm up, and traced one sharp, broken nail over the lines. "I don't have to look deep to know." She shook her gnarled bent finger at him. "Drink the tea."

"I'll have Pavel—"

She suddenly stilled, and her attention snapped from Bridger to the door, and her whole demeanor changed from a warm, gentle teasing to a frigid, stiff stance in seconds flat. She dropped Bridger's hand as if burned her.

The door opened. Summer Lore waltzed in with Matt the cameraman on her heels, and Bridger groaned. He ran a hand over his brow. His pulse ticked up, and everything good about his day vanished. Nausea swept over him, and his school lunch threatened a reappearance on Grandma Alice's nice hardwood floor. It was amazing how the atmosphere could change from jovial to pressure cooker in a matter of moments.

"My," Summer said, eyeing the shelves lined with jars full of things that probably shouldn't be in jars. "This is quaint."

Bridger rolled his eyes. "This is stalking."

"This is a public establishment," she countered.

"This is bordering on harassment. Are you following me now? What next? The school bathroom? Are you going to crash my graduation?"

She shook her head. "You have a wild imagination and—" Her reaction the moment she caught sight of Grandma Alice would forever be seared into Bridger's brain. She let out a squeal, and her mouth dropped open, and her expression shifted through emotions so fast it was difficult to discern what they were, but Bridger was certain he caught horror, then disgust, wrapped in a burrito of recognition.

"*You!*" Eyes wide, she pointed a shaking finger at Grandma Alice, and Bridger reveled in the way her complexion drained of color and all professional pretense vanished. He propped an elbow on the counter and relaxed to enjoy the show.

Grandma Alice became downright gleeful. Her violet eyes sparkled. "Me," she agreed.

"You're the Witch of the Woods."

Grandma Alice waved her hand, scoffing at the moniker. "I'm not a witch. I'm an apothecary. And I was on vacation."

"You *chased* me through the woods while screaming."

Grandma Alice's laugh bordered on maniacal. Bridger couldn't decide if he should run or grin, because the sound sent a shudder down his spine, but Grandma Alice was clearly having the time of her life.

"You interrupted me, jabbering on about witches, scaring away all the good beetles and moths. How am I to catch frogs with you crunching through the leaves? Hmm? Were you going to grind blood worms to dust for my customers?"

Summer gagged. "Certainly not!"

"Then you shouldn't have been out there making a ruckus. And as I understand," she said with a huff, while her thin shoulders shook with suppressed giggles, "it was your best-rated episode. You should thank me."

"You watch TV?" Bridger asked.

Grandma Alice shrugged. "I'm old, not dead."

Wrinkling her nose, Summer pressed her lips together before acquiescing. "You're not wrong. It was our most-watched episode of all time. But I do not owe you. If anything, I should sue you for emotional distress."

Cackling, Grandma Alice shook her head and waved away the threat. "You don't belong here, missy. Move along and don't bother my favorite customer." She ran a gnarled hand through Bridger's hair. "Or I'll have to hex you." She cackled again, stepped from her stool, and toddled off to the back of the shop with the hem of her dress dragging behind her.

"Is that a threat?" Summer called after her. Grandma Alice didn't respond and left Bridger with his crate of supplies and Summer standing in his way to the door. She narrowed her eyes at him. "Of course, you'd be her favorite customer. Bridger Whitt. Friend of ghosts and crones and black owls. Is there anything creepy not drawn to you?"

"It's part of my charm," Bridger said.

"I wouldn't call it charm." She placed her hand on Bridger's arm. The pink of her nails clashed with the blue flannel he wore. "I'll figure you out sooner or later, Bridger. Might as well mitigate the damage and give me an interview. Tell me what you know about what else is out there terrorizing Midden, and I'll make sure your reputation stays intact. It'd be awful if your friend and boyfriend decide to ditch you because of a silly TV show."

Bridger yanked his arm away. His skin prickled with sweat. Annoyance tinged with fear welled like a tide, but he swallowed it down. She was trying to get him to crack. He'd faced down a literal hag. He could deal with a figurative one. "Lady, you are *bent*. And you're blocking my exit." He hefted the crate. The jars rattled. "Unless you want black blister beetle all over your dress, move out of my way. And I wouldn't ignore Grandma Alice's warning. She doesn't play around."

Summer stepped to the side, bowed slightly, and opened her arm. "Of course. After you."

He wasn't expecting Summer to follow him out, but she did. Matt was on her heels with his camera firmly aimed at Bridger's back. He fished his phone out of his pocket and with one hand shot Astrid a text to come pick him up. He tacked on a *hurry*.

"What's with the crate of supplies? Summoning a demon? What about that black dog that came to your rescue the other day? Was that one of your creatures as well?"

Bridger bit his lip. He didn't respond, but every atom of his body trembled with anger and frustration and annoyance.

"I saw that cute picture of you and your boyfriend in the school paper. There was one floating around the baseball field while I caught a snippet of practice today. I heard there are some very important school games coming up including possibly the state tournament, all because of him. He's an outstanding player. Good catch."

Bridger tamped down on all his impulsive instincts, because "good catch" was a bad romantic baseball pun, and he needed to *say something*. But instead he turned away. She was trying to get a rise out of him. That was all. He needed to ignore her.

"Prom's coming up, huh? I know Luke used the money from his interview to be able to ask out your best friend. That must sting, the interconnectedness of it all."

"Don't you have somewhere to be?" Bridger clutched the crate.

She shrugged. "I could be interviewing a few more of your friends. They were so eager to talk about you and your boyfriend."

Bridger swallowed.

"We could shoot more background shots. But I think I will go back inside and talk to your Grandma Alice a little bit more."

"I wouldn't. She's frightening on a good day. I'd hate to see her annoyed."

"She doesn't scare me. Plus, she's old. She'll let something interesting slip."

Bridger exploded. "What is your problem? Huh? What happened to you? Your first season was great, despite the low production values. You gave an actual shit. But now? You stalk high school students? You make fun of people? You exploit them? And for what? Another season of cable ratings and a lackluster paycheck?" He set the crate at his feet, hard enough for the glass to wobble and clink together. "It's hard enough being me; I don't need you breathing down my neck too. So get on with it." He spread his arms. "Bring it. Film me. Mock me. Threaten me. Ask me questions to which I have no answers. Get it over with, Summer. Because I have prom to worry about. And a research paper. And graduation. And a dad I haven't talked to in a decade wants to have dinner with me."

Summer didn't move. Her jaw worked, and her face went red to her hairline.

"Well?" Bridger demanded. "Come on! Matt, are you rolling? Did we lose the light? What's stopping you?"

Summer's teeth ground together. "You heard him, Matt. Grab my microphone out of the van before he backs out and runs away."

Oh, no. What had he done? *Shit. Shit. Fucking shit.*

Of course, that's when Bridger heard the distinctive sound of a tear in space-time and thanked his lucky stars.

Pavel appeared from around a fence near the corner of the parking lot in a flurry of his long coat and with the crunch of gravel beneath his shoes. He stalked, black hair wind-whipped, clothes smelling of ozone. *The portal.* Pavel had used the portal. Bridger wondered how urgent the toaster had sounded. Pavel's expression was fierce: lips in a thin line, eyes glittering with annoyance. It was as if Bridger's discomfort summoned a dour angel. Pavel was Azriphale. All he lacked was wings and a flaming sword. He had the vengeance though. His back was straight, there was not a stutter in his step, and the usually confident Summer shuffled away from Bridger when Pavel wedged between them.

Pavel crossed his arms. "What's going on here?"

She raised her eyebrows. "And who are you? Are you the dad? The one that's been missing for a decade? Is your son's obsession

with cryptids and folklore a cry for attention due to your abandon-
ment of him?"

"I'm not his father. I'm his boss."

"Wait." Summer peered at Pavel the way someone would if
they realized they knew the person from somewhere but couldn't
place them. She snapped her fingers. "You're the man from the
beach. I saw your picture." She pointed at Bridger. "You saved
him. You pulled him from the water."

"I did."

She smiled sweetly. Her attitude changed from obnoxious
to sultry in a blink. She pressed her hand to Pavel's lapel; her
fingernail slid under the fabric of his collar.

"You must really care for him, to risk your life. Diving into a
lake filled with creatures to save your favorite employee. Strong
too." She squeezed his bicep. "To pull a waterlogged teen from
the lake and provide first aid. You rescued him. He's alive because
of your bravery."

Bridger rolled his eyes so hard they almost fell out of his head.

"Others assisted."

"Yes, but you, *you* are the true hero. Would you consent to
interview? Would you be willing to talk about that day and gush
about your employee?"

Bridger bent his head and covered his eyes with his hands to
avoid the oncoming train wreck. This was not good. Pavel was
going to go all weak-kneed and blush at the physical contact.
Summer was touching him and flirting with him. Who knew what
Pavel would do? Stutter? Flush? Age backwards into a hormone-
fueled mess ala Bridger himself?

"Stay away from him."

Snapping his head up, Bridger stared with wide eyes. Pavel's voice was steely; his accent was deep and harsh. His hand clasped Summer's wrist and held it away from his body.

"What?"

"Stay away from him. Please."

She wrenched out of his grasp.

"Or you'll what?" She lifted her chin and crossed her arms. "Call the cops? We both know you don't want that. You don't want the attention, or your name and picture would have been in the paper when they wrote up the beach event. But it wasn't. You vanished. Oh, yeah," she said with a nod, calculating Pavel's expression. "I've talked with a few of the kids. You showed up. Walked straight into the water with the little boyfriend. Pulled your assistant out, then disappeared minutes later, before the ambulances arrived. Sounds fishy to me."

Another pun. Oh, she was pushing every one of Bridger's buttons. Maybe use of bad puns was one of her strategies to get Bridger to break. Well, it worked. And she was not wrong. He kept forgetting she was an investigative reporter. She'd looked this shit up.

Pavel's jaw worked. The air around him dropped a few degrees, and Bridger grasped the sleeve of Pavel's coat to ground him, to remind him that he couldn't allow his anger and frustration to show in his expression, or, well, his whole being. Pavel's appearance shifted on occasion and revealed the turmoil beneath his usual placid veneer, and this was the exact wrong time for that to happen.

Glancing to his side, Pavel gave Bridger a nod.

"I've asked nicely."

She huffed. "And what? You've said 'please,' so I'm supposed to drop everything and leave? Yeah, right."

"Leave my assistant alone." His tone brooked no argument. "Leave his friends alone."

"You've yet to provide any consequences to me if I don't."

Pavel smiled, a mean little twist of his mouth. "I won't threaten you, but I am warning you."

"You think you're intimidating." Summer huffed. "You're nothing. You think I've gotten this far by playing nice? You aren't the first two guys who haven't wanted me around and you certainly won't be the last. But in the end, I always get the story. This will be no different. Whatever you're hiding will be brought to light even if it's just an affinity for black blister beetles." She kicked the crate at Bridger's feet.

Bridger shivered and gripped the fabric between his fingers tighter.

Pavel shook his head, and black hair fell across his eyes. He sighed heavily. "Fair enough, Ms. Lore. But remember, I did warn you."

For some reason, that brought Summer up short. Her self-assured persona wavered, and her bravado dimmed. Her crossed arms went from a defiant position to a defensive one. "Noted."

Pavel turned on his heel and strode across the parking lot and toward the street. "Come along, Bridger."

Hefting the crate, Bridger scrambled after Pavel. He cast a glance over his shoulder at Summer. Mouth turned down, she watched him. She tapped her jawline, considering Bridger with a pinched look.

Ducking his head, he focused forward, because the last thing he needed was to trip or run into something and break bottles of who-knows-what all over the concrete. He turned a corner and found Pavel in front of the portal—a shimmering oval of magic, which blended into the landscape and was only visible to those familiar with it.

"Pavel, what just happened? I don't get it."

Pavel gestured for Bridger to hand over the supplies, and he did so.

"I need to talk with my mentor. Go home now. I'll mirror you tomorrow."

"What? Pavel? No. I'm sorry, okay. I lost my cool. I know this is all my fault. I should've stayed away from her like you said. Okay? I know that now. I'm sorry." He dragged a hand through his hair. "I'm sorry, but don't fire me, okay? Let me fix it."

Pavel's forehead crinkled. "Bridger, calm down."

"No, I can't. She literally said she's going to keep looking into everything. I fucked up. Please let me help you."

"Bridger, I'm not mad at you. And I'm not firing you. I promise." Pavel nudged Bridger with his elbow. "I will include you in any plan that I make. But I must confirm Intermediary Guidelines in this case. I will talk with you tomorrow. Until then, go home. Relax."

Bridger sucked in a breath. *Relax? Yeah, right.* "Okay," he said, chin dipping to his chest. "Okay."

Pavel waited with Bridger until Astrid arrived, which Bridger was grateful for, but which also made him feel he was back in kindergarten and couldn't be left without adult supervision. But he was an adult, technically. He didn't feel like one.

Astrid didn't say anything when he slid into the car empty-handed and Pavel disappeared in an ooze of light and sound. Bridger studied his hands as she drove.

"Want to talk about it, Cap?"

"Not really, Buck."

"Okay."

They rode in silence. Bridger studied his hands and picked at his fingernails; his thoughts were a whir; his anxiety was at an all-time high. Knowing how to handle his moods better than he did, Astrid let him stew. She really was his best friend, but the Marvel nicknames didn't quite fit any more. He didn't feel like Captain America—maybe pre-serum Steve Rogers, always jumping into things he couldn't handle—but not the upright paragon of truth and justice. But to be fair, all Astrid and Bucky Barnes shared was their badassness and their ability to wear killer eyeshadow.

When Astrid dropped him off, she gave him a sympathetic look and an awkward side-hug before he exited the car.

"I'll see you tomorrow. You'll be okay."

"Thanks."

Using his key, he opened the door and dropped his backpack at the foot of the stairs.

"Answer your father's text!" His mom yelled from the kitchen as soon as he entered, followed by the sounds of pots and pans clanging and the stove hissing. "He's been driving me crazy."

Oh, yeah. Bridger pulled his phone from his pocket and checked his texts.

Dinner, tomorrow?

Ugh. No. He really didn't want to, but this was Dad making an effort--too little too late, maybe, but at least effort.

Sure. Time & place?
7pm. I'll pick you up at home.
Great. Not really. C u then.

"He wants to have dinner tomorrow. I told him yes."

"Okay. That's fine!"

"I have homework. I'll be in my room."

Bridger fled before his mom could answer. He threw his bag in his computer chair and slumped on the bed, falling back onto the pillows. He draped his forearm over his eyes.

How had everything become such a mess? All he wanted to do was be happy, graduate, have a job and a boyfriend, and exist in something other than chaos and panic. Was that too tall an order?

Marv padded out from beneath the bed, jumped up next to him, curled under his chin, and purred.

"Thanks, Marv," he said, scratching behind the kitten's ears. With her comfort and with the exhaustion from the day, he fell asleep.

CHAPTER 10

"I don't know how you do it, Whitt," Taylor said.

Bridger raised an eyebrow. He checked another name off the list of pre-sale yearbook pickups and handed a freshman her magical book of memories.

"Do what?"

Taylor hovered over him, supervising as he unenthusiastically passed out yearbooks at a table in the cafeteria.

"Not constantly break in half from jealousy."

Bridger raised an eyebrow and handed a sophomore guy his yearbook. The kid blushed when they knocked hands, and Bridger shook his head at his own awkwardness.

"I have no idea what you're talking about, Taylor."

They slapped their hand on his shoulder. "Over there."

Bridger looked up from his list and spied Leo across the room. He had a group of admirers around him, all fighting to sign his yearbook. Leo laughed, clutched the book to his chest, and waved off the crowd.

"What?"

"Your boyfriend is the hottest guy in school and is fawned over constantly. How are you not a ball of nerves?"

Oh, little did they know. Bridger *was* a constant ball of nerves. In fact, Bridger had traded in his bones, muscle, and brain for extra nerves and, as such, was one massive, twitching mess with no direction, self-control, foresight, or body. But seeing Leo across the room, being his genuinely awesome self, wasn't anything nerve-wracking. In fact, it was a comfort knowing that Bridger's mess was not affecting Leo and his happiness.

"Why would I be? Leo and I are together, but that doesn't mean I have to be with him every second of the day. He has a life. I have a life. He has friends. I have friends."

"You're not worried about breakup week?"

Bridger rolled his neck. He was developing a crick from constantly looking down at the list of names. "Breakup week? Never heard of her."

"The week after prom and before graduation. All the couples break up. They wait until after prom to make sure they have a date, and then break up before heading off to college."

Bridger had never heard of breakup week. It wasn't something he'd ever thought would be on his radar. Having a boyfriend or girlfriend his senior year hadn't been in the hand of cards Bridger assumed he'd been dealt. "That's unfortunate. But I'm not worried."

"Huh. Okay then. Good for you, I guess."

Bridger shoved another book across the table and tried not to scowl when he spied a girl trying to tug Leo's yearbook out of his hands.

Leo shook his head and held on, though he wielded a pen and signed a page for the girl. He dropped a few more signatures for the group. He smiled as he did so, his eyes crinkled. Then he extricated himself from the group and made his way to Bridger.

He plopped down in the empty seat beside him despite Taylor's sniff.

"This side of the table for yearbook staff only."

"Do I get to leave then?" Bridger asked. "Because I'm technically not yearbook staff. And I'd rather not spend my limited after-school time here."

Taylor grumbled something uncomplimentary but allowed Leo to stay.

"Hey," Leo said, knocking his shoulder into Bridger's. "Will you sign my yearbook?"

"Yeah. Of course."

Bridger accepted the book and flipped through the pages, hoping to find an empty space where he could write a cute message. All the signature pages were blank. No message or scribbles to be found. No hearts or smileys or jokes. Nothing.

"I wanted you to be the first to sign it." Leo leaned on Bridger's side and handed over a sharpie. "It was a battle, but, you know, you may not have been the first friend I made when I moved here, but you're certainly my favorite."

Bridger's throat went tight. "Will you sign mine?"

Leo's grin blinded him. "Yes. But shouldn't Astrid be the first?"

"She was the first…" and only "…person to sign it last year. I think it's safe for you to be the first this year." Bridger grabbed one from the stack and handed it over.

"Have you even looked in it yet?" Leo asked.

"Not really. Why?" Bridger didn't see the point of looking through it. He'd already seen his own senior picture. It was unflattering at best. And Astrid's wasn't much better, since her mother had made her remove all her piercings and have only her natural hair color—light brown—in the picture. It made Astrid look not like Astrid, but like a watered-down version of herself. Leo's was, of course, perfect.

Chuckling, Leo flipped to the section about homecoming and held it up. There they were, on the sidelines during the homecoming game, kissing. Bridger cupped Leo's cheeks, and Leo's helmet dangled from his fingertips, and the scoreboard was lit up behind them.

"Oh," Bridger said, flushing. He laughed awkwardly. "Oh."

"Yeah." Leo said with a grin. "Isn't it awesome? Our first kiss is immortalized in the yearbook."

"It is, isn't it?" Bridger should be mortified, but he wasn't. He was *giddy* with the fact that his big, old, coming-out kiss took up half a page. He ran his hand over the glossy finish. "It's amazing."

"You really didn't know?"

Bridger shook his head. "No. I didn't."

"I'm glad I got to show you then." His cheeks dimpled. "Hey, I have to get to practice. You keep that." Leo tapped his yearbook. "I'll get it back from you later. And I'll keep this one and write something nice and sweet in it."

Finding it hard to speak, Bridger nodded. "Sounds good." Bridger gave him a quick peck on the lips. "I have dinner with my dad tonight, so I probably won't get to talk to you until really late."

Leo's expression turned fierce. He had a glint in his brown eyes Bridger had only seen on the sports fields. "I can be on standby if you need me to swoop in again. I can borrow my mom's car. I'm sure she'll let me if I explain the situation."

Bridger could've hugged him. As it was, his belly filled with butterflies. He laced his fingers with Leo's and rested his forehead on Leo's shoulder. "Nah. I should be okay. But thank you. That means a lot."

"Hey, you'd do it for me."

"In a heartbeat."

Leo softened. "I know." He tightened his hold on Bridger's hand. "I have to go now though. Coach will be upset if I'm late. If we win tomorrow, we have a good chance at the state tournament."

"Okay. Hit a hundred home runs."

"That's not how the game works, Bridge," Leo said on a laugh. "But I'll try."

They disentangled, and Leo slid Bridger's yearbook into his bag, then looped it over his shoulder. "I'll talk to you tonight."

"Okay. Later."

Bridger watched Leo walk away, admiring both the view and the way Leo cast a lingering glance over his shoulder and waved, before turning the corner for the locker room.

"You should've asked him if he knew about breakup week," Taylor said, looming over Bridger's shoulder.

Bridger let his head fall foreword until it thumped on the table.

AFTER THE CAFETERIA HAD MOSTLY cleared and he'd handed out more yearbooks than he had ever wanted to touch, he raised his hands above his head and stretched his back, then promptly had a heart attack when the sound of every piano key mashed at once came from his backpack. He avoided Taylor's raised eyebrow and scurried to the nearest secluded corner. He flipped open the compact and snorted. Pavel's idea of a text message stared back at him. He'd trained the compact to ring once, then aimed it at a handwritten note, propped up on the small table in the living room.

Come to the house when you can was written in Pavel's tiny, messy script on a piece of torn parchment.

Bridger snapped the compact closed. "Ridiculous."

He shoved it into his bag and looped the strap over his shoulder. "Later, Taylor. I have to get to work."

They waved as Bridger left the building. A quick look satisfied him that Summer wasn't lurking, and he headed to the bus stop. He nodded to the route driver, whom Bridger had come to know fairly well, plopped into his usual seat, took out the yearbook, and flipped through the pages until he landed on the shot of him and Leo kissing. The caption was about the game, a quick wrap-up about the loss despite heroic efforts. Bridger snorted. Heroic efforts indeed.

He continued to look through the yearbook until the bus stopped at Pavel's neighborhood. His shoulders were a tense line, and his kept his hood up and head down, just in case Summer lurked nearby. She wasn't allowed in the school building, so Bridger was safe there, and she couldn't enter Pavel's house, but all spaces in between were fair game. He was on edge the entire walk to Pavel's and broke into a jog once it came into view.

He bounded into over the threshold. When magic buzzed over his skin as he passed through the warded door, Bridger was finally able to relax. Standing in the foyer of Pavel's house, he felt the cramp in his muscles ease and the racing of his pulse slow.

"Hey, Mindy," Bridger said, sidling over to the desk. He took stock of the bobbleheads and noticed more were missing. He picked up a sheep wearing sunglasses, hat, and a wolf's tail. *A sheep in wolf's clothing. Hilarious.* "Why so many casualties in your bobblehead army?" Bridger asked, shaking the sheep slightly so the head wobbled. "Is there some kind of bobblehead migration going on? Are you making room for more? Please tell me you are gradually switching out the old ones for new ones to creepily stare at me when I'm down here."

Mindy blinked; her orange eyeshadow swept like flames across her eyelids. Her expression didn't change when she slid a piece of paper across her desk. "Sign your sheet."

"A woman of few words. I admire that."

Her frosted lips pulled into a tiny smirk. Mindy tapped her orange nail on the blank space for Bridger to write down his times and sign. Dutifully, Bridger clocked in and signed his name with a flourish worthy of John Hancock.

"Mindy, are you going to tell me why your figurines are slowly disappearing? Is it a plague? A relocation program? Did they witness a crime? Oh, oh, don't tell me Bran made good on his threat and is trying to find a way to make the cute cat with wings come alive."

Mindy sighed heavily and went back to her phone.

"Fine, don't tell me. But I'll find out," Bridger wagged a finger at her and turned to the stairs.

"You're a good kid."

Bridger stopped short. He craned his neck to see Mindy watching him with an expression other than bored disinterest. It unnerved him.

"What?"

"You're a good kid. Don't let anyone tell you otherwise."

Weird. "Mindy?" Bridger clutched the straps of his backpack. "Is something wrong?"

"No."

Bridger frowned. "You're okay, right?"

Back to her clandestine self, she didn't answer or look at him. Instead, she clacked away on her keyboard, effectively ignoring him.

He cleared his throat and headed for the stairs. "Thanks though. I needed to hear that."

Mindy's typing paused, for only a second, then resumed.

Bridger continued his trek to the second floor and Pavel's study. Nia greeted him as he stepped onto the landing. Her wings fluttered; her movements were perceivable only as a flash of pink as she zipped around the room. In a corner, a cauldron bubbled, balanced on a hot plate that was plugged into the wall.

"What's cooking?"

"Nothing that concerns you," Nia said, all business, as she dropped a handful of *something* into the pot. "Thank you for the shipment from Grandma Alice. Shame about the black blister beetles. I need them for the hand lotion."

Bridger reined in a gag. "I can't believe you sell this stuff."

"Believe it, human." She stirred the thick concoction with a long-handled spoon. "I sold out of the anti-aging cream. We'll need more unicorn donations soon. And the acne treatment is flying off the shelves."

Bridger flopped into a high-backed chair. "I've heard. Pavel told me he was helping you ship packages."

"Yes. It's hard work, and Pasha is the only one who can travel to the post office." She fluttered to a bookcase filled with jars and pulled one out. "We've been forbidden."

Stifling a grin, Bridger rubbed his hand over his mouth. "But do you enjoy it?"

Nia smiled, all sharp glinting teeth. "Yes. Now that Pasha has you, I am able to pursue other interests. Such as potions and cosmetics. It's fulfilling."

"That's great. Glad my existence is useful sometimes." Bridger propped his elbows on his knees. "Have you talked to Pavel today? Did he tell you about stuff?"

Nia upended a jar of powder into the cauldron. The bubbling increased, and plumes of green and pink smoke rolled over the sides and slid to the floor. Nia stirred madly, grunting with effort; pink sparkles shot everywhere.

"No. He hasn't mentioned anything special."

Dragging a cloth bag, Bran buzzed into the room. "Three pig hairs, a crow feather, and a moth wing," he said, dropping the bag next to Nia's supplies.

"Thank you, Bran. You may now eat a Pop-Tart."

Bran pumped his fist and let out a squeaky sound as he dove into the kitchen cupboard. He emerged with a cookies-and-cream Pop-Tart in his hands, and his mouth, and his hair.

"Hi, Bridger," Bran said. Flecks of chocolate and frosting went everywhere.

Bridger flinched. "You're gross."

"You're gross," Bran retorted.

"You're all gross." Pavel leaned over the railing from the third floor. "Bridger, up here."

"Why? Aren't we going to talk? Shouldn't Bran and Nia be in on the conversation? I mean, we're coming up with a plan, right?"

"We're not worrying about Summer Lore today," Pavel said, beckoning Bridger to the third floor. He held a bouquet and had a bag looped over his shoulder. "We have other duties."

"Really? Pavel, I don't think we should be ignoring the lady that could literally ruin your life, my life, and the lives of the myth community of the Midwest."

"It'll keep."

"Pavel," Bridger rubbed his brow, "you are stressing me out. All of this is stressing me out."

"Exactly."

Frustration, thy name is Pavel Chudinov. "I don't think—"

"Bridger," Pavel cut him off. "Trust me."

Bridger wilted. "Fine. Okay. Whatever."

"That's the spirit." He slapped the glossy railing. "Come along."

Bridger climbed the stairs to the topmost floor. He spied the blue door down a hallway to his right. They passed the headless mannequin, which Pavel really needed to address because *creepy.*

"I know. I know," Pavel said. "I'll do something with it later."

They ducked into a room, literally ducked, since the ceiling slanted in odd places.

Pavel straightened the high collar of his jacket—a leather thing that looked appropriate for a James Dean movie—and opened the closet door. At first glance, the closet was empty. The shadows coalesced into a gleaming mass of swirling chaos, semi-sentient, and pure magic. Infinite space and time, stars and black holes and nebulas, beginnings and endings, births and deaths, the first breath and the last gasp—the enormity of existence manifested in the enclosed area of a closet. Bridger peered at the undulating viscosity of the portal, and it peered back at him, waiting, humming, expectant.

"Hello, we'd like to visit Ada, please." Pavel touched the surface and it slithered up to his wrist. "Thank you. Yes. The cemetery is perfect."

Pavel reached back and offered his hand. Bridger took it. Pavel's long spindly fingers wrapped around Bridger's palm. They stepped through.

Though Bridger had used the portal several times, he never thought it'd become normal for him to be squeezed on all sides, disappear into the ether, then pop out somewhere miles away. This time, they appeared on a sidewalk in front of a fence proclaiming Findlay Cemetery in black wrought iron.

"Where are we?"

"Ada, Michigan," Pavel said. He walked to the entrance and waved at a groundskeeper. She waved back as if a tall, thin, fine-boned intermediary was a common sight at the cemetery. He probably was, knowing Pavel.

Shoulder to shoulder, Bridger walked beside Pavel as they leisurely traversed the walking paths of the cemetery. Tall trees, swaying gently in the late afternoon breeze, offered shaded patches and solemnity to the ground, which was dappled with grave markers and tombstones. The spring air was crisp, and Bridger was glad for the sleeves on his hoodie. He kicked a pebble, and it rolled down the ribbon of path which cut through the rolling green lawn.

"What are we doing here?"

Pavel strolled, one hand in his pocket, the other clutching the bouquet. "Fascinating, isn't it? All these people, generations of families buried together, their lives marked by a slab of stone with two dates and a dash, their stories unknown, save by the people who loved them."

Bridger bit his lip. He'd have a stone one day. That was part of being human. He hoped it was later rather than sooner, but no one could know. "What about you?" He glanced at Pavel, who had his face tipped toward the sun. His eyes were closed, expression peaceful as he ambled in the sunlight.

"Not for a while. Magic prolongs life. All who knew my story, my real story, are gone, turned to dust decades ago."

"I'm sorry."

He shrugged. "I didn't bring you here to wax maudlin. I wanted to give you a day to relax. I wanted you to see that my work, *our* work, isn't always one crisis after another. Some days, it's a stroll in a cemetery to see a friend."

"I hate to say this, but I don't have time for friendly visits. Seriously. I have a paper to finish, a boyfriend I hope doesn't break up with me after we go to prom, a best friend who wants to make sure we're color-coded, a dad who has decided to reappear out of nowhere and, oh, a lady who wants to expose us to the world."

Sighing, Pavel turned off the path. "Bridger, our lives consist of a sequence of decisions. Sometimes we make good decisions and sometimes we make bad ones. Sometimes what we think is right is wrong and sometimes our decisions have outcomes we'd never expect. Everyone makes mistakes, Bridger. I've made plenty in my life."

"Is this a lecture? Because I really don't want one. I know I screwed up, Pavel. I should've stayed in my lane. I should've stayed away when you told me too. I shouldn't have antagonized her. I should've kept my head down and my mouth shut."

Pavel shook his head. "No. You did what you thought was right. I'd rather you act when you see a wrong than sit on the sidelines. You thought she was going to hurt your friend, and I'm proud that you intervened. I only wish you'd done it less conspicuously."

Bridger shook his head. "Okay, then why are we here?"

"To pay our respects. To correct a mistake." Pavel paused in front of a tombstone. The grave was overgrown, and bare of any decorations or flowers, but the stone was new, not weathered like the others around it, though *witch* had been sprayed across it in red paint. "Have you heard of the Ada Witch?"

Bridger blinked. "I read about her in the field book." He twiddled his thumbs. "She cheated on her husband with another man. The husband found them and killed her. Then the other man and the husband fought and inflicted enough damage on each other that they ended up both dying. A prime example of toxic masculinity. And now the Ada Witch roams the area where she was murdered and appears as a woman in a blue dress with long, flowing hair. She's not really a witch. She's a ghost, like Ginny."

Nodding, Pavel kept his gaze firmly on the grave in front of them. "That's correct. Several individuals have seen her over the years. Around dusk, she sorrowfully walks the length of the road and gives drivers a scare. She's quite popular, and people flock to Ada from all around to catch a glimpse of her."

"Sounds about right. We're nothing if not nosy."

Pavel agreed, grimly. "About twenty years ago, a monster-hunter of sorts supposedly solved the mystery of the identity of the Ada Witch. The individual stated they'd done research and found a woman who died at the correct time in history and in the right area. That researcher gave the Ada Witch a name. They gave her the *wrong* name."

Bridger gulped.

Pavel knelt at the grave and placed the bouquet. He opened the satchel at his side and removed a pair of clippers, a cloth, and a bottle of what smelled like turpentine. He set to work scrubbing away the paint.

"Is this her? Is this the Ada Witch?"

"No," Pavel said. "This is a woman who happened to perish in this town near the same time that the myth began." He brushed a pale hand over the name and the cause of death added beneath the dates at the bottom. *Died of typhoid fever.* "Since then, this poor woman's grave has been desecrated. Her stone was broken, and pieces were sold on the Internet. She's believed to be something she's not, and she cannot defend herself. Thankfully, someone looked further and realized this woman was not the infamous Ada Witch. A new headstone was placed, and the township has worked on correcting the mistake since."

"And you come to tend the grave why exactly?"

Pavel sat back on his heels. "Because I was asked to."

He looked up and stared to the left of Bridger's shoulder. Turning slightly, Bridger caught a glimpse of a woman with long, flowing hair wearing a blue dress. Bridger startled, tripped backward, and fell on his ass. He clutched his heart and clamped down on the curse which almost burst forth.

The apparition moved slowly, purposefully; her gaze roved over Bridger before settling on Pavel. She floated a few inches above the ground. Her shoes peeked out beneath the fabric of her long dress. "Hello, Intermediary Chudinov," she said softly. "Thank you for coming."

"Hello, Lizzie." Pavel sat back on his heels and ran his hands down his thighs, wiping dirt on the fabric. "I apologize. I didn't warn my assistant."

She pressed a hand to her throat and touched a necklace which rested in the hollow. "No apologies needed. I enjoy visiting with youth when they aren't vandalizing." She turned sorrowful eyes to the grave. "Thank you for fulfilling the task I've asked of you. She doesn't deserve to suffer the consequences of my actions."

"You're not responsible for the actions of others, Lizzie." Pavel used a cloth to wipe away dirt on the edges of the marker.

"No. I am not. But it pains me. I am grateful for your assistance."

Bridger sat, eyes wide and fixed on the transparent, blue-tinged woman in front of him.

"I brought my assistant to learn the task you've set for me so that he may be able to complete it in the future in my stead if needed."

Lizzie, the real Ada Witch, observed Bridger with a blank expression. Her hands were folded across her abdomen; her long hair lay still despite the breeze.

"As long as he understands the purpose."

"I do." Bridger blurted from his sprawl on the ground. "I do. I promise."

"Then it is acceptable."

Pavel continued to scrub at the red letters; the turpentine cut through the grime and the paint. "Thank you, Lizzie."

"Thank you, Intermediary Chudinov."

She gave him a nod, then disappeared, as if she hadn't been there at all.

Bridger stayed on the ground, curled his legs beneath him, and sat, staring at the grave. Pavel scrubbed the stone until it gleamed, then used the clippers to cut back the tangle of grass. After his task was completed, Pavel joined Bridger at the edge of the grave and folded his long legs beneath him. He rooted around in his bag and pulled out a small pack of cookies and a flask. He nudged Bridger's arm, and Bridger took a cookie. His stomach rumbled. He'd yet to eat anything since leaving school later than usual.

"What's in the flask?"

Pavel handed it over. "Grandma Alice's tea and honey. She mirrored me to ensure I made it for you."

"I'm certain she enjoyed talking to you. She says you're handsome."

Pavel blushed and fidgeted as Bridger took a sip.

"What do you think this will do to me?"

"I think it's meant to comfort you. Like hot drinks and soup have, anecdotally, for centuries."

Bridger nodded toward the grave. "Was this a lesson?" he asked around a bite of the cookie. "A metaphor for what's going on in my life right now? Because I don't get it. I mean, I understand the importance of this duty, and I understand that this person…" He gestured toward the headstone. "…got the raw end of a deal. But I don't know how this applies to me."

Pavel shifted beside him, threw the strap of the bag over his shoulder, and shoved his hands into his pockets. "No lesson. I just like coming here sometimes to take a break. It's peaceful."

"Peaceful." Bridger swiveled his head, peering at the graves that surrounded them. "Even with the ghosts?"

"Yes, even with the ghosts." He waited a beat. "I know you're overwhelmed right now. I wanted to give you a break, since I'm sorry that this job has added stress in an already stressful time in your life."

Bridger shook his head. "No. Don't. I think even if Summer and her show weren't in Midden right now, there would be something else that would send me over the edge. I'm the master at dedicating energy to a crisis to avoid another crisis."

"What crisis are you avoiding now?" Pavel asked. His black hair ruffled in the breeze.

Bridger plucked a blade of grass. "All of them. Though my paper is almost finished, so one crisis averted. Prom, but Astrid and Leo are helping me. And that leaves graduation looming in front of me. And my dad."

"That's good. You're doing well. You have help in your friends and in your family."

"I know. I forget that sometimes."

"What about your father?"

"Yeah. That one I'm not doing too well with."

"I'm sorry." Pavel fiddled with a button on his jacket. "He made bad decisions, Bridger. And his mistakes affected you. And it's not fair. To use your words, it sucks. But now you have to decide how you're going to handle him being back in your life."

Bridger ran a hand through his hair. "Can you make that decision for me?"

"I wish I could. But it's not my place, and I don't think your father—"

"Oh, crap!" Bridger said, perking up. "What time is it?" He yanked his phone out of his pocket. *7:45!* He had three missed texts from his dad. *Oh, no!* "I have to go! I was supposed to meet him at seven for dinner." Scrambling to his feet, Bridger flailed his hands. "I am so late!"

"It's all right. Come on, we'll take the portal to your house."

"He's going to be so angry. I know it."

Pavel's hand was heavy on Bridger's shoulder, but it wasn't a reassurance. Bridger didn't know how his dad would react. He didn't know him well enough to gauge his feelings as to tardiness.

Bridger squeezed out of the portal and landed on the sidewalk around the corner from his house. Pavel appeared right behind him, and together they walked briskly, turning the corner in the fading light.

His dad sat on the front porch under the lamp, with his elbows propped on his bent knees and his phone dangling from his fingertips. His Audi was parked in front along the curb. He looked up at the slap of Bridger's shoes on the pavement. Yep, he looked angry.

"Where have you been?" he demanded as he stood. "You're almost an hour late. You didn't answer my texts."

Bridger winced. The feelings surrounding his dad were intense in a way that made his insides ache. He didn't want his dad to be angry, but fuck his dad for being angry. If anyone had a right to be angry, it was Bridger, not his dad. But, ugh, his dad was angry at him and it made him feel ashamed and small.

"It was my fault," Pavel said, smoothly, stepping up beside Bridger. "I kept him late for work for an important task, and we lost track of time. I apologize for the inconvenience."

Bridger didn't like the way his dad sized Pavel up. He could see it in the head-to-toe sweep his dad gave Pavel, the change in his body language, and the small smirk of his mouth. They couldn't be more different people, standing opposite each other on Bridger's tiny patch of lawn like a study of light and dark. His dad was tall and muscular, blonde-haired, blue-eyed, the epitome of

Midwestern, cornfed beefcake. Pavel was tall as well, but willowy, with dark hair and a muddled accent that marked him as foreign as clearly as the odd aura that enveloped him. His dad would blend into a crowd and assimilate with ease, while Pavel would always stand out as strange, not because of his appearance, his propensity for bad fashion, or the way he spoke, but because of the oddness that clung to him, the impression that he was not fully of this world.

"You're his boss? What kind of work do you do?"

"I help people."

"Like a therapist?"

"In a way. Kind of like a therapist. Definitely not a hit man."

Bridger barely stopped himself from smacking his forehead. His dad huffed a laugh.

"Well, you're an hour late. If your boss wasn't vouching for you, I'd think you were getting me back for being an hour late to your birthday."

Bile churned in Bridger's stomach. He trembled beneath Pavel's steadying hand on his arm. "I'm sorry. It really was work."

"I know, Bud. I'm glad Mr.— "

"Mr. Chudinov. Pavel Chudinov."

"Well, I'm glad Mr. Chudinov is teaching you the value of hard work. It's a good lesson to learn."

"Bridger is an excellent assistant. And on that note, I've taken up far too much of his time this evening. I'll see you after school tomorrow." He released Bridger's arm and walked down the street, leaving Bridger with his dad.

"Hungry?"

"Starving."

"Well, we're too late to go where I wanted, but we can order in. Might be easier to catch up in the kitchen than in a restaurant anyway."

Bridger forced a smile. "Yeah."

He stepped around the imposing figure of his dad and let them into the house. He pocketed his keys and led his dad to the kitchen. He opened a drawer of menus and plucked them out, dropping them on the table.

"So that's your boss, huh? He's weird."

"Yeah. He is. But he's really nice and he pays me well."

His dad's eyebrows twitched. Hands in his pockets, he sauntered around the small kitchen. His gaze trailed over the walls, the few framed pictures of Bridger and his mom, the stack of reminders on the refrigerator for bills and doctor's appointments, the unwashed dishes in the sink, the hand towel that had seen better days, the peeling wallpaper near the electrical outlet, the coffee ring on the counter where his mom always set her mug.

"Not much has changed in here," he said.

Bridger tapped the pile of menus and pulled out his phone. "We have some great options. It really depends on what you're hungry for. And most of the restaurants know us pretty well and will give us discounts. I have all the numbers programmed; just tell me which one to call."

"You order out a lot?"

"Well," Bridger said, voice unsteady, "Mom works nights."

It was weird to talk about his mom to his dad. Bridger had a sinking feeling that anything he said may be used later in an argument, but it was no secret his mom worked nights at the hospital. He cleared his throat and kept his gaze averted.

"Are you left alone a lot?"

"It's fine."

His dad hummed and trailed his fingers over the kitchen table, until they snagged on newsprint. "Look at you on the front page of the school newspaper." He picked it up, and Bridger went cold. "'Hot Race for Prom Court,'" he read. "Wow. Popular enough to be considered for prom court. That's great, Bud."

Bridger froze. He should've snatched the paper from his dad's hand, but his limbs locked up as he did his best impression of a deer in headlights.

Don't look too closely. Don't look too closely. Don't look too closely.

But his dad squinted, picked up the paper, and held it to his face to get a better view.

Bridger saw the moment his dad realized who was in the picture with him, and what it meant. There was no other way to interpret him and Leo, their arms around each other, their laughter, their smitten expressions. His dad's brow creased, then his expression went hard, his jaw set, and his lips pressed into a thin pink line. The paper shook, then his dad dropped it back to the table as if it burned him. Tense silence settled over them, and Bridger gripped his phone, held onto it like a lifeline. He was terrified and hopeful in the same moment, on the verge of tears no matter the outcome.

"Do you, uh…" His voice came out thick, a choked whisper. "…want Chinese or pizza? We could also order sandwiches. Sal's delivers. They have great meatballs."

His dad didn't answer. He stared at the paper on the table. His gaze trailed along the headline, as if to memorize the picture and the words for an exam he needed to pass about his estranged son. After a year-long minute, Bridger shakily cleared his throat.

"Dad?"

He didn't know what he was asking. Were they going to talk about food? Was the elephant in the room going to be addressed? Or would it continue to sit on Bridger's chest, restricting his breathing, until he died from lack of air and attention?

His dad tried a smile, but it fell, and he tried again, plastering on something as fake and as forced as Bridger's had been a few minutes earlier. He didn't look at Bridger at all, didn't raise his gaze from the newspaper on the table. When he did, he stared off in the distance, at the kitchen wall and the wooden rooster where the rarely used spatulas dangled.

"It's late," he finally said. "I have to go. We'll do this another time."

Bridger bit his lip. "Are you sure?" Is avoidance the way they'd play this? Would his dad just disappear again? The way he had ten years ago? Was this it? Or would there be a delayed conversation like the one he'd had with his mom? Did he need a minute to process?

"Yeah, Bud. I'm sure."

"It's not that late."

"It is." He shook his head. "Maybe next time you'll be on time."

It was a verbal slap. "Yeah. Okay."

His dad didn't acknowledge him when he left, merely walked out of the kitchen. The front door opened, slammed, and Bridger was left alone, holding his phone, standing at the kitchen table.

Like a zombie, he pulled out a chair and sank into it.

His mind was blank. His thoughts blissfully void, he flipped his phone in his shaking fingers as he replayed the last few minutes over and over again in his head. Strangely hollow, he didn't know how long he sat there. It could've been an hour. It could've been forever. He didn't wake from his daze until he heard a car door slam. Soon after, the front door opened, and his mother appeared.

"I thought you were at work," Bridger said. His voice was flat, and his words were slurred.

"I was. But your dad called and I..." she trailed off. "How long have you been sitting there, Bridge?"

He shook himself. "I don't know. Since he left." He swallowed. "He left," he said again. "He saw the picture and he left."

Nothing felt real. There was a distance between him and everything, and he didn't like it. But he didn't know how to stop it, and he knew, if he moved, if he acknowledged it, he'd cry. He didn't want to cry, not in front of his mom.

"Oh, sweetheart," she said, crossing the room. She wrapped her arms around his head and pulled him close. His cheek pressed into her stomach, one of her hands threaded in his hair, and she rubbed his back with the other. "You're okay."

"Why did you leave work?"

"Because I wanted to be with you. I needed to be with you. I talked to your dad and he, well, he saw the picture. He had questions. I answered them, and we talked. And we'll see what happens."

And that was it then. And for some reason, his mom leaving work, holding him, and confirming that his dad wasn't pleased, wasn't happy for him, wasn't sure if he was going to come back—that made it all real.

Real.

Bridger crumpled. He squeezed his eyes shut, but tears leaked out anyway and slid down the side of his nose. He stifled a sob, because why was he crying over a man who didn't know him anyway? Over someone who hadn't wanted him for the last ten years? How could he hurt so sharply when there was nothing between them but a vague promise of a relationship?

He was eight all over again.

"Oh, honey," his mom said, squeezing him. "I'm sorry. I'm so sorry."

Bridger cried. His shoulders shook, and his nose clogged with snot, and his breathing went ragged. He clutched at his mom's scrubs and sobbed into the fabric.

Fuck.

Fuck, it hurt.

His mom whispered phrases and words that he couldn't make out, but her voice was low and soothing. She held onto him, held on even though he was eighteen and an adult and smearing tears and snot all over her shirt. She held on until he finally could inhale and nothing else shuddered out of him. Even then, when he started to pick up the pieces of himself and slot them back into place, exhausted and worn, she held on.

"Bridger." She bent to his eye level and put her hands on his shoulders. Her expression was earnest and kind as she stared into his eyes. "You have done nothing wrong." Bridger wiped his nose on his sleeve. "Except that," she said. "That was gross. Let me get you a tissue."

"I love you, Mom."

"I love you, too, Bridger. To the stars and back and everywhere in between. You are my everything and I love every bit of you."

"Even the weird parts?"

"Especially the weird parts."

Bridger reached over and tapped the paper. "Even this part?"

"Yes, Bridger. Don't ever question it. I love you. And I will love whoever you love as long as they love you."

"Okay." He sniffled and used the tissue she handed him. "I, I don't know where that came from. I don't know why I reacted like that."

His mom didn't answer, but she didn't keep a poker face either. She was angry. Not at him, but Bridger could guess how well the phone call between her and his dad had gone, especially since she felt compelled to leave work and come home.

"Have you eaten?"

Bridger shook his head. "We didn't get that far."

"Okay. Good. It's late, but I think Sal's is in order. And I think we should watch some TV and maybe you take the morning off from school tomorrow."

"That sounds good."

FEET PROPPED ON THE COFFEE table, belly full of a warm meatball sub, his mom next to him, Bridger breathed.

"You okay, kid?"

"Yeah." His eyes heavy-lidded, he sprawled deeper into the cushions. "I think, I think if someone had reacted like that six months ago, it would be a different story. But you didn't. Astrid didn't. Pavel didn't."

She wrapped her fingers around his. "I'm so sorry."

"Don't apologize for him. I'm just saying this because I'm not ashamed of who I am. And I'm not going to stop being who I am because of him." He rolled his head so he could meet his mom's worried gaze. "Don't worry. I have no plans to run away to Florida this time."

She wiped tears from her cheeks. "I'm glad to hear that."

"And if he wants to talk, I'll talk. But I'm not hiding."

"Okay. You're the bravest kid I know. The best kid."

Bridger turned up his nose. "I'm not a kid. I'm a mature adult now."

"Oh really? I guess the mature adult doesn't want chocolate sprinkles on his ice cream."

Bridger mustered a grin. "Not that mature."

"I figured." She patted his knee. "I'll be right back."

His mom disappeared into the kitchen, and Bridger's façade cracked. A few new tears dripped down his cheeks, and he hastily sopped them up with his sleeve. Mature adult or not, he felt like shit. He tipped his head back and studied the ceiling. He felt bruised in a way he never had before, sore and stretched thin, as if his spirit had doubled as a punching bag. But he wasn't going to dwell. Maybe for tonight. But tomorrow was a new day, and he had friends and he had a life and he had people who loved him. Grandma Alice had seen it in his marrow. He only needed to remember that, cling to it, and he'd be fine.

He'd be fine. He'd be fine.

He *was* fine.

He was living as himself, and no one could take that away from him. He wouldn't let them.

CHAPTER 11

THE WEEKEND SNUCK UP ON Bridger.

Summer Lore had either taken Pavel's warning to heart and gone into hiding or she was around and causing trouble out of sight. Bridger put his money on the second option. There were plenty of folklore and myths in the area, and she could be traveling to the Upper Peninsula or across the state to report on any of them. At any rate, he hadn't seen her since their encounter at Grandma Alice's shop.

Bridger worked on his paper. He agonized over what to write in Leo's yearbook, then settled on something he wasn't ready to say out loud and that he might regret later. He did more homework. He handed out yearbooks. He voted for the prom court and ignored the pointed glares Lacey sent his way when the subject was brought up at the lunch table. He got fitted for his cap and gown in the gym along with the four hundred other seniors in the school. He procured more unicorn poop for Nia and visited Ginny and drank Grandma Alice's tea, though he wasn't quite sure what it was supposed to be doing for him. He met with Pavel and talked through a few more crises. He also received permission to use the portal for something not myth-emergency related.

He didn't hear from his dad. He didn't reach out either, though one night he hovered over his dad's contact number, debating whether to call him or remain silent. In the end, he decided to let his dad come to him.

Suddenly it was Saturday, which meant prom night. Bridger had known it was coming. He'd rented a tux. He'd paid his share of the limo. He'd suffered through another sex talk with his mom. But when Saturday rolled around, Bridger wasn't ready.

"You're fidgeting," Astrid said, leaning close to the mirror in the hallway bathroom. She swept eyeliner over her lid in a perfect line, wing and all. "What's wrong? It's Leo. You've been with Leo for months now."

"Yeah. Well. I'm nervous."

"I'd raise my perfectly plucked and arched eyebrow, but it'd mess up my makeup."

Bridger huffed. "I may have something planned."

She turned, dropping her lipstick case. "Oh, really?"

"Yeah. Nothing like, nothing like a teen movie okay? So get your mind out of soft-focus hotel scenes."

"I said nothing."

"You looked like you were going to say something."

Earlier that day, Astrid had an appointment to have her hair styled into something elaborate and gorgeous. She had consulted Nia about cosmetics, and Bridger had kept his mouth firmly shut when the topic of ingredients came up. Now, Astrid stared at him through the reflection in the mirror, beautiful and amused.

"Okay, spit it out."

Bridger shrugged. "Leo's been, well, he's been really understanding and compassionate and basically the best boyfriend ever. I want to do something nice and romantic."

"Oh, you're cute. Do you need help?"

"Nah, I got it. I just wanted to let you know if we disappear from prom for a minute not to worry."

She winked. "Got it."

The doorbell rang. Soon after, his mom's voice carried up the stairs. "Luke, Leo, and the limo are here!"

"How alliterative," Bridger said, slipping his tux jacket over his crisp shirt and vest. His bow tie was crooked, but he'd left it like that to give his mother something to do.

"Stall for a minute while I slip this dress on. Okay?"

"Yeah."

Bridger thundered down the stairs in his glossy and squeaking shoes and stopped at the foot. Leo waited, dressed in a gray, fitted suit with a skinny tie and with his hair styled in his usual spikes and swoops. Luke danced nervously at his side with a corsage in his hands. His vest and tie were blue to match Astrid's dress.

His mom had promised not to be too embarrassing, but she clasped her hands and was unsuccessful in stifling a gasp. She straightened his tie and smoothed down his vest. "You're so handsome," she said, brushing his hair from his eyes. "I almost can't stand it."

"You're embarrassing," he said, playfully. "But thanks."

"Together the three of you are stunning. I need a picture."

"Mom," Bridger said, "you promised."

Leo elbowed Bridger in the side. "I hate to tell you this," he said, smile playing around his mouth, "but my mom and dad are waiting outside to pounce with, like, actual camera equipment. It's going to be super-humiliating."

Bridger's pulse raced. "Really? Sounds awesome. I can't wait."

"Squeeze together," his mom said, wielding her phone. "And straighten your tie again, Bridger."

Leo did the honors of tie straightening, and his mom took pictures of that too. She also took pictures when Astrid descended the staircase and when Luke put the corsage on her wrist. She took pictures as they walked outside, and, sure enough, Mr. and Mrs. Rivera waited next to the limo. The four of them posed together, then as couples, and then as friends, and in front of the limo, and in front of a tree, and in front of the house, and they were going to be late for their dinner reservation.

Leo rolled his eyes and spoke in Spanish to his dad, who kept posing them and snapping pictures.

"They're going to miss dinner and prom if you keep going," Mrs. Rivera said, gently placing a hand on her husband's arm.

Mr. Rivera was a large man, former military, and probably the nicest dude Bridger had had the pleasure of meeting. He seemed constantly amused when Bridger was around, though Leo reported that he could be strict when it came to rules and grades. Mr. Rivera gathered Leo in a large hug, kissed his hair, then roped Bridger in as well; his muscular arms wrapped around the pair of them and squeezed them together.

"My boys," he said. "Have fun."

Warmth blossomed through Bridger. "We will, Mr. Rivera."

"Good."

The four of them piled into the limo and waved goodbye. The parents took a picture of that too.

Dinner was great. They ate and laughed and pretended to know what fork to use for each course. They rode to the hotel ballroom and, when they arrived, the three guys scrambled out and snapped pictures as Astrid emerged as if she was a movie star at a premiere.

The prom theme was something about fairytales, which hit a little too close to home for Bridger. He kept his mouth shut, though he and Astrid snickered at the cutouts of fairies all around the room. The rest of the ballroom was decorated with trees in random positions to recreate a magical forest, and in a corner sat a net of blue and white balloons with mermaids along the walls.

"I swear, if someone in a sasquatch suit pops out from behind one of those trees, I'm leaving," Bridger whispered in Leo's ear.

"I'll protect you. I promise."

"My hero."

Leo's mouth quirked up. "Literally."

The DJ played, and they danced and drank punch. The senior class crowned Leo prom king and Lacey prom queen, and they danced for half a song until Leo bowed out and all but ran away. He grabbed Bridger and yanked him to the dance floor from where he stood on the edge. Lacey didn't seem to mind as she swung Carrie—from the field hockey team—from the crowd and into her arms. The song finished with the four of them on the dance floor and with Bridger and Leo awkwardly wrapped around each other, because Leo clutched him and Bridger didn't know where to put his hands while the chaperones watched.

"I don't know if I should bow to you or order a burger."

Leo adjusted the crown; a faint blush crossed his cheekbones in the flashing lights. "I wasn't expecting it. And I panicked. Does it look that bad?"

How the hell was he so endearing? How was that possible?

"No. It doesn't look bad, just, okay, so it looks ridiculous, but you wear it with honor. Seriously. Don't take it off until I get a picture."

They took selfies and danced again and drank even more punch, and it was the best night Bridger had with Leo and with Astrid.

About halfway into the dance, Bridger checked his watch, then nudged Leo's side with his elbow. He leaned close. "Want to get out of here for a minute? Get some air?"

Brown eyes sparkling, Leo drained his cup. "Yeah."

Wiping his sweaty hands on his rented trousers, Bridger laced his fingers with Leo's, and together they left the hotel ballroom and meandered to the parking lot. Listening for the familiar hum, Bridger guided Leo to where the portal hovered near the dumpsters at the back of the building.

Leo raised an eyebrow. "What do you have planned?"

"Something." Bridger's middle fluttered. "Do you trust me?"

"Of course."

"Okay." He tugged on Leo's hand. "Follow me through. Keep holding on to my hand." Bridger stepped up to the inky blackness and touched the surface. "To where we discussed, please."

The portal climbed up his arm and, with one backward glance at Leo, Bridger stepped through.

They came out on the other side in a small meadow. The Upper Peninsula was chillier than Midden, but otherwise it was perfect. A blanket was spread on the ground, and a string of white lights hung from the branches of the tree above them. A picnic basket sat on the blanket with two champagne flutes on its top.

"What is this?" Leo asked, beaming and blushing. "Did you plan this?"

"The pixies helped immensely. And Pavel recalibrated the portal for us both. But the idea was all me."

Leo squeezed his hand. "This is awesome." His cheeks dimpled. "You're a closet romantic."

"Sometimes."

They sprawled on the blanket. The spot overlooked a misty ravine. Bridger handed Leo a glass and pulled a bottle from the basket. He poured Leo a glass of sparkling white-grape juice. He poured his own glass, and they clinked them together.

"This is better than the punch," Leo said. "We should've ditched sooner."

Laughing, Bridger reclined, propped on his elbows. "No way. And miss your coronation?"

"I still don't think it should've been me, by the way." Leo had abandoned the crown on a table before they left. "I thought it would be Zeke."

"You're too humble. You've charmed everyone in the school. Even the lunch ladies. All you have to do is flash your million-watt smile, and everyone is putty. It's gross and an abuse of power. I don't know why I even like you."

Leo playfully kicked Bridger's shin. "Good to know my charms don't work on you."

"Pfft. They work the most on me."

Shaking his head, glass dangling from his fingertips, he slid closer. "Good. Because your charms work on me as well."

Bridger snorted. "What charms? Like the tripping over everything? Or the fact that I freak out all the time? Or where I overanalyze every little interaction or tidbit of information?"

Leo brushed a wayward strand of Bridger's hair behind his ear. "All of it."

Ugh. This guy. So cute. So perfect.

"Do you know where we are?" Bridger asked.

"Not a clue."

"Paulding, Michigan."

Leo crinkled his nose. "Is that important?"

Bridger gestured at the lightly wooded area in front of them. "Just watch."

They sat in silence, cuddled together, under the sliver of moon. On a wisp of a breeze, the light appeared, bobbing along the length of the ravine. It was greenish-yellow, small, round, and beautiful. It moved slowly, hanging in the mist, casting a glow along the trees and the thick vines and wildflowers. The atmosphere became heavy with the feeling of the supernatural, the otherworldly, that Bridger felt often around Pavel and the pixies: comforting and still, thick like a blanket, but alien, existing beyond the natural laws.

"What is it?" Leo asked, breathless.

"The Paulding Light. Don't worry. It's harmless. I totally wouldn't test your hero abilities with something that could hurt us."

Leo squeezed Bridger's torso. "I'm not worried. It's beautiful. What's the story?"

"There are several different stories, and all of them are kind of sad. Some say it's a father looking for his lost kid, and the light is the flame from a lantern. Other say it's a conductor who was decapitated on railroad tracks, looking for his head. But there aren't tracks around here, and that seems a popular story for ghost lights." Bridger ran his fingers through Leo's hair. "I don't know what it is, but I thought it would be cool to share with you. I know you know about everything now, but we haven't, I mean, other than Grandma Alice, you haven't gotten a chance to experience any of it. I thought this would be a good place to start, a phenomenon to witness together."

Leo kissed him.

Bridger wasn't expecting it, but Leo wrapped his arms around Bridger's shoulders, hauled him close, and cupped the back of Bridger's head. Leo tasted like grape juice and heat and enthusiasm.

With an oomph, Leo rolled Bridger to his back and hovered over him on the blanket.

"You're disheveled," Bridger said, cupping Leo's cheek. He rubbed his thumb over the line of Leo's blush. "And flushed. People are going to think we're a prom cliché."

"Let them think it," Leo said. He tugged on Bridger's tie until it came undone, then ruffled Bridger's hair. "There. Suitably debauched."

"That's a big word."

Leo laughed. His forehead rested on Bridger's chest, so the sound was muffled by Bridger's vest. "I wouldn't mind it, you know."

"What was that?"

Leo lifted his head, his brown eyes shining. "I said, I wouldn't mind being a prom cliché."

"I thought… we had a whole conversation."

Leo propped his chin on his hands, which, in turn, pressed on the buttons of Bridger's shirt. "We're having a new conversation."

"I'm not ready to have a new conversation," Bridger admitted.

"Okay," Leo rolled off and lay next to Bridger on the blanket. He was a line of heat down Bridger's side. Their shoulders touched; their hands tangled. "Thank you. This was romantic and special, and the grape juice was awesome."

"You're welcome. Thank you for being a totally awesome boyfriend."

"No problem. It's easy because I'm with you."

Bridger snorted. "We're venturing into George Lucas-dialogue territory."

"Hey. I can't besmirch the Princess of Genovia, but you can drag George Lucas? I don't know how I feel about that. I think I'm offended."

Bridger poked Leo's side. "Have you listened to the dialogue in the prequels? It's mind numbing."

Leo put his hand over his heart. "I take every nice thing I've ever said about you back. All of it."

"Nerd," Bridger said, propping up on his side. "You have everyone fooled that you're this cool guy and really you're just a massive geek."

"Takes one to know one."

"Oh, it's on."

They rolled around on the blanket, playfighting; Leo emitted gales of laughter, and Bridger did his best to tickle Leo while avoiding being kneed in the gut. It was all fun and games until someone ripped their rented tux, so they stopped and just kissed for a while.

Leo broke away. He snuggled into Bridger's side, head resting on Bridger's shoulder.

"So, what do you think it is?"

"Think what is?"

Leo poked him in the side. "A few kisses and you lose all brain power. The light. What do you think it is?"

"Well," Bridger laced his fingers behind his head. "Past Bridger would say it's a trick of the light. Swamp gas? A reflection of a streetlight? Something mundane." Past Bridger lacked imagination and supernatural-life experience. Past Bridger was also kind of lonely and wouldn't have put himself out there to even consider the existence of a ghost light much less be vulnerable enough to share it with someone as important as Leo.

"What does current Bridger think?"

"I'm not sure. I know what's it's not. It's not a pixie or a ghost or a Goatman."

"Thank everything for that." Leo propped his chin on Bridger's chest. "I may be a hero, but I'm not here for an axe-wielding Goatman. Just FYI."

Bridger threaded his fingers through Leo's thick dark hair. "Me neither. I'd run away, very quickly."

"You know what they say," Leo said, expression solemn. "You don't have to run faster than the monster, only faster than your friend."

Bridger barked a laugh. He jabbed his fingers into Leo's side. "Oh, my God. Don't *even*. You know you'd totally let me get away then you'd figure out how to disarm the Goatman and convince it to stop its axe-wielding ways. You'd use your ineffable charm and by the end of the interaction, he'd abandon his murdery profession and choose to live on a farm raising chickens. He'd bake pies for his neighbors and volunteer at a kitten rescue on the weekends."

Leo snorted. "You have the wildest and weirdest imagination."

"You like it."

"I adore it." Leo's flicked Bridger's ear. "I adore you."

Bridger's heart raced. "I don't know why, but hey, not questioning your judgment. You *are* a hero. You should have good critical-thinking skills."

"So I've been told." Leo sighed. "Pavel says I'm a hero. But I don't feel it. I'm not perfect." He shrugged. "I'm just a guy."

Beautiful and humble. Ugh. Bridger couldn't deal with the perfection. Affection suffused every crevice of Bridger's being. He gave Leo his best cheesy grin. "You're my guy."

"Now *that* is bad dialogue."

Bridger turned up his nose. "I have it on good authority that you adore it."

Leo kissed Bridger's cheek. "I do. God help me, but I do."

They indulged in another round of kissing, but this time it was Bridger who pulled away when it became a tad too heated. He kissed Leo's forehead. "We better get back," Bridger said, chest heaving, lips tingling. They'd been gone a while and had to return before a chaperone noticed. "Now that we really look debauched."

"Yeah. I want to dance some more." He tugged lightly on Bridger's tie. "And then I want to go to the school gym and play stupid games during the after-prom and eat all the ice cream."

"Sounds like an awesome plan." Bridger stood and grabbed Leo's hand, hauling him to his feet. "Oh, almost forgot." He flipped the top of the basket and pulled out Leo's yearbook. He'd agonized for days over what to write and in the end went with something simple and soppy and as heartfelt as Bridger was capable of. He slapped the book against Leo's chest. "Don't read it now. Please."

Leo beamed. He clutched the book. "I won't. Promise."

"Okay. Because it's, well, just…" Bridger blushed.

Leo took his hand. "I'm sure it's perfect."

They left the mess behind for the pixies to clean up, because if Bridger can hunt unicorn poop for them, they can pick up a blanket and grape juice.

Stepping through the portal, Leo's hand tight in his, Bridger was happy. He was well and truly happy, and his only worry was sneaking back into the hotel ballroom as discreetly as possible. But even that didn't matter much, because there were worse things than being caught with his boyfriend after rolling around on a blanket in the grass.

They landed on the sidewalk near the line of limos. The silence of the night was broken by the sound of a long slurp when Leo popped out behind Bridger. Before he could take one step on the concrete in his tight, shiny shoes, he heard a squeal. Glass broke, shards skittered across the asphalt in the moonlight, and pieces came to rest at his toe. He snapped his head up. Summer stood right in front of them.

"Where the fuck did you come from?" Eyes wide, mouth hanging open, Bridger saw the moment she spotted the magic portal behind them. "And what the fuck is that?"

Oh, shit.

CHAPTER 12

"WHAT ARE YOU DOING HERE?" Bridger asked, grip tight on Leo's hand. He willed the portal to disappear, but it didn't. It hummed behind them, expectant and shimmering and completely magical. "I thought my boss made it clear when he warned you about stalking me. In fact, I'm pretty certain he said to stop."

Summer narrowed her eyes, then she swayed. Her bathrobe fluttered, cinched tight over pink silk pajamas, one leg of which was doused in a strong-smelling liquid. She wore strappy high heels, which scared Bridger. The thin points were easily sharp enough to stab someone. And she might snap an ankle given how uncoordinatedly she moved.

She pointed a wobbling finger at him. The sharp smell of alcohol wafted from the slick asphalt and the shards of glass. "Public street."

"Yeah, right next to the hotel where we're holding our high school prom. How convenient."

Snorting, she flipped her hair. It was a tangled mess, so blond strands flopped into her eyes. "You self-centered little jerk. It's the only nice hotel in town, where I've been staying for the past few weeks because you Michiganders love your folklore."

"Oh."

She took a step, and glass crunched under her shoes. "Now. How in the hell did you appear out of thin air?"

"We didn't. We were in the woods," Bridger said, jerking his thumb over his shoulder toward the copse of trees by the sidewalk. He picked a blade of grass from Leo's hair. "See?"

"Uh huh." She pushed her face close. "I know what I saw. I saw you—" She interrupted herself with a fierce, wet, burp.

Bridger gagged. "Have you been drinking?"

"Have you?"

"No."

"Then no."

"Liar. It smells like what I imagine a frat house does. What was in that bottle? Paint thinner?"

"You..." She dug the tip of her finger into Bridger's sternum. "...have been a thorn in my side since I arrived in this one-Target town. Now, you're going to tell me why the sky is humming and blurry."

"Because you obviously have had way too much of whatever you were drinking. And you're super-embarrassing yourself. We are at prom. We are boyfriends. We went into the woods to have alone time. Okay? Now, please leave us alone before we call the police and tell them all about your voyeuristic tendencies." Bridger stepped backward. "Come on, Leo."

She may have been on the wrong side of tipsy, but she was still fast and strong. Summer lashed out and grabbed Bridger's arm. Her grip was bruising; her fingernails dug into the fabric of his tux.

"Oh, no. You're not brushing me off. I know you know more than you're telling me."

"Let go."

"No."

"I said—"

A loud sucking noise sounded behind them, and Bridger rolled his eyes to the sky. Because *of course*.

"Bridger!" Pavel yelled. "I heard the toaster and—"

Summer gaped at Pavel.

Pavel stared at Summer. His face drained of all color, leaving him translucent.

Stomach sinking to his knees, Bridger looked at them. There was no way he could bullshit his way out of this one. He wrenched his arm out of her grip and stumbled into the solid, stable presence of Leo. Leo hooked his hand in the crook of Bridger's elbow to steady him.

Hand tucked at his side, hidden by the flap of his coat, Pavel snapped his fingers. The action was discreet. The portal was anything but. It collapsed in a flash of light and with the sound of a vacuum snagged on ripped carpet.

Well, that wasn't helpful *at all*.

"Holy fu—" Summer trailed off. "I thought, I thought— " Her hand trembled in front of her open mouth. Bridger was certain she was either going to scream or puke. The odds were fifty-fifty.

"We really need to talk about subtlety when this is all over," Bridger said under his breath to Pavel as Summer stumbled.

He gave a sharp nod in return. "Noted."

Leo coughed into his fist, unsuccessfully hiding a laugh.

"I thought it was a *hoax!*" she screeched.

Bridger flinched, but then his brain caught up, and his eyes widened. "What?" He impressed himself with his ability to be deadpan. "You what?"

"But it's *real*! Isn't it? It's all real!" She put her hands on her head and spun around in the parking lot; her impractical shoes slid across the debris of her bottle. Her bathrobe flapped, and her pajamas swished.

"Miss Lore, I think you may need to go back to your hotel," Pavel said. "I'd be happy to escort you to ensure your safety, or maybe I can call your assistant to help? Either way, you clearly need to go inside and perhaps sleep this off."

Bridger held up a hand. "Wait a minute! Before you go anywhere, explain the hoax bit!"

She laughed, drunk, and close to deranged. She stopped spinning, but she staggered and clenched her arms around her stomach.

"You have no idea how many times I've gone to backwoods, dingy little towns to find teenagers bored to tears and making crop circles. The number of fake footprints I've followed to the laughter of those little jerks would make your head spin more than mine is right now." She flailed, almost smacking Bridger in the face. "And you," she whirled, "were obviously the ringleader here. That fake voice on the EVP. The crap about being the witch's best customer. The *bullshit* speech about *believing*."

"First off, shows what you know, my life may resemble a circus, but I've never been the ringleader of *anything*, and second, what was with all the following and the waving the microphone in my face?"

"To put pressure on you to tell the truth!" She wiped a hand over her eyes, smearing her makeup. "If I could get you to break and confess to all the shenanigans, then I could go home! Back to Georgia and back to trying to find a way off this stupid show. But no! No! You had to be interesting and it all has to be real!"

Oh. Oh, no.

Oh, no, no, no.

Nope. Nope. Nope. Nope.

"When you said you wanted me to crack—"

"There's always one spineless clown who will spill the beans about the pranks when I put enough pressure on them. And you..." She shoved her finger in his chest again. "...you were a tougher nut than I thought. You panicked when I talked to Luke and you ran at the bakery, so I thought I could get to you. But no, not Bridger-freaking-Whitt, sarcastic asshole, and generally beloved teenager."

Bridger flushed and resisted the urge to ostrich or turtle or gazelle. He wanted to run, but Leo's grip on his arm tightened. This whole time, Bridger was working on the basis of knowing everything was real and he'd thought she was trying to get him to spill about how the paranormal was alive and well in Midden, but that wasn't the case. Summer worked from a perception that everything was *fake*, and she was trying to get him to admit to a long prank.

"The break between season six and seven," Bridger said, realization dawning.

"Now he gets it!" Summer threw out her arms again. "I tried to leave then, but they pulled me back in, promising me more money, more gravitas, fewer forests, and less mud. But no. No!" She stomped her foot. "Now I'm here, preparing for season eleven. I've been through five different camera operators!" She held up her hand, fingers spread, and shoved it in Bridger's face; her palm was an inch from his nose. "Five! They've all left for better gigs. Our ratings are in the toilet. Our expenses are over the top with all the travel. I hoped that if Midden tanked, then the show would tank. And that'd be the end of it." She thrust a finger to where the portal had hovered minutes before. "But now it's real!"

She hiccupped, then sobbed, and her mascara leaked down her cheeks.

"You're right. It was all a hoax," Bridger said. He disentangled from Leo and stepped away from Pavel, distancing himself. "They had nothing to do with it. It was all me. You are correct. I'm the ringleader. I set it all up."

Summer wiped a hand over her face; her black makeup made a bruise-like smear from her eye to her ear. "Liar. You're a liar."

"Yes. I mean, no. Not as much as I used to be, but you're right. It was all a senior prank, orchestrated by me. You caught me enlisting Grandma Alice's help that day. I screwed with the EVP recorder. That day at the beach was a joke that went horribly wrong, but that was also me. I'm behind it. All of it."

"Bridger, what are you—"

"My boss is an awesome, caring dude and didn't know. He defended me because he thought you were harassing me—which, let's be honest, you were. And my boyfriend knew nothing. He's so busy with baseball and school there was no way he could be involved."

"Stop!" She raised her hand. "Stop. I know what I saw. There was a distortion in the air, and you stepped out of it."

Pavel cleared his throat. "You're drunk, Miss Lore."

"I may be drunk, but I know what I saw. Okay, I don't know what I saw, but I saw something, and you three know what it was." She wobbled, then stumbled and went down on one knee.

The three of them lunged to assist her, but she pushed them away. She gained her feet just as her cellphone rang. She pulled it from the pocket of her robe and answered.

"What?" She squinted. "In the parking lot. No, the one with all the limos. Yeah, wait, where are you?"

Matt appeared down the sidewalk with his cellphone pressed to his ear and utter relief on his face.

"I'm right here, looking for you!" He ended the call and shoved the phone in his pocket. "Thank goodness, Summer. You went to the liquor store an hour ago. What the heck happened?"

"We found her here," Pavel said, smoothly. "She's quite impaired. She's been raving about seeing things and she smells of liquor. She accosted my assistant again, and I did warn her last time about harassing him. Next time, we will call the police."

Summer scoffed and, if glares could kill, Pavel would have been a corpse, as would Bridger—one in a tux, but still a dead man walking. A prom zombie.

Matt sighed and gently took Summer by the arm. "Let's get you back to the suite."

"There was a glowing oval!"

"Uh huh." Matt steered her toward the back door of the hotel. "You can tell me all about it in the morning after you sober up a little."

Summer glared at the trio while Matt escorted her away.

Bridger stood frozen in the parking lot until Summer and Matt were through the back door of the hotel. "As much of a pain as she is, Pavel, I don't feel good about that."

Leo frowned and rested his hand between Bridger's shoulder blades.

Pavel sighed. "I don't either. But we must protect the myths at all costs." He leveled Bridger with a significant gaze. "You know that."

Bridger did. He remembered their conversation last fall, when Leo's life was the price to bring peace and balance back to the myth cycles, the solution to keeping the supernatural world from being revealed. Fortunately, Leo's hero death was a metaphorical one, but there were a few days when Bridger and Pavel were on opposite sides of a huge divide, and there didn't seem to be a way to meet in the middle that didn't involve a fight. Maybe he was more like Captain America than he'd thought, but that would make Pavel Iron Man, and that made Bridger's brain short-circuit.

Bridger shivered. "Still doesn't mean that I feel awesome about gaslighting Summer."

"I know." Pavel shook his head. "Go back to your dance, Bridger. Enjoy your night with Leo. I'll see you Monday."

"Pavel?" Bridger fidgeted. He tugged on his loosened tie. "Are you okay?"

"I'm fine. Thank you."

Pavel was a bad liar, but Bridger let it slide, even if he could see the aging in Pavel's posture and the lines forming around the downturn of his mouth.

"Okay. I'll see you Monday."

Waving, Pavel disappeared into the night.

Leo draped his arm over Bridger's shoulders. "Do you still want to dance? We don't have to stay. We could go home if you want."

"Are you kidding?" Bridger managed a smile. "I think there is a fake Vegas roulette table at the school gym that we have to hit up. And I need at least one more dance with the prom king. I mean, how many guys can say they're dating the prom king? Only one. Me. It's me. I'm dating the prom king."

"You don't have to pretend to be okay for me, Bridger. The whole situation is…"

"Shitty," Bridger supplied. "It's awful. And makes me feel like a bad person. And I feel all mixed up inside about it, but I don't feel mixed up inside about you. Let's go dance and drink the bad punch and go to the after-prom and gamble with raffle tickets."

"And eat all the ice cream."

"Yes. And eat all the ice cream." Bridger nodded. "I agree with this plan. It is a good plan."

"Even if you came up with it."

"Hey! I'll have you know that my plans have gotten better than they were before. I know they couldn't get much worse, but there has been marked improvement."

Chuckling under his breath in the way that made Bridger's heart double-thump and his cheeks flush, Leo led Bridger back to the ballroom. "I know. You did just pull off an amazing prom surprise."

"Exactly! I should get at least some points for that."

Leo rolled his eyes. He dug his fingers into the indent of Bridger's waist. "Not everything is a contest."

"Says the prom king who plays all the sports."

Leo shook his head and glanced at Bridger through his eyelashes. "Speaking of sports, the next home game is for the chance to play in the state championship. I'd love it if you came to watch."

"Of course. I'll be there. With pom poms and a huge sign declaring that you are the best player in the entire universe."

Leo kissed his cheek. "Please don't."

Snorting, Bridger knocked his shoulder into Leo as they entered the hotel. The music from the dance careened down the hallway, the melody was muffled, but the beat thumped in the floor. Determined to enjoy the rest of the night, Bridger gritted his teeth and hooked his fingers in the side pocket of Leo's jacket.

Bridger's life was destined for change, and everything around him was in a tumult. He would graduate and be forced to face the next chapter of his life. His dad circled him in a Plutonian orbit. His job was unpredictable bedlam. His feelings on all those subjects were a tangled mess, but at least he had Leo for the night. And he had Astrid. And the next few hours stretched out in front of him in a needed predictable pattern of too-loud music, bad dancing, spontaneous laughter, and weighted kisses. He clung to it, as he clung to Leo as they snuck back into prom, because everything *was* changing, and he was certain he couldn't handle it alone.

*   *   *

BRIDGER SLEPT THROUGH MOST OF Sunday. He didn't wake up until late afternoon. He ate, worked on schoolwork, then went back to sleep.

He went through the motions on Monday. All anyone could talk about was prom, which was a relief from talking about anything else. Bridger went to classes. He had lunch with Astrid. Luke had moved from his spot on the other end of the table to one beside her. She blushed at Bridger's raised eyebrows.

After lunch, Bridger handed out yearbooks and avoided making eye contact with the underclassmen because it invited conversation and he was not in the mood to make small talk. He hadn't heard from Leo about the note Bridger had written in his yearbook and that meant either he hadn't read it yet or he didn't have anything to say. Leo had yet to return Bridger's yearbook, so maybe he was agonizing as much as Bridger had. Anyway, it wasn't something Bridger wanted to dwell on, and he pushed it to the back of his mind.

At the end of the day, with his hood pulled up, he hopped into Astrid's car.

"We're kind of dating," she said to Bridger before he could ask. "He likes me, and I like him but he's going to Ohio State for school."

Bridger made a face.

"I know," Astrid said, shaking her head so her piercings glinted in the spring sunlight. "Of all places."

She pulled out of the parking lot and drove toward Pavel's house chatting away about prom night and graduation.

"Hey," Bridger said, "Leo wants me to come to the baseball game this week. You in?"

"Definitely. I'll invite Luke."

"Sounds good. Maybe we can go out after."

"Awesome."

They lapsed into silence. If Astrid noticed his extra moodiness, she didn't comment, and he was grateful for it. She stopped in front of Pavel's house.

Bridger grabbed his bag from the floorboard. "Hey, can you proofread my paper for me? It's almost done."

"Yeah, sure. Print it out and bring it to me at school."

"Print it out? There are like five other easier ways for me to share my paper with you than to print it out."

"Yeah, but I like to read it on paper. I catch more mistakes that way. Plus, I like using a red pen."

Sighing, Bridger opened the car door. "Fine, Grandma. I'll get it to you this week."

"That's a funny way to say thank you!" she yelled from her open window.

"Thank you!" Bridger yelled back to her from the front porch. She flicked him off.

Caught off guard, Bridger burst out a laugh; his mood lifted. Still chuckling, Bridger waltzed into the house. He tipped an imaginary hat to Mindy at her desk but stopped short when he looked at her desk.

"You're down to one?" A lone bobblehead sat on the corner. It was a spider with a clown hat, and it eyed him as if he owed it money. She shrugged and slid a terrifyingly long, sharp pin through her pile of hair. "What's going on?"

She blinked. Her eyeshadow was deep purple and matched the purple on her pursed lips and fingernails. She leveled him with a stare. "I needed a change."

"Oh," Bridger said. "So, like, are you moving on from bobble-heads? You're going to invest in something equally as unsettling to spread over your desk? Is it porcelain babies? Or a giant tank filled with bug-eyed fish and weird plants and a pineapple under the sea?"

"Something like that."

"Oh, okay. Awesome. Thank goodness. That is a change I can handle. Honestly, I miss cross-eyed Postman Rover, but I look forward to his replacement."

"Boss is on the large mirror upstairs. Be quiet when you head up. If you're capable."

Aghast, Bridger pressed his palm to his chest. "Rude."

Smirking, Mindy went back to her phone and tapped away at some game.

As quietly as possible, Bridger ascended the stairs and went to the large mirror in the living area. Usually it was hidden behind a curtain, and Bridger had never seen Pavel use it, though he knew it was how Pavel contacted his mentor and Intermediary Headquarters. He poked his head around the corner.

Pavel stood in front of the mirror with his head hanging, the heel of his hand pressed to his forehead, and his eyes focused on a worn spot on the floor.

In the reflection was a person Bridger had never met, but who was vaguely familiar. He had white hair that fell to his shoulders, and his wrinkles had wrinkles. He wore a sweater and jeans and he looked like someone's farmer grandpa, except that he exuded the same otherness that Pavel did, the aura of someone not quite of this world. He stared at Pavel with a disapproving expression, and, when he spoke, his voice was deep, in such a low register that Bridger had trouble hearing it.

"You are not suggesting you reveal the myth world to *Summer Lore*," he said, tone incredulous and angry. "Have you hit your head?"

Pavel winced. "I thought if we revealed something small, then it would satisfy her curiosity and she'd move on."

"Why? Because your assistant is uncomfortable with lying?"

Pavel snapped his gaze to the mirror. "Because I'm uncomfortable with the situation. She saw our portal, and I used her drunken state to take advantage."

"And that is your fault. You should know better than to leap into a portal without knowing what is on the other side."

"The toasters rang, and my assistant needed—"

"Where was his familiar?"

"I don't know. It doesn't matter."

"It does matter. I warned you Midnight Marvel needed retraining and was not disciplined enough to be assigned. She is inattentive and rebellious. You must send her back to be disciplined."

Bridger recoiled. Pavel clenched his jaw and stared at the floor. "Midnight Marvel is not the problem. The situation required my immediate attention. My assistant—"

"Your assistant is a liability. And if was up to the Intermediary Council, he'd no longer be part of your team. It's only the rule that intermediaries choose their assistants that has allowed him to continue as your subordinate for as long as he has."

"He has been the only one who has lasted—"

"Again, Pavel, this is all the product of your actions and, dare I say, mistakes."

Sagging, Pavel shoved his hands into the pockets of his striped trousers. "Understood, Aurelius. I will strive to do better."

"Get Summer out of your region. Do it quickly. The Council doesn't care about the means, only the result."

"I will see what I can do."

"No, you will accomplish this task. Or they will make you quit."

Pavel paled, lips parted in a gasp. He nodded and tugged at his collar. "I understand."

Bridger gulped. Quit was a powerful word. When Bridger was on the verge of leaving himself, Nia had pinched his lips shut with her tiny arms before he could utter it. The house had a mechanism for those who chose to leave: pitching the individual out via the side door and erasing their memory of all magical knowledge. The person would believe they'd been working at a boring office job instead of running errands for pixies. The side door was a failsafe, a way to keep the number of people who knew about the magical world to a minimum.

"Good. Mirror me again when the job is done. Until then, keep a better eye on your assistant and ensure his familiar is doing her job."

"Yes, Aurelius."

The mirror winked out.

Pavel drooped, and sat heavily in the chair.

"He's the guy from the portrait downstairs, isn't he?"

Startling, Pavel hit his knee on the underside of his table. His tea cup toppled, hitting the carpeted floor with a thunk.

"Sorry." Bridger sheepishly retrieved the cup. "I'll make you some tea."

Pavel didn't argue, merely squeezed the bridge of his nose with his fingers. Having watched Pavel make tea a hundred times, Bridger could make a decent cup—at least he thought he could. Pavel took a sip, and his expression remained neutral. At least he didn't spit it out.

Bridger sat across from him and scrubbed his hands over his jeans. "What's the deal with Marv?"

"Oh, well, um, Midnight Marvel is easily distracted. She wasn't very good at her last assignment and forgets that she's a familiar at times."

"Oh. Are you going to send her back?"

"Of course not! This is her third assignment. If she fails this one, then…" He trailed off. "Anyway, don't worry. She's fine."

Bridger rubbed his hands on his jeans. Marv had been a great comfort to him thus far, and he couldn't really picture her failing at being a kitten. "And they want me fired?"

"Huh? Oh," Pavel waved the question away. "It doesn't matter. They can't make me fire an assistant. It's in the bylaws."

"But they can make you… They can make you leave."

"Yes. And if they do. then I lose my memory and my magic."

"Yikes." Bridger winced. "Would you, you know, since you're a century old…"

Pavel winced. "What would it matter? I'd lose everything else." He gestured around him indicating his home, and it hit Bridger like a ton of bricks.

"You'd lose your family."

"Yes."

"Oh, shit, Pavel. I didn't realize."

"And my replacement would likely bring or hire their own assistant."

Bridger shivered. "Really? I… Fuck. What do we need to do? Tell me what I need to do."

Pavel remained silent and still, staring at a spot on the wall. He was quiet for so long, Bridger thought he might have to repeat the question.

"Do you have your book?" Pavel asked, coming to life as if someone had unpaused him.

Bridger nodded quickly. "Yeah. Yeah, I carry it with me all the time. You told me to keep it nearby."

"Good. I want you to look through it and make notes on what might be a small element of our world that we could reveal to Summer. Something that would satisfy her curiosity but also not spur her onward toward other revelations. Make a list."

"Like an offering? Something to appease her?"

"Yes." Pavel tented his fingers. "Yes. But only if she continues to hound you. We won't need to use it if she decides the portal was a figment of her imagination."

"Um, not to be a jerk but, uh, wouldn't you be better at that?"

"No. I'm too immersed. You would have a better eye for it. Write down your suggestions and I'll look them over tonight."

"Okay. Yeah, I can do that." Bridger yanked the book out of his bag and flipped it open. "I guess it needs to be local and small, maybe the Paulding Light or the Ada Witch, though I'd hate to bring more attention to that cemetery and—"

"Quietly, Bridger," Pavel said; a small smile teased the corner of his mouth. "Make some notes. I need to talk with Mindy."

In a flurry of cheap fabric and thin limbs, Pavel shot to his feet and left the room.

Bridger frowned, fairly certain that the assignment was busy work to keep him mollified and out of the way while Pavel did the real work. But research had come in handy before, and it wouldn't be a bad idea to do what Pavel asked. Doing the opposite was what had got them into this mess—and put Pavel and his family at risk.

Bridger grabbed a notebook and a pen and set to work.

He worked until it was time to go home. Pavel hadn't returned. Bridger tore the information from his notebook and left it on the table in the study. He waved at Mindy when he left, then rode the bus home. He oozed into his house and texted his mom that he'd arrived home from work.

Feeling like a slug, Bridger took a shower, then dressed in pajamas. He made a soggy grilled cheese and ate while responding to texts from Leo and Astrid that had accumulated over the day. He climbed the stairs to his room and printed his paper for Astrid to review.

His phone rang just as he was contemplating going to bed. His dad's number flashed over his screen. *Of course.* His day wasn't shitty enough as it was, might as well add a conversation with his homophobic dad into the mix. Eyes squeezed shut, Bridger swiped over the screen and accepted the call. "Hello?"

"Hey, Bud," his dad said. "Look, I wanted to talk—"

"I don't go by that anymore," Bridger said, interrupting. "I haven't since I was eight. You can call me Bridger. Or you can call me Bridge if you feel like shortening it, but not Bud." Bridger was met with silence. He swallowed. "Dad?"

"Yeah, sorry, I'm here. I just... okay. Bridger. I'll stick to it."

"Thank you."

"So anyway, I wanted to talk. Do you have a minute?"

"Yeah. I do."

"I want to apologize for leaving the other night. Your mom pointed out to me that it was a dick move and that I should've stayed and talked."

"Yeah. It was."

Another pause. His dad was obviously waiting for absolution, but Bridger had had a bad day and was feeling a bit like a dick himself. Maybe it was hereditary. He kept his mouth shut and allowed his dad to flounder. He could drown for all Bridger cared.

He wasn't going to be throwing out the proverbial life raft. He was eighteen. His dad was forty. His dad could deal.

His dad cleared his throat. "I still want to come to your graduation. Would that be okay with you?"

Bridger bit his lip. "Yeah. That would be cool."

"Great. Well, I have to run—"

"Are you going to ask me about my boyfriend?" *Wow, way to make it awkward.*

"I, I don't know what to say. What do you want me to say, Bud? Bridger. Sorry. Bridger. Old habits."

"I want you to tell me why you left the other night?" Bridger sat on the edge of his bed.

"Did your mom talk to you?"

"Yes. She left work to come sit with me after you left. Because she's a good mom. And she talked to me. But I want to hear it from you."

"I didn't know how to react. It's not like I have a problem with gay people. I have a female coworker who has a wife."

Bridger refrained from rolling his eyes and then remembered his dad couldn't see him, so he did it anyway.

"But you're not cool having a son who has a boyfriend."

"I didn't say that."

"Then why did you leave?"

"Because I didn't know how to react, okay? Is that what you want to hear? I see you on the school newspaper with another boy. Right there on the front page."

"What does that mean?"

"I don't know. It wasn't subtle."

Subtle? "What? Am I supposed to live in the closet?"

"No. No, Bud. That's not what I'm saying. I just… you blindsided me. Okay? I didn't grow up with that lifestyle being out and open. And it definitely wasn't in the school paper. But I'm learning. And I'll do what I need to do to understand you better."

Lifestyle. In the open. Bridger rubbed his temple. His dad was playing "all the wrong words" bingo. His tension headache grew with each passing second.

"I don't have time for this," Bridger muttered, chin dropping to his chest.

"What was that?" His dad's voice went sharp.

Bridger cringed. "Let's just start over and pretend the last few minutes didn't happen. Okay? Yes, come to graduation. After that, when I'm off school for the summer and don't have a million things to worry about, we can talk more."

There was another lengthy pause, long enough for Bridger to start formulating his dad's response in his head. He had managed *What do you have to worry about? You're only eighteen* when his dad finally spoke.

"Okay. It's taken me longer to deal with my mom's estate anyway. I should be around for a few weeks of the summer."

Oh. Bridger hadn't realized reconciliation had a time limit. *But, whatever.*

"Sounds good. I'll see you at graduation."

"Text me the details. I don't trust your mom to send the correct ones."

Oh, for the love of— "Sure, Dad. I will."

Bridger hung up and fell backward onto his bed. Marv jumped up next to him and curled under his chin; her fluffy tail hit him in the eye. He scratched between her ears.

If Pavel was made to quit, he'd lose his home and his family. Bridger would lose them too. He'd lose Pavel and Elena and the pixies and Mindy and Marv and Grandma Alice. Would he lose Leo? Would his memories of their relationship be wiped away when he was pitched out of the side door? Would he be reset to back where he started in the fall—lonely and unsure?

Throat tight, Bridger squeezed his eyes shut. As much as it would suck, he'd still have Astrid and his mom. Pavel would have no one. He couldn't let that happen. He wouldn't let it happen. But with experience comes wisdom, and he knew he'd need help.

CHAPTER 13

"DAMN, BRIDGER, HOW DO YOU get yourself into these situations?"

"It's a gift," Bridger said, deadpan.

"I'd go with curse." Astrid took a sip of her pop. "You have any idea how you're going to get out of this one?"

"Literally, no." Bridger slouched in his seat at the diner. They had agreed to have a quick dinner before heading to Leo's game. As with all important events, it was being held at the community college's field. Bridger poked halfheartedly at his fish tacos. "I wouldn't be asking you if I had any plan other than making things look like an accident."

"I wouldn't joke about that."

"Yeah." Bridger tapped his foot. "I possibly wasn't joking."

Astrid grimaced. "Do you think that's Pavel's plan?"

"No. I hope not. I haven't talked to him since I left on Monday, but at that point the plan was to give her a hint. Something tiny to satiate her curiosity and have her think that's the extent of what we're hiding."

"That's a crappy plan."

"I'm aware."

"Is this like last time when Pavel's plan was to let Leo experience his hero death and you tried to go around him and screwed everything up? Thus causing a massive folklore fight in the parking lot of the homecoming game?"

Bridger slumped. "Yeah. Something like that."

Sighing, Astrid checked her phone. "Okay, well, we have a baseball game to watch and then we can dive into this further. Leo is going to win us a state championship."

"That's not how the sport works. It's a team effort. That's what he says anyway. I think he could win it singlehandedly."

"You would."

"Of course, I would. He's my boyfriend."

She quirked an eyebrow. "Is that the only thing he can do singlehandedly?"

"Oh, my God, you're the worst." Bridger said with a soft chuckle. "I'm offended."

"But you're laughing, so my job here is done." She bowed theatrically, waved to her audience, and accepted pretend flowers.

Bridger gave her a flat look but applauded.

They paid for their meals. Bridger's fish tacos were not sitting quite right in his stomach. On the drive to the game, Bridger kept an eye out for Summer's van, but he didn't see it. Maybe she had sobered up and bought the bullshit Bridger had tried to sell her—probably not, but he could hope. Optimism wasn't normally his thing, but Leo had rubbed off on him. Not literally. Seriously, not literally, not yet anyway, though not for lack of enthusiasm. Bridger shifted in his seat. Okay, he needed to stop thinking along that line.

"Stop thinking about it," Astrid said, pulling into the lot. "You have to focus on this game and on Leo. And you can't do that with all those other thoughts running through your head."

Ha! If she only knew. "You're right. Pavel told me to enjoy this stuff. So I'm going to take his advice."

"For once."

"You really are no help at all."

They approached the stadium and flashed their school ID cards to be let through the entrance without having to pay a fee. Bridger and Astrid took seats right behind the home team dugout on the third base line. Bridger waved at Leo's parents, and Mr. Rivera returned the wave and held up his camera. Bridger and Astrid posed for the picture.

"Mr. Rivera is the cutest dad."

"Yeah, he's pretty awesome," Bridger agreed.

"How's the whole situation with your dad?"

Bridger groaned. "Let's not talk about that either."

"Fair enough."

Bridger had never been a sports guy. He knew the basics of most of the popular ones but didn't seek any out to watch on TV. He knew about the Michigan versus Michigan State rivalry and he guessed he'd be more into that once he went to college in the fall. He definitely knew that Michiganders had it ingrained in them to hate Ohio State, and thus how weird it was that Luke was going there for school. But, with the little knowledge that Bridger did have, he knew that Leo was amazing at baseball. Watching him play was absolutely mesmerizing, and once the game started Bridger had difficulty looking away when Leo was on the field.

After the first inning, Luke joined them on the bleachers and sat close to Astrid. Zeke followed as well.

"Hey, Zeke," Bridger said with a nod. "Lacey not a baseball fan?"

"We broke up," Zeke said, voice flat.

Bridger winced. The whole conversation he'd had with Taylor about breakup week echoed in his brain. "Oh, that sucks."

That was not a great response, if Astrid's elbow to his ribs was a clue. He really shouldn't be allowed to socialize. He was a disaster.

"She wanted to explore other options." Zeke shrugged, then narrowed his eyes, watching Bridger with intense consideration. "You're not going to break up with Leo, are you?"

"What?" his voice cracked. "No way. Not ever. Why? Did he say something? Is he going to break up with me?" The knee-jerk fear was real for an intense second, then Bridger remembered prom and rolling around on the blanket and holding each other while the Paulding Light bobbed in the ravine, and yeah, Leo wasn't going anywhere for at least the summer, and after that, well, that was a problem for Future Bridger. Until then Present Bridger didn't have to worry about relationship drama. He had bigger things on his mind.

Huh. For once he wasn't freaking out about Leo. That was a first. Score one for maturity and character development.

"No. He hasn't."

"Okay. That's good. Because I don't plan on breaking up with him at all. I'm in it to win it, or whatever people say."

"They don't say that," Luke said. "At all. Ever."

"Thanks, peanut gallery."

"They don't say that either, Bridge," Astrid said, her arm hooked through Luke's. "Where do you get your vocabulary?"

"Jeopardy. You know that." At Luke's raised eyebrows, Bridger scoffed. "Don't even pretend you didn't know how big of a fan I am. I had a picture of Alex Trebek in my locker all through middle school."

Astrid placed a hand over her heart. "Long may he reign."

"Long may he reign," Bridger echoed solemnly.

Luke's gaze darted between them. "You two have too many inside jokes."

"Don't worry, Luke." Bridger waved his hand. "Stick around a while and you'll catch on. Leo is able to decipher about seventy-five percent of what we say now."

Astrid blushed brilliant red. "Oh, look," she said, focusing on the field. "Leo is on deck."

Bridger didn't know what that meant but he turned his attention back to the game. Leo was next to bat and, though he didn't hit a home run, he did smack the ball into the outfield in an impressive display of athleticism. He rounded second and headed to third as the other team tried to make a play on the runner at home. Leo slid into the base, kicking up red dust, and the crowd cheered as Leo and the other runner were both declared safe, giving Midden High the first run of the game.

The game continued with the lead changing hands several times over the next few innings. Zeke bought popcorn and shared it among the four of them. Bridger drank a blue slushy while Astrid and Luke shared a red one. Going into the bottom of the ninth, Midden had a two-run lead with the visiting team at bat, and between Leo in the field and the closing pitcher, a freshman phenomenon, the other team went three up and three down.

The crowd erupted. Midden High would play in the state championship for the first time in the school's history. Bridger cheered and jumped up and down on the bleachers with the rest of the crowd. On the field, Leo and his team threw their gloves in the air and tackled the pitcher on the mound. Chaos reigned for a few minutes as everyone celebrated.

With Astrid hanging onto his hoodie, Bridger maneuvered out of the bleachers. Luke and Zeke trailed behind them until they congregated on the edge of the parking lot waiting for the players. Milling around, they talked about graduation and school and carefully avoided the topic of Lacey as the minutes dragged on.

"What is taking so long?" Astrid asked.

"I thought I saw something happening on the field when we were leaving, but I didn't see what."

"I'll go check," Bridger said.

He walked to the enclosed dugout, where he found a group of players and parents talking with the coach. Bridger squeezed through the crowd until he found Leo standing with a bunch of other players. His baseball cap sat crooked over his sweaty hair, and he had dirt smeared across one cheek and a mixture of dirt and chalk from his ankle to his hip from sliding.

Despite winning the most important game in school history, Leo was not smiling, in fact, his whole posture was subdued. No one was talking.

"What's going on?" Bridger asked, standing hesitantly on the outside of the clump of angry baseball players. "You guys won. Shouldn't there be celebrating?"

One of Leo's teammates let loose a torrent of rapid Spanish that Bridger didn't understand at all. Leo responded, measured and even, and whatever he said calmed the guy down, though he crossed his arms over his chest and forcefully spat a sunflower seed on the ground.

"Okay. I understood nothing. What was that?"

"Some assholes on the other team wouldn't shake Leo's hand after the game," another teammate explained.

Bridger's stomach flipped, and it wasn't the fish tacos. He went still. "Did they say why?"

The team exchanged uncertain glances.

The freshman phenom raised her hand. "Well, they also said something pretty mean about, well, they know Leo has a boyfriend. So—"

"Guys," Leo said, hands out, shrugging. "It's okay. Coach is going to talk to their coach. If they want to be classless homophobic jerks let them. It was just three guys. The rest of their team was really nice."

"They're angry they lost," another guy chimed.

"That doesn't excuse it," Bridger said sharply. The guy bowed his head, cowed, and scratched his cleat through the grass. "Sorry." Bridger ran a hand through his hair. "That wasn't... Sorry. That wasn't directed at you. I'm mad."

"It's okay. You're Leo's boyfriend. We expect you to be protective and we'd be worried if you weren't pissed off."

The side of Leo's mouth lifted.

"Well, good. And on that note, if you're done with my boyfriend, I'd like to talk to him for a minute."

"Bye, guys. Good game." Leo picked up his bag and slung it over his shoulder.

Bridger held out his hand, and Leo took it. Guiding Leo through the group of concerned parents and past the gate, Bridger eased them to the back of the darkened concession stand. "That must have hurt," Bridger said, once they were out of earshot. "I'm sorry."

Leo shrugged. He focused on the grass. "Honestly, it didn't feel great."

"I'm so sorry."

Leo leaned against Bridger's body. "I've been surrounded by such a supportive family and community that sometimes I forget there are still people who will hate me for being who I am."

Bridger folded Leo into a hug. His emotions were a scribble. That was the only way he could describe the anger and sorrow and shame and defeat that painted over each other inside him, looping and blurring into a mess of feelings hopelessly entangled.

Leo rested his forehead on Bridger's collarbone and sighed, loud and long; his shoulders were tight. Seeing Leo upset just made Bridger angrier. Leo was extraordinary. He was kind and gentle and confident and the pinnacle of goodness. And it pissed Bridger off that someone could make him feel less than, could shake the core of someone so grown and secure with who they were. He wanted to cry and punch things in equal measure and he clutched Leo tighter.

"Fuck them," Bridger said, cupping the back of Leo's neck. His dark hair was damp with sweat, and granules of dirt ground beneath Bridger's fingers. "Seriously. Screw those guys." Bridger's voice was tight. "You're amazing. You're the best player on the field. You're the best person I know. They're small and petty and yeah, they are angry they lost, and they want to make you feel the same. So, fuck them. And fuck anyone who agrees with them. You make everyone around you happier, and the entire school adores you, and your family loves you, and I can't imagine a world without you, and yeah. Keep being you. Because you're awesome."

Leo's shoulders shook.

"Are you crying or laughing. I can't tell."

Leo lifted his head. "Both? I don't know." He wiped at his eyes, then took Bridger's face in his hands. He shoved a hard kiss against Bridger's lips. It happened so fast, Bridger only registered the wet, bruising force and the smack of sound before Leo pulled away. "Both," he said with a shaky exhale. "When did you get so smart?"

"I don't know if you know this, but I do watch a lot of Jeopardy." Leo laughed outright. "But also, I happen to be dating this guy who is pretty smart himself and has taught me a lot about being true to who I am."

Beaming, Leo threw his arms around Bridger's shoulders and squeezed. "Thank you," he said, low and heartfelt. "I needed to hear all that."

"You're welcome."

Leo held on a few seconds longer, then released Bridger from his death grip. "I need to find my parents and talk to them. I'm going to have to calm my mom down. I'm scared she's going to write a strongly worded letter or something." He used the sleeve of his uniform to wipe away the stray tears and smeared more dirt across his nose. It was ridiculously endearing. "We're still going out?"

"Definitely. Meet me at Astrid's car."

"Okay." He kissed Bridger's cheek. "See you in a minute."

Bridger wandered back to Astrid. He felt weird: happy that he could help Leo, angry that he needed to.

"Hey, everything okay?" she asked. "I heard from one of Leo's teammates what happened."

"Yeah. It's okay now."

She knocked her shoulder into his. "It sucks that crap like that still happens. Are you okay?"

Hands in his pockets, Bridger walked toward Astrid's car. "Yeah. I guess. Just thinking." His talk with Leo had his mind whirring—thoughts about his own fears and insecurities, his dad, his future—and maybe he needed to take his own advice.

"Oh, yeah, now I see the smoke."

"Hilarious. You're hilarious."

Most of the fans had cleared out right after the game. Bridger could see where they'd left Astrid's car, even in the growing dark. His steps slowed. The dome light in Astrid's car cast a soft glow. "Uh, Astrid?"

"Yeah?"

"Did you kill your battery by leaving the interior light on?"

"No. I never turn the light on."

"Did you leave your door open?"

"No." She quickened her steps, and Bridger matched her. "What the hell?"

Astrid's car sat between two empty spaces, and even from the distance, they could see that the driver's side door was propped open.

Bridger broke into a jog; Astrid was right beside him.

"Someone broke into my car!" She stopped at the side, hands on her hips. Gently, she pulled the door open from the top. "Shit. What did they take?"

Bridger went around to the passenger's side. His door was open as well.

"Um, whatever they did, they opened this door too."

"Don't touch the handle. Maybe the police can dust for prints."

"Do you think they're going to dust for prints when we don't even know if they took anything? Obviously, they didn't want the car. Or my backpack because…" Bridger's bag was on the seat. He'd left it on the floorboard. The zippers were open, and Bridger always made sure to close everything after a middle school disaster involving an open flap and a pudding cup.

"Well, they didn't take anything out of the center console, which is not surprising, since there's only charger cords and gum. How about over there?"

Bridger stared at his bag.

"Bridge?"

"They moved my bag. They, they went in my bag." Bridger's heart skipped a beat. He took a breath, and it got stuck in his throat as he reached for the car door with a trembling hand. Swinging it open, he went from the speed of a sloth to that of an agitated pixie. Bridger dove for the bag and pulled open the main compartment, the zipper tearing in his haste. He shoved his hand inside. His heart sank.

Oh, no. Oh, no. No. It was gone.

"Bridger?"

"Oh, no. Oh, no."

"Bridger? What's wrong?"

The book was gone. "The guidebook is gone."

Saying it out loud made it real, and panic slammed into him. His teeth clenched, and sweat broke out on the back of his neck. And despite shoving his hand deeper into the bag and wishing with everything he had that his fingers would brush the familiar leather and parchment, they didn't.

The book was *gone.*

"*What?*"

"The book. The guidebook. The abridged version of the magical world." Freaked, Bridger upended his backpack onto the seat and shook out the contents. His pens, notebooks, books, a smooshed pack of gum, and a crumpled dollar fell onto the seat. "The rules and regulations. The confirmation of magical existence." His compact bounced on the floorboard and cracked onto the pavement. It wasn't there. It wasn't there. "It's gone. Oh, shit, it's gone."

"Bridge," Astrid said. She sounded far away, as if she spoke through a tunnel, or water, or over an EVP from the other side of death.

Rifling through the contents, Bridger flipped through his notebooks just in case it was lodged in one. It wasn't. He threw his textbooks onto the floor. He picked through all of it and then shoved his hand back in his bag, feeling in all the pockets, skimming his fingers along all the edges. It wasn't there. He dropped his bag onto the asphalt.

"Bridge?"

He pushed his fist into his chest. He couldn't breathe. Why couldn't he breathe? His lungs were useless, deflated balloons, and no matter how much he gasped he couldn't pull in air. It was like trying to breathe through a straw with his nose plugged. He pushed harder on his sternum; black spots danced in his vision. His legs shook and he fell hard to the concrete curb in front of the car.

"Bridge!"

Oh, fuck. The fish tacos swam in his stomach, then washed up bitter and acidic in the back of his throat. He was going to puke. There was going to be vomit. There would be fish taco vomit.

He'd never learn. And there would be popcorn kernels in it and bile and blue slushy. It would be foul, and Astrid was going to murder him. Pavel was going to murder him.

There would be a murder of him.

"Bridger!"

He'd lost the book. He'd fucking lost the book. No, he didn't just lose it. Someone broke into Astrid's car and stole it. Only one person came to mind who would go through his bag, one person who was on the verge of discovering the myth world. It had to be her. She stole it. Summer stole the book, the travel version of the encyclopedia of the myth world.

She'd know *everything*.

He clutched his legs and dropped his forehead to his bent knees. His chest hurt. His fingers dug into the fabric of his jeans, like frozen claws. His tendons strained; his whole body went rigid. His heart raced. He gasped like a fish on land, and his whole world zeroed down to the burning in his lungs and the pounding in his head. He was going to die. He was going to die right there in the parking lot. His heart was going to rupture, and he was going to drown on land because his lungs wouldn't work, and he'd become a cautionary tale about the hazards of eating fish tacos from the diner and dating hot baseball players and carrying ancient books around in his backpack.

He registered tugging on his arms and hands rubbing his back, and his world tilted when someone manhandled him out of his crouch. They unfolded his legs and eased him back. He went from staring at the blue of his jeans to staring at the darkening sky, as his head thudded back onto someone's hard shoulder.

"Bridger," Leo's voice was gentle as he pressed a hand to Bridger's chest. The heel of his hand pushed on the medal of Saint Dymphna—some help she was. "Breathe. Come on. Follow me." Leo sat behind him, cradling him; his chest was molded to Bridger's back. "There you go. Just like me. Breathe in. Breathe out." His body rose and fell with Leo's even breaths, and Bridger did his level best to follow Leo's example. It was tough, especially at first, when each breath was stuttered and thin, but, after a few attempts, he didn't feel as if his heart was going to burst from his chest alien-style.

Astrid appeared, her face pale, but her jaw clenched. He'd appreciate her stoicism when he could breathe again.

"Bridger," she said. "You're doing great. You're going to be okay." She took one of his claws and pressed her thumbs into his palm, then spread the pressure out into his fingers. Gradually, the clench eased. "That's it. Relax."

Easier said than done, but, enveloped by his two favorite people in the world, Bridger inhaled, and it wasn't a harsh staccato and it didn't catch on a high whine. He blew out in a long, albeit shaky, exhale.

"Perfect," Leo said, his voice a whisper on the shell of Bridger's ear. "And again."

Bridger found it easy to follow Leo's orders and he focused on Astrid's touch. Just as quickly as the panic attack started, it ended, and Bridger's spine went from unyielding steel to liquid. Bones and muscles as solid as jelly, entire body trembling, he slumped into Leo's arms.

"Holy fuck," he said, when he could finally speak again.

"There he is." Leo tucked his nose into Bridger's neck. "Bridge, tell me five things you can see."

Bridger blinked. His world came into sharp focus. "Astrid, a pen that rolled under the car, the car door, your baseball cap on the ground, and a green leaf on the asphalt."

"Great. Now four things you can touch."

"You, the pavement, the dirt on your uniform, my jeans."

"Good job, Bridge. Do you need to keep going or do you think you're okay?"

Bridger was not okay, but the panic attack, because he was certain that was what he'd just experienced, ebbed, and he was more embarrassed than anything else. "I'm good." His voice was a rasp.

"Lie." Astrid patted his knee. "But we'll let this one slide."

"Is he okay?" And that was Luke.

"Bridger?" And Zeke. "You all right, man?"

"He's good," Astrid yelled back. "But stay on that side of the car for a hot second." She leveled her gaze, eyebrows drawn together. "Do you need anything?"

"Water. Definitely water."

"Can you guys find a bottle of water?" Astrid yelled.

"Yeah, sure!"

Bridger saw their feet scamper off.

"What happened?" Leo asked.

Bridger craned his neck to stare at the sharp line of Leo's jaw. "The book—" His throat went tight again; the words were strangled.

Astrid held up a finger. "Don't even think about it, Bridge. Give yourself a second." She turned her focus to Leo. "The guidebook is not in Bridger's bag, and my car was broken into."

"That's... not good."

"No, it's not. But we're fine. Bridger is fine."

Leo rubbed his hands up and down Bridger's arms. "Yeah. We're fine."

The sound of a hundred construction vehicles backing up emanated from beneath Astrid's car. From where he sat in the cradle of Leo's body, Bridger spied the compact mirror vibrating against the blacktop.

"Can you answer that?" he said to Astrid. "You know what happens if we ignore it."

"Yeah, and the last thing we want is this thing to get louder."

Astrid crawled on her hands and knees and reached one long arm under her car. Once she had the mirror in hand, she scooted to Leo and Bridger on the curb.

Flipping it open, she angled the mirror so the three of them were reflected. Face pale, eyes squinted, Pavel appeared, wearing horrid pajamas.

"Bridger, are you all right? Your toaster has been ringing like mad. I would've used the portal, but, well, we know what happened last time… And it's gone off before and stopped so I didn't know if you needed my help."

"I'm fine, Pavel."

Astrid frowned. Leo's grip tightened.

"Okay, I'm not fine, Pavel. I had a panic attack."

Pavel grabbed a robe, slid his arms in, and cinched it around his waist. "Do you need me to come pick you up? I know my vehicle isn't your favorite, but I would be able to be there in a few minutes."

Maybe it was from being worn out and shaky from the adrenaline, or maybe it was the situation with his dad, or maybe it was that Bridger had doomed Pavel's magical life and family, but tears gathered in the corners of Bridger's eyes.

"Thank you for offering, but I'm okay. I have Leo and Astrid."

He needed to tell him about the book. He'd lost the book. Summer had the book. She had the book. She had the book. She had the book. She had the book. The four words beat though his head in time with his heart.

Pavel's expression was one of fond concern, but he nodded to Leo and Astrid. "Just let me know if you need anything."

"I will," Bridger said. "I promise."

"Okay. Good night then."

"Night."

Bridger clapped the compact shut.

"Why didn't you tell him?" Leo's chin dug into Bridger's shoulder. "He deserves to know. It's technically his book."

"I, I, didn't want to disappoint him."

"Bridge," Astrid said softly, "Pavel's not your dad."

"I know," Bridger snapped.

"No, I mean, he's not going to be disappointed in you. Did you hear him? He'd show up here in that mucus-colored robe in his battered car if you asked him to." She bit her lip. "And it's his life that's going to be shattered if she does anything with that book. More so than yours."

Hauling himself upright, Bridger rubbed his forehead. "I know. I just need a chance to fix this on my own." Gaining his feet, he swayed, and Leo scrambled to grab him.

"What do you mean?"

"I know where she's staying. I know what the van looks like. I'm going to get that book back."

CHAPTER 14

"I TOLD LUKE AND ZEKE that you're sick and couldn't hang out and that I was driving you both home," Astrid said as she adjusted her mirror. Bridger had knocked it askew in his mad search for the guidebook. "I don't like lying, Bridge."

"Consider it a half-truth," he said, face pressed to the window. "You technically are taking me home, and I did get sick, just with panic. And almost vomit. It was a close call."

"If you throw up in my car, you're walking home."

Bridger's stomach churned. "Noted."

Leo leaned forward, elbows on the middle console, chin propped in his hands. "What's the plan?"

"Find the van. Find the book. Save the world." Bridger bounced his leg against the floorboard. "Preferably in that order."

Leo turned the brim of his hat to the side. He was still dressed in his uniform and smudged with dirt. "Are we in a movie? Because that sounded like a tagline."

"I hope not," Astrid said, taking a turn. "Because that sounds like a sci-fi thriller. I'm more a romcom fan myself. As is Bridger." She smirked.

"We've established that." Bridger scanned the streets. "But I think I could handle sci-fi. More *Star Trek*, less *Alien*."

"As long as it's not horror, I'm in," Leo said, squeezing Bridger's shoulder. "We all know what happens to the love interest and the plucky comic relief in horror movies."

"Which one am I?" Bridger asked, craning his neck to look at his boyfriend. Passing streetlights and headlights illuminated Leo's fond grin.

"Do you have to ask?"

"Does that make me the final girl?" Astrid slowed at a red light. "Because I could live with that. Literally."

"Exactly. Bridger and I would be dead, and you'd be the one taking down the ax-wielding bad guy."

Bridger shivered, remembering the Pope Lick Goatman. "Can we not talk about death and axes? And focus on the task at hand, please?"

"Find the van. Find the book. Save the world," Astrid and Leo said in unison.

"Mock me. I see how it is and for the record—" Bridger caught sight of the white van idling in a corner convenience store lot. "There!"

Astrid turned sharply, tires screeching. The car went up on the curb, and several horns honked. With two hands gripping the wheel, Astrid jerked the car into a parking space near the van.

Bridger was out of the car in a heartbeat, striding with a purpose, spurred on by incandescent and righteous rage.

Summer stepped out of the store, hotdog in one hand, candy bar in the other, and a diet pop precariously balanced in the crook of her elbow. "Hey, Matt, they have those nachos you…" She trailed off when she caught sight of Bridger thundering toward her.

"Well, hey there, Bridger," she said with a wink. "Aren't you supposed to be at an important baseball game?"

Bridger wasn't in the mood for snark and word play. He blocked her path to the van. "I know you broke into Astrid's car and I know you took it. Now, give it back."

She blinked. "I don't know what you're talking about."

"I'm talking about how you snuck into the parking lot at the baseball game and broke into Astrid's car, rifled through my backpack, and took something."

"You're so creative. It's almost as impressive as the bullshit you tried to pull on me with your boss when you stepped out of the glowing magic oval."

Bridger glared. Two could play at this game. "I don't know what you're talking about."

"Of course not. Now, where's your boss? Is he going to appear any minute and save you from the mean lady with the microphone and the hot dog?"

Bristling, Bridger gritted his teeth. "I know you have it. I want it back. Hand it over, and I won't have to call Pavel."

"Oh, please do. He's quite cute, and I do love a good warning." She tapped her toe on the curb. "No? Not going to happen? Great. Can you step aside and let me get back to my dinner?"

Bridger crossed his arms. "I'm not moving. I know you have it."

"Oh, really? You know that for a fact?"

"Yes."

"That's a hefty charge. Breaking and entering and stealing. What's your evidence?"

Technically, he had no evidence other than a missing book and scratches on Astrid's driver-side door that possibly, maybe, highly probably, were not there before the game—and the fact that his magic guidebook was missing. Pavel told him to always carry it. And he did. In his backpack in case of emergencies. It was the one rule he actually followed.

"Your fingerprints on the door."

She laughed. "Oh, my. Forensic evidence. Good job. Well then, Detective Boyle, I hate to break it to you, but I don't have anything of yours. Now, if you'll excuse me."

She moved to step around him, but Bridger was undeterred and darted in her way. She elbowed him in the chest, and her pop dislodged, falling to the ground with a thunk and an impressive spray.

"*Brooklyn Nine-Nine* reference aside, I'm not letting you get away with this."

"You owe me a soda."

"Yeah, and you owe me a—"

"Bridger!" Astrid's voice sliced through the confrontation. She stood by her car with Leo next to her, and Bridger didn't realize he was nose-to-nose with Summer until he had to fumble backward to be able to turn his head.

"Yeah?"

Astrid held up the compact. Even across the parking lot, Bridger could hear the sound of two thousand European ambulance sirens. "This isn't over. I'll be right back." Sprinting away, Bridger took the compact from Astrid's hand and scrambled into the back seat. He flipped open the mirror.

"Bridger," Nia said, tiny arms crossed over her chest, lips pursed in her already-pinched face. "What have I told you about leaving your things lying around?"

"Uh, Nia? Is this an emergency? Because if not, I'm in the middle of something."

"You better hope you're not in an emergency." She shot out of frame, leaving a wake of pink sparkles, before she appeared hefting an old book, leather-bound with parchment pages. "You left this on the table." She held it in her tiny arms, thrusting it toward the mirror. *The Rules and Regulations for Mediating Myths and Magic: A Comprehensive Guide to All Documented Myths and Cryptids and the Rules and Regulations for Intermediary Interaction* filled the screen in flowing gold script. "I'd hate for you to encounter anything without it. Don't you remember the first time with the unicorn?"

"Oh. Um. Oops?" Oops indeed. A big oops. Kind of a massive oops. "I'll be by tomorrow to pick it up."

She dropped it back to the table. "Fine. Don't do any work until then, because we want our human in one piece. Also, I won't tell Pavel. This time."

"Thank you, Nia."

She studied him. "Are you okay? You look pale. Paler than normal."

"It's the lighting. I'm in Astrid's car."

"Oh!" Nia said, wings fluttering. "Are you out? Any cafes or bakeries nearby? I'd love a—"

Bridger shut the compact. He'd totally pay for that later and he did owe her something sweet for not ratting him out to Pavel about the whole book situation, but he didn't have time to listen to her ramble about the decadent consistency of dark chocolate.

Bridger sheepishly emerged from the car, dodging the expectant looks from Leo and Astrid.

"Bridge? Who was it?"

"Nia. I, uh, she found the book."

Leo sucked in a quick breath. "Oh. Wow."

"Yeah."

"*Dude.*"

"Yeah."

"Where was it?"

"In Pavel's study. Where I left it. After doing research."

Astrid winced. "Wow."

"Yeah." Bridger looked to where Summer stood by her van taking small bites of her hotdog.

"What are you going to do?"

"Eat crow and buy her a pop, I guess."

Trudging across the parking lot took the longest thirty seconds of Bridger's life. Okay, technically not true, because thirty seconds was thirty seconds, and would always be thirty seconds, but time was also relative. Apparently. Sometimes. Whatever.

"Yes?" She raised an eyebrow. "Do you have something else to accuse me of?"

Bridger wrinkled his nose. "I'm sorry."

"What was that?" She tugged on her ear. "Say it again."

"I said I'm sorry. I'll replace your drink."

The jingle of the bell above the shop door rang, and Leo appeared at Bridger's side. "Here," he said, handing over an empty cup. "They said to just come back in and fill it up with what you want."

She took the cup. "What a thoughtful young man. What are you doing with this guy?" she said, jerking her chin toward Bridger.

Leo's eyes narrowed. "That's not really any of your business. But he is my boyfriend, and you've been making his life stressful, which I don't appreciate. I hope from this point forward you'll leave us both alone as well as our other friends."

"Is that a polite way of telling me to back off?"

"No. It's me saying that I think it's best if we stay out of each other's way from this point forward. Finish filming. And we'll focus on school."

"Well, I can't argue with that. Cute and articulate and athletic. He's really out of your league, Bridger."

Ugh. She really knew how to poke at a wound.

"Your opinion has been noted and placed in the appropriate receptacle," Leo said, twining his fingers with Bridger's. "Which is the trash, if you didn't get that."

Bridger's mouth dropped open as Leo tugged him to the car. But he gathered his wits quickly. "Let me know if you need any cream for that burn," Bridger said over his shoulder. "I know a great cosmetic line."

Leo snickered as they tumbled back into Astrid's car.

Astrid dropped them off on their street. After a long kiss goodnight, which left Bridger a little breathless and warm, Leo retreated to his house, citing an intense need for a shower, which yeah, because Leo smelled like sweat and still had dirt and chalk smeared across his skin.

Bridger's mom was at work, and he settled in for a night of homework and watching TV and hopefully not ruminating on his social faux pas of accusing someone of stealing an ancient guidebook to magic and myth and, quite frankly, mayhem.

However, a question still nagged him about the situation. Someone had definitely broken into Astrid's car, but nothing was missing. Summer's van was nearby, and she mentioned the baseball game. It could've been her, but it could've been any of the student body that was there. And his backpack had been tampered with for sure, but the contents were intact. Not even the crumpled dollar that resided in the bottom for vending machine emergencies such as needing a caffeine jolt at the end of the day had been taken.

Bridger wrestled with calling Pavel and was turning the compact mirror over in his hands, when there was a knock at his door. Slipping the mirror into his pocket, he heaved himself from the human-eating couch and opened the front door.

Leo stood there in fresh clothes, hair dripping from his shower, brown eyes wide. He clutched a yearbook.

Oh, yeah. *That.*

"Did you mean what you wrote?"

"You've only just read it? I gave it to you at prom."

Leo blushed. "Yes. I've been busy and kind of forgot about it. But I did. Just now. Did you mean it?"

Bridger stared at his toes and cleared his throat. "Which part?"

"All of it."

"Well, yeah, I—"

"Me too," Leo said, cutting him off. "Me too. All of it. Back at you."

Bridger's pulse pounded. "Really?"

"Yeah. Of course."

Bridger didn't know whether to smile or cry. He tried a smile, but the edges felt all wrong, and it fell despite his entire being brimming with happiness. Tears gathered as he laughed lightly, and he felt as if he vacillated between that pair of theater masks.

"I, uh, I..." He couldn't complete a thought, much less a coherent statement.

He didn't have to. The book clattered to the stoop, and Leo barreled over the threshold. He cupped Bridger's face and kissed him, hard and demanding. Surprised, Bridger clutched Leo's hips to keep them from falling backward. He kicked the door shut. It slammed as Leo propelled Bridger into the house, kissing and kissing, as if Bridger was air and he was drowning.

The back of Bridger's ankle hit the bottom step, and he jerked away and pressed his palms to Leo's shoulders. "Hold on. Hold on. I don't want to fall. And I, I have questions." His voice was husky and low. His chest heaved.

"Okay. But yes. Whatever the question, the answer is yes. Okay? I can write my response in your yearbook, but I thought I'd express it like this, if that's okay?"

"Yes. Yes. This is good. Great. Amazing. Thank you."

"Good. Because I want..." Leo trailed off. His cheeks flushed. His dark hair was a mess. His mouth parted as he breathed. His muscles flexed beneath his T-shirt, and he was literally the most incredible person who had ever looked at Bridger as if he wanted to pounce on him. Okay, the only person who ever looked at Bridger like that, but it was the sexiest Leo had ever been, which was saying a lot.

Bridger's heart pounded. His blood rushed to every part of his body, some more than others. "Are we having a new conversation?"

"Can we? Please?"

"Yeah. Definitely. Right now. In my bedroom?"

Leo responded by dashing around Bridger and vaulting up the stairs. At the top, he looked over his shoulder. "Bridger? You coming?"

Warmth suffused Bridger, and he smiled, walking up the stairs to join Leo instead of running, lest he injure himself—which would be his luck. And he didn't want to chance spoiling anything that was about to happen.

He took Leo's hand. His own hand trembled; his palm was sweaty with nervous anticipation, but with a certainty he rarely felt, he led Leo to his room and closed the door.

His and Leo's conversation had been wholly private and amazing and a little awkward at first, but then there had been other conversations that were just as awesome, because there was more than one way to converse. Bridger looked forward to learning them all.

Anyway, despite Astrid being the best friend in the universe, Bridger didn't say a word about what had transpired after she dropped them off, though he bounced through school the next day and she shot him questioning looks, and even Taylor raised an eyebrow when Bridger was significantly cheerier than usual when fourth block rolled around.

"Can you believe graduation is only two weeks away?" Astrid asked as she waited in line to leave the parking lot. The sky above them held the promise of thunderstorms; thick gray clouds hung low and moved slowly. "Like, how did we manage it? How did we make it through high school? In two weeks, we will be high school graduates in hot scratchy gowns holding diplomas with our embarrassing middle names on them. And then on to college. College? How is it possible?" She paused, then looked away from the road to her passenger. "Bridger?"

"Huh?"

"What is with you? You look like your face got stuck in an anime smile."

"Nothing's wrong." Bridger adjusted his backpack in his lap. "Everything is great actually."

She narrowed her eyes. "Wait. Wait a minute. What happened last night after I dropped you off?"

"Nothing." *Obvious lie.* He couldn't stop the grin if he hung weights to his lips.

Astrid gasped. "Oh, my God! Are you no longer unicorn-friendly? Is that what happened?"

Uncanny. Astrid found the one thing that could put a damper on his mood. "I should have never told you about that."

"Answer the question, Bridge!" Over-excited, she slammed on her brakes at the stop sign. Bridger's seatbelt snapped across his chest.

"Ow!"

"Did you and Leo…"

"I shouldn't answer that because I am a gentleman who does not kiss and tell."

"Bridger!"

"Fine. Yes. Okay. Yes. Neither one of us are going to be petting unicorns ever again. Maybe. I don't know. I actually need to ask the unicorn this question because I am unsure. But if we're going with the traditional sense of things, I am no longer a friend to the unicorns."

Astrid's happy squeal was ear-splitting and unholy. She smacked her palms on the steering wheel. "Oh, my God!"

"Why are you so happy about this?" he asked, laughing.

"Because you're happy about it!"

"Of course, I'm happy about it. It was *amazing*."

She held up a hand. "I do not want details. I know we're best friends, but I don't want to know anything. I love you but there are some things that are a road too far."

"Aw, I love you too. Also, Leo and I kind of said that to each other in a roundabout way. So that happened too. It was a big night."

Astrid leered and opened her mouth, but Bridger beat her to it.

"Don't! Seriously. If I'm not sharing details, you can't make jokes."

She bit her lip. "Fine. Fine. No jokes."

"Thank you."

"You're welcome."

She parked in front of Pavel's house. "I'm happy for you though. And proud. Honestly. Look at how far you've come."

Bridger nodded. "Past Bridger was a mess, a bit of jerk, and sad and lonely. And while I'm still a few of those things, at least right now I'm happy. I'm not lonely. I still have problems, but I have good things going too."

"Was that wisdom? Actual wisdom? You've leveled up. Evolved. Like a Pokémon."

Snorting, Bridger grabbed his backpack. "If you call me Pikachu, we will no longer be friends."

"Is Squirtle acceptable? Charmander? What's the brown eggplant-looking one?"

"Diglett." Astrid pressed her lips together, eyes crinkled, as if it took everything to keep words from bursting forth. "No jokes! You promised!"

"Okay." She swallowed. "Okay."

"That looked excruciating." He shook his head. "In other news, have you had a chance to proofread my paper?"

Astrid gave him a blank look. "You never gave it to me. I thought you decided to turn it in as is."

"I gave it to you. I printed it out the other night."

"Um, no. Has one night of sex deprived your brain of blood?"

Brow furrowed, confused, Bridger opened his bag. "I know I put it in here. I checked before the..." The baseball game. He'd had it in his bag before the baseball game.

"Uh? Checked before what?"

"The game." He turned in his seat. "Astrid, are you sure you didn't see it in here after the game? Did it fall out when I upended my bag on the seat?"

"No. You didn't give it to me, and I didn't find it. I cleaned my car out. I'm certain I'd remember seeing a paper about the Michigan Dogman."

Bridger's eyes widened. "Oh, shit."

"What? Just print it out again."

"No! Astrid." He turned to face her. His mind whirred; events clicked into place like an intense game of Tetris. "Someone broke into your car. We thought they didn't take anything, but they did. They went through my bag, and my paper is missing. Who would steal a paper about the Michigan Dogman?"

She paled. "Oh, shit. Summer took your paper? Why?"

"Because! She thinks I know things! She thinks the paper is legit!"

"Is it?"

"Kind of? Not really? Elena told me to write half-truths, so I did! That paper is *dangerous* to someone who thinks it's accurate information."

"Well, what can she do with it?"

"Oh fuck! Is today Thursday?"

"Yeah."

Bridger bolted out of the car and ran up the driveway. He heard Astrid cursing and running behind him.

The door swung inward, and Bridger leapt over the threshold with Astrid hot on his heels.

"Hey, Mindy," Bridger yelled as he took the steps to the second floor two at a time. "Hope your day has been awesome!" he yelled. "Because it's about to suck!"

At the last step, his foot caught, and he fell to his knees on the landing. It was a good thing Astrid was somewhat graceful, or he would've been a pancake. As it was, when she sidestepped him to keep from tumbling herself, she stepped on his hand. He let out a strangled yell. If the rhythmic thumps of their ascent hadn't alerted Pavel to their presence, that certainly did.

He popped out from behind the doorway to the kitchen.

"Bridger? Astrid? What is going on?"

From his place on the floor, Bridger clutched his hand to his chest. "Summer stole my paper about the Michigan Dogman, and it's *Thursday*."

Pavel blinked.

"I hope that means something to you," Astrid said, hands on her hips. "Because it makes no sense to me."

"I am not sure. Larry hates Thursdays."

"Yeah, he couldn't get the hang of them." Bridger grabbed the banister and hauled himself to his feet. His knees ached, and his hand throbbed. "Anyway, the important thing is, that is when most of his sightings happen. On Thursdays. And I wrote that in the paper. With a statistical analysis!"

"And Summer has the paper. We think. She broke into my car and went through Bridger's backpack."

Pavel made a panicked noise in his throat. The cup of tea in his hand wobbled. "Did she find the field book?"

"No, as luck would have it, I accidentally left it here. Not the point though. Totally not the point. The point is that if she goes to Wexford today because of that stupid paper—"

A toaster rang.

It sounded like an old rotary phone from a black and white TV sitcom. The toaster danced along the counter until it fell off the edge. Frozen, the trio watched as it vibrated along the floor. With mounting horror, Bridger stared as a picture flashed across the polished reflective surface. Another toaster twitched, rang out, fell, then another, and another.

Paling, Pavel grabbed one from the counter, and held the convulsing toaster in both hands. Brow furrowed, lips pressed into a thin line, he examined it.

"Well then, either she is going to meet an irritated and potentially homicidal Dogman, or, judging by the number of alarms, she already has." Pavel dropped the toaster. "Bridger, to the portal. Astrid, call Elena on the mirror and stay here. We will need both of you before the night is over."

Bridger grabbed his mirror from his bag and slid it into his pocket. He tossed his backpack through the door of Pavel's study, then followed Pavel up the stairs and to the portal's resting place. The mannequin stood in the corner but now wore a jacket and scarf and a hat jauntily tilted on its neck stump.

"No less creepy," Bridger said, as Pavel flung the door open.

"Really? I thought the clothes gave it a kind of charm."

"No. Anyway, to Larry."

Pavel addressed the portal as he shrugged on a dark blue jacket and shoved a baseball cap on his head. "To Larry. Please. Wexford County."

The terrifying, magic, liquid mass of swirling darkness quivered. Pavel grabbed Bridger's hand, and together they stepped through.

Bridger didn't think he'd ever get used to traveling via portal. It was the same experience each time, warmth and pressure, and then being squeezed out the other side with the sound of a champagne cork.

Popping into the middle of a cornfield into a summer rainstorm was not Bridger's idea of a great time, especially when what awaited them were the bright headlights of a car. The weather was worse in Wexford, and the clouds rolled above them, blocking out the sun and casting the entire area in apocalyptic low light—except for the headlights, which blinded him.

He threw up his hands just in time for Pavel to tackle him to the ground. They landed with a squelch.

"Ow!" Bridger's shoulder screamed in pain, while Pavel scrabbled to standing, placing his body between the car and Bridger on the ground. "What the hell was that for, Pavel?"

"I thought it was headed straight for us. Except..." His long coat whipped around his thin, jeans-clad legs in the rising wind. "...it isn't moving."

Bridger pushed to his knees. "Is it even running?"

"I don't hear the engine."

Between the rain and the blinding effect of the headlights, it was difficult to gauge the distance, but the car appeared to be on the other end of the field. Bridger gained his feet and followed Pavel as he trudged across the landscape. Pavel approached the vehicle as he would a wild animal, slowly, turning as he inspected it, hands in his pockets, lightly stepping between low, green cornstalks. "No, it's not idling. But the door is open." He reached in and turned the key, killing the lights.

Blinking away the bright spots, Bridger rubbed his eyes. "Thanks. Why is there a car in the middle of a cornfield?"

"I don't know. But the portal brought us here for a reason. Larry must be nearby."

"Hey!" Summer appeared between the rows of fledgling corn, batting the stalks away as she thundered toward them. Her hair was pulled into a ponytail, and she wore overalls and thick-heeled boots. And as she tore her way through the field, in one hand, slowly dampening in the spring rain, was a stapled bundle of white paper.

"Hey yourself!" Bridger shouted, and thunder rumbled above them. "That's my folklore paper."

She ignored him. "Why did you turn off the lights?" She waved the paper in Pavel's face. "I'm trying to disorient it."

"Him," Pavel corrected. "Him. And you are in grave danger, Miss Lore, and need to leave the area immediately."

"Oh, no," she shook her head and wagged a manicured finger in Pavel's face. "No, no. I am here to see the Dogman. I know it exists. Just like that magic oval did. Just like the ghost at the bakery. And the Ada Witch? Am I right? Because a cemetery attendant described a man who visits every month and that description matched you down to the tassels on your loafers."

Bridger smacked his face.

"Miss Lore, I know this all seems very exciting and—"

"Oh, cram it, Doctor Who. I'm not leaving until I catch this beast on my cell phone camera." She held up her phone. Rain beaded along the case. "Now, if you'll excuse me."

"Wait!" Bridger yelled. "You don't understand. That paper is not true. Okay? It's full of half-truths, and you can't trust it."

"Oh, really? Like I can trust you two?"

"No. I wouldn't trust us either," Bridger said. "I'd get in my car and leave."

"Yeah, that's *exactly* what you want me to do."

Pavel nodded. "Yes. Precisely."

The rain increased as Pavel and Summer continued their verbal sparring, and Bridger went from damp to soaked, even with his hood up. No amount of rubbing his sleeve across his face could catch all the drops. Amid the sound of raindrops on the fat green leaves of the corn, Bridger caught a frantic rustling noise to his right. He went still, listening, his hair standing on end. He inched closer to Pavel and elbowed him in the side.

"Pavel," he said, jerking his chin. "There's something over there."

A bright flash of lightning forked through the sky, and a few seconds later thunder boomed across the flat landscape. A rabbit shot out from the stalks and zig-zagged across the field.

Bridger exhaled and wilted.

Summer smirked. "What? The confidant of witches and ghosts is scared of a little bun—"

An inhuman scream rent the air.

Bridger jumped and grabbed Pavel's arm. Summer yelped, then clapped her hand over her mouth. Her pink fingernails dug into the skin of her cheeks.

The sound came again. The ground under them shook like an earthquake. The corn leaves rattled. Something shot through the stalks in front of them, then behind them, and on both sides. Bridger squeezed closer to Pavel as the creature circled, running around them again and again, coming closer with each pass. The creature was like the wind creating a tornado funnel, spinning and spinning, flattening the rows of corn. In a flash of lightning, Bridger caught a glimpse of The Michigan Dogman, his black fur, the shadow and shape of his human torso and canine body, and the bright blue of his eyes. Bridger's heart lodged in his throat.

"Bridger," Pavel said, low, even, calm, despite the fact that an irritated supernatural creature ran around them, tightening its circle every time it passed. "When I tell you, take Miss Lore and run. To the portal."

"Pavel," Bridger's voice was a breath, barely heard over the sound of the pounding rain. "That's all the way across the field."

"Then run fast."

Bridger grasped Summer's wrist in his clammy hand. "What are you going to do?" he asked.

"Magic."

Larry came closer, his huge body tearing through the corn. Bridger could only see a black blur in the storm, but he could hear the way his body slashed through the crop and the heavy pants of his breath. He ran in front of them, circled to their left, and must have forgotten the car was there.

Larry slammed into the rear quarter-panel just as another fork of lightning tore through the darkening sky. The car spun and juddered in the mud; suddenly as dangerous as the creature itself, it became a sliding vehicle of death.

"Run!"

Bridger took off. He dragged Summer through the flattened corn toward the portal.

"The car is that way!" Summer screeched.

"So is the Dogman!"

"But your research," she said, flailing the paper next to Bridger's face, "says we should stand our ground."

"Don't cite my own dumbass paper at me! Pavel said to run. We're running."

Summer wrenched out of Bridger's grip. "No! You lied to me last time." She turned on her heel, slipped on the wet ground, and ran back the other way.

"What are you doing?" Bridger scrambled after her. His face and hands stung from the pelting rain; every muscle was coiled like a compressed spring. He caught up to Summer just in time for them both to witness Pavel use his intermediary magic to create a shield between him and Larry.

Larry swiped a massive claw at Pavel's head only to bounce off a shimmering bubble and fly backward. The bubble reminded Bridger of the ward on the front door of the house: a protective measure, for defense not offense.

"What the hell? You can wield magic?" Summer yelled over the storm.

Pavel looked behind him. "I told you to run!"

Larry gathered his legs beneath him, and his attention turned from Pavel to Summer and Bridger.

"For the record," Bridger said, tugging on the back of Summer's overalls, "I don't have magic defenses."

"Oh," she said as Larry stalked forward. "Do you have any ideas?"

"No!"

Pavel shot out his hand and sparks flew from his fingers into Larry's eyes. Larry roared, claws tearing at his snout and face, but the pyrotechnics fizzled quickly. It was enough to distract Larry long enough for Bridger to shove Summer to the side.

"Split up!"

She took off in one direction and Bridger the other. He tore through the young, green stalks of corn; the leaves whipped him in his knees and thighs. He ran with no direction in mind other than safety. He'd have to curve around, head back to the portal and Pavel. He hoped Summer would run for her car, but he couldn't count on it, not when she was hellbent on catching Larry on her camera.

Pumping his arms, heart racing, Bridger snuck a glance behind him. Two ice-blue eyes followed him in the dark, as did the sound of growling and the beat of paws on sodden ground.

Oh, shit. Think, Bridger. Think.

Okay, outrunning a Dogman was not going to happen. He steadily gained and left a wake of flattened corn. Bridger was going to have to do something drastic and stupid.

Well, here's goes something. Bridger skidded to a stop and spun around. Larry barreled toward him, all fur and muscle and a snout of sharp, pointy teeth.

Oh, crap. He hoped Leo would remember him fondly, because this suddenly was a no-good, very-bad idea. No time to rethink. Larry's strides ate up the distance in a blink.

Joints locked, muscles trembling, Bridger gripped his slick phone and waited. At the last second, he brandished it and switched on the flashlight. He shined it in Larry's eyes—just a flash. Larry howled. He stopped, paws sliding in the mud, momentum carrying him forward, but now slowly enough for Bridger to get out of the way.

Bridger rolled to right, careening, Larry clipped his shoulder hard. His claws raked down Bridger's side. Bridger tumbled over and over in the mud, destroying corn, legs flailing, arms tucked into his sides. He was the equivalent of a runaway train without a track, all kinetic energy and destructive force, until he finally slid to an ungainly stop.

Every inch of his body was bruised, and his side was on fire, but at least he wasn't being chased. Raising his head, Bridger swiped away the mud on his forehead and surveyed the landscape. A flash of lightning revealed no sign of Larry, but that didn't mean much. He had to get back to the portal. He had to find Pavel.

Pushing to his hands and knees, Bridger fished out his compact. He flipped it open.

"Call Pavel, please."

Ears straining, he didn't hear Pavel's ring, but his reflection wavered, and the mirror glowed. Pavel appeared, a worried furrow between his brows, face paled and smeared with mud.

"Bridger, where are you?" he whispered.

"I don't know. Not anywhere near the portal. What about you?" Bridger kept his voice low as he stood, head swiveling in hopes that Larry had decided chasing teenagers was boring for a Thursday night and had left.

"By the car."

"I don't know how to get back."

"Hold on." The view in the mirror tilted, and Bridger spied the damage to the car—a mangled quarter panel and a torn-off bumper. He heard the engine, both over the mirror and echoing across the corn and saw lights flashing. "Do you see the lights?"

"Yes."

An inhuman howl broke through the distant rumbles of the passing storm. Bridger startled. The howl wasn't too far from where they had collided. His heart stuttered.

"That caught Larry's attention," Pavel said. "Meet me at the portal as soon as you can."

"Okay. I'll be there in a flash."

Based on the location of the lights, Bridger figured out the general vicinity of the portal, and sprinted in that direction. Everything hurt, especially the gashes along his ribs, and he was going to have a pointed conversation with Elena about her friend, Larry the *dick*. He needed a bath and maybe stitches and some of the pixie's magic salve to soothe away his aches.

He dodged a particularly thick clump of corn and plowed over a cowering Summer. He kept his feet, somehow, but jarred his side. Sucking in a painful breath, he disentangled from her.

Wet strands of hair hung in her face. Her eyes were wide; her complexion was ashen. She shook as she clutched Bridger's hoodie.

"You ran," she accused.

"Yeah, like my boss said to, genius."

He pried her hands off his arm.

"You pushed me."

"And he followed me, not you."

She grabbed his hand again; her nails dug into his skin. "Don't leave me."

"I'm angry, not an asshole. Just come on."

Annoyed, Bridger dragged Summer with him, tugging at her to keep up as he jogged. Soon he heard the comforting hum of the doorway through space-time and relaxed when he saw the oval of magic floating a few yards away.

Of course, Larry was smarter than Elena had given him credit for and he stalked the line between the portal and the car. He lumbered on all fours, waiting for their inevitable arrival.

Summer whimpered, gripping Bridger's shoulders as if he was a life preserver and she was a passenger on the Titanic. However, no amount of fear would keep Summer from getting her story, apparently, and she raised her phone next to Bridger's ear.

He smacked her arm down. "Are you serious," he hissed.

Larry's head snapped up, and he zeroed in on Bridger and Summer. He snarled and prowled toward them—a dangerous mass of brute force and sinew. He stood on his hind legs, backlit by the gloomy sky, and loomed over them. His muscled human torso flexed; water droplets hung from his coarse hair. His claws gleamed in the flashes of lightning, and his blue eyes burned in the darkness. His lips pulled back over his sharp, white teeth; strings of saliva frothed along his jowls.

They were going to die. There was no way around it.

And, in their last moments, Summer raised her phone and took a picture. The flash sputtered in the darkness. If they hadn't been about to be murdered, Bridger would have seriously considered doing it himself.

Larry flinched, and growled, long, low, and terrifying. He spoke, the words indecipherable, guttural, and furious.

Bridger took a step back, and his heel caught on a trampled corn stalk. His ankle rolled, and his other foot slipped in a mud puddle, and, despite latching onto Summer's arm, he fell. She toppled onto him; her elbow dug into his sweaty armpit. *Delightful.*

This was it. Despite running and hiding and his daring action-movie move, Bridger was going to be mauled to death by an angry werewolf wannabe, all because of a research paper he had to write for folklore class—and a reporter, who squirmed next to him in a soggy cornfield.

Larry raised a massive paw. Summer yelped. Bridger squeezed his eyes shut.

He heard a cut-off howl and a thump.

Jolting upright, Bridger watched with wide eyes as he saw Larry wrestling with a bear. Was that a massive black bear? It was! And it was *angry.*

A blur of fur and fangs rolled in front of them clearing their path to the portal. The sound of snarls and howls and yelps was ferocious, and Bridger watched, stunned, as Larry was absolutely *owned* by the completely random but appreciated bear.

"Bridger!" Pavel yelled, standing in front of the portal. "Come on!"

Staggering to his feet, Bridger hobbled toward Pavel, Summer a burr stuck to his back.

"What, what happened? I'm so confused."

"You're bleeding," Pavel said, gesturing at the wounds on Bridger's side. He peeled back the shredded cloth of Bridger's hoodie. "We need to get you to the pixies."

"There's pixies?" Summer muttered, dumbfounded, probably in shock, still clutching her phone.

"You first." Bridger jerked his thumb over his shoulder. "Is that a bear? What the hell? Did you summon that thing with your magic?"

Pavel cocked his head; his forehead creased with concern, and his lips thinned. "It's Midnight Marvel."

"Marv? That's Marv? Marv!"

The black bear paused its assault on Larry and eyed Bridger with bright yellow eyes. Larry squirmed beneath Marv's massive paws and slipped from beneath her, scurried away, then abruptly turned and charged toward the trio.

Pavel shoved Bridger to the portal. "Go through!" Pavel yelled. "I'll hold Larry off!"

"No way! I'm not leaving you!"

Pavel scowled, but didn't argue. Grabbing Summer by the elbow, Pavel pushed Bridger hard, and he stumbled through the inky swirl of magic. Squeezed on all sides, warmth rushing over him, Bridger went from the middle of a cornfield in Wexford to the familiar surroundings of Pavel's attic. Popping out of the closet, Bridger fell into Astrid's arms. Dragging Summer, Pavel appeared right behind him. The closet door slammed shut.

Astrid stared. "Uh? What?"

"Don't ask," Bridger slurred, using Astrid as a crutch. He fingered the wound in his side and raised his hand. His fingertips were stained with blood. "Oh," he said, his side burning. His head swam as adrenaline left him in a rush. He took a small step, then promptly passed out.

CHAPTER 15

BRIDGER WOKE TO SHOUTING. A cacophony of voices, all clamoring over each other, each trying to be louder than the next, assaulted his slowly burgeoning consciousness. It wasn't the greatest way to wake up, but considering he'd taken damage from sharp claws and a free-wheeling tumble, shouting was better than, say, a really sore body.

But yeah, there was that too. *Oh fuck.* There really was that. Everything *hurt* in a way that Bridger hadn't hurt before. His side throbbed. His joints ached. His muscles burned.

He twitched, then groaned, because—holy hell. *No. Don't move. Do not pass Go.* Do not collect the more than two hundred dollars Pavel owed him for this. Because this had crisis pay written all over it. *Wait. No. Do collect the money.* He needed it for school. And maybe he should sit in jail for three turns to rest while everyone else took their chances on the board. He hoped Summer landed on Boardwalk with three hotels. It would serve her right. Pressure on his chest quieted his thoughts.

"Don't even think of moving," Leo said. "Not until Nia and Bran say you can."

Bridger opened his eyes to slits and stared at the concerned face of his boyfriend and the black puff of fur that was his magical cat, both of which hovered over him. Tail curled around her paws, large ears pricked forward, Marv sat on his chest. Leo smiled softly, but he looked like hell, uncharacteristically disheveled. His hand splayed across Bridger's collarbone.

"Leo?"

"Yeah."

"What are you doing here?"

"Watching over my boyfriend while the pixies work their magical healing and everyone else fights it out in the study."

Bridger lifted his head. He was stretched out on Pavel's couch, the one that smelled a little weird and had cushions that were divine. Literally. They'd been blessed by some minor deity whom Pavel knew well. Lying there was what sleeping on a cloud must feel like.

"What's going on?"

Leo shrugged. "All I know is that you stumbled through the portal bleeding and covered in mud, then passed out. The pixies cleaned and bandaged your side, and I helped change you out of your wet clothes."

Bridger peered down at his body. An old blanket was tucked around him, obscuring his wounds from view, but he didn't need to see them to know they were there. The sharp and noticeable pain was enough evidence.

"What does the yelling sound like?"

"Intense. And I'm glad I'm not involved. Astrid and Elena are a scary team."

Bridger winced at the picture in his head and pitied Summer for a hot second before remembering her taking video on her cell while they were running for their lives.

"I told you to call me when he woke up!" Bran's blue, tiny body shot into Bridger's line of sight; sparkles trailed after him.

"He only woke up a few seconds ago. Don't worry. I was going to tell you."

"He needs to drink Grandma Alice's fortifying tea. And he needs more salve." Bran flew close to Bridger's nose, and Bridger's eyes crossed.

"What's going on in there?"

"Don't worry about it." Bran darted around, picking up another blanket and unfolding it across Bridger's legs. "Are you warm enough?"

"Yeah."

Bran gave a sharp nod. "Good. I don't want our human to get too cold." He fussed with Bridger's pillow, then sped off in a shower of blue. His tinny voice echoed after him. "He's awake! Now, stop fighting before you upset him!"

"Is Bran a pixie or a mother hen?" Leo asked.

"Both. Pretty sure they're not mutually exclusive." Bridger squirmed. "Can you help me up?" Leo looked doubtful, but Bridger gave him his best pleading look. "Please?"

"Fine. But when Bran comes back, tell him it was your idea. I don't want to be yelled at."

Gritting his teeth, Bridger struggled into a sitting position with Leo's assistance. Marv meowed, then jumped onto the back of the couch, curling around Bridger's neck. He would've petted her but didn't think he could lift his arm. Leo piled pillows at his back and draped another blanket over his shoulders, tucking it around Bridger with sharp jabs. Marv's tail curled around Bridger's ear; her face pushed into his cheek.

"Better?"

No. His head swam. His body was one huge bruise. But Bridger wasn't going to admit to it. "Yeah."

Leo smoothed the corner of the blanket. "So are you going to tell me what led to a panicked phone call from Astrid? Or do I have to guess?"

Bridger groaned again; his head thumped onto the back of the couch.

"Are you in pain?" Features drawn in concern, Pavel appeared in the doorway. He entered the room, followed by Elena, Astrid, and Summer.

Bridger shrank back into the cushions, feeling small and vulnerable, and not all that happy to see anyone. He clutched the blanket, grateful someone had found him a T-shirt and pajama bottoms, not grateful that they obviously came from Pavel's wardrobe.

"Yeah, I'm in pain. I was mauled by a very large Dogman."

"You weren't mauled." Summer crossed her arms. She was still caked in mud, and her hair had come loose from the ponytail and was falling, sodden, in her face.

Elena growled at her, eyes flashing. "You don't talk to him."

"Yeah," Astrid echoed, eyes narrowed. "Pipe down, Reporter Barbie."

Pavel pinched the bridge of his nose. "This is what I was trying to get across to you, Miss Lore. Magic is troublesome. Myths are dangerous. You can't tromp over centuries of work and research and not expect to experience consequences. This time the consequences were a scary evening and a banged-up assistant, but next time, it could be much worse."

"Hey!" Bridger sat up straighter, then winced. "This is worse enough, thank you."

Summer frowned. "If you'd been truthful with me from the beginning, this wouldn't have happened."

"Maybe," Pavel admitted. "Or something worse would have. We can't guess at alternate realities. I can only do my job. And it's my job to protect cryptids and myths and magic-folk, and I take it very seriously. Exposing them to the world would only end in chaos and in their destruction. I won't allow it."

"I think what Pavel is trying to say," Leo said, hand clasped with Bridger's, "is that you may be strong enough to know and accept the truth, Miss Lore, but there are others who aren't. Others who would react in ways we can't predict. We'd be risking lives if the information we know became public." Bridger squeezed Leo's hand. "Maybe in the future the world will be ready, but it isn't now, and, really, that's not Pavel's call to make. In the end, it would be a choice of the individuals themselves, and, if or when that happens, you'll be one of the people to call."

Bridger couldn't have been prouder of Leo. His heart swelled, and if he could've bent at the waist without ripping bandages, he would've kissed him. As it was, he clutched Leo's hand to his chest and smiled widely.

"Also consider that, if the myth world is exposed, Pavel loses everything." Elena gestured to the house around her. "His job. His family. His *life*. From one bitch to another, you surely can't be that cruel."

The stubborn clench of Summer's jaw softened. "I didn't see it that way. Tonight has been eye-opening in more ways than one. Reporters are taught to uncover the truth no matter the cost. I haven't much thought of how it would affect others." She swiped at a streak of mud on her overalls.

"You should continue to do that when it comes to politics," Astrid said. "Seriously. But on this, maybe a half-truth would work best?"

"I think we can work something out," Summer said. "I have plenty of footage and interviews. We can develop a few half-truths that will be fair to everyone." She rested her hand on Pavel's arm. "Thank you for saving me tonight."

Pavel gulped. "You're welcome."

Clearing his throat loudly, Bridger pointed to himself. "Excuse me? What about me? I literally pushed you out of the way and then dragged your ungrateful ass through a cornfield."

"Thank you too, Bridger. And I apologize for making the last few weeks of your life hell."

"Apology in consideration." Leo pinched him. "Fine! Apology accepted. Kind of. I'm tired. And I'm injured. And I have school tomorrow, and my folklore paper is due."

Pavel's frown returned, chasing away the nervous smile he'd worn when Summer touched his arm. "Nia is brewing tea, and, after you drink it, you should sleep."

"I'll proofread your paper," Astrid said. "And I'll cover with your mom."

"Let's leave the teens to their romcom," Elena said. "The three of us will convene in the study." Despite her words, Elena trailed her fingertips over Bridger's shoulders before she sashayed out of the room. Summer followed, leaving a trail of drying mud, and casting a glance over her shoulder.

"Bridger?" Pavel asked, fingers knotted. "How are you feeling? Do you need anything else? Another blanket? Snacks? Pizza with pineapple?"

"I'm fine, Pavel. Really. I'm sore and tired, but I know how the pixie salve works, and if you give me another blanket I'm going to drown in fabric."

"All right, then. I, I'm proud of how you handled yourself tonight."

Bridger blushed. "It was nothing."

"No, it was everything. You listened when you should have and you kept your wits about you and you saved Summer and yourself. You did everything correctly. And I'm proud to have you as my assistant." Marv squeaked. "I'm proud of you too, Marv. You performed your duty admirably."

Bridger rubbed his cheek on Marv's fur. "Pavel, if I could stand, I'd hug you."

"No," Pavel said, raising his hands. "Stay where you are. We'll hug later. Maybe."

Bridger laughed, then wished he hadn't when his whole body twitched in pain. "Okay. Later."

"Oh, if you want to contact your mother, you'll need to step outside." He looked at the ceiling. "The house is blocking signals right now. I felt it was a needed precaution."

"The house can do that?"

Pavel nodded. "The house has a few magical settings that can render technology useless."

"Huh. That's clever." If Summer wanted to upload her shaky camera footage to the Internet, the house wasn't going to let her.

Pavel winked then left.

A second later, Nia flew in, a cup of tea balanced on her head. She shoved it in Bridger's face. "Drink."

He did. And seconds later, his eyelids began to droop, and his entire body relaxed into the couch. Leo lowered him to the pillow. Nia shooed both Leo and Astrid to the door, though Bridger held Leo's hand until the last minute.

He had school tomorrow. He had graduation bearing down on him. He still hadn't figured out his dad dilemma. But at least, the myth world was safe.

*   *   *

"RISE AND SHINE," PAVEL CALLED as he flung open the musty curtains. Sunlight poured into the small room with the couch, and Bridger grabbed the edge of the blanket and pulled it over his head. Marv let out a loud meow when she was dislodged from her place in the crook of Bridger's arm. "Astrid will be here in thirty minutes to take you to school. You need to eat breakfast and to freshen up before then."

"Go away," Bridger said through the fabric. "I'm injured."

"Yes. You are, but you also have a paper to turn in, one that you need to graduate, if I remember correctly, so up and at them."

"Why are you so cheery? Don't you sleep until noon most days?"

"My sleeping habits are not your concern."

"That's a yes if I ever heard one." Pavel tugged the blanket from Bridger's grasp, and Bridger squinted against the sun. "Seriously? Just let me skip today. I can afford an absence."

"No. The last days of your high school career are important, and you shouldn't miss them." Pavel tossed a towel at Bridger's head. "Astrid is bringing clothes. Let the pixies attend you, then hop in the shower while I make breakfast."

"Ugh." Bridger sat up and immediately slumped forward. "What happened? Did you and Summer…" He made a face. "Never mind. I don't want to know what happened between you and her."

Pavel rolled his eyes. "Nothing, for your information. Other than that she agreed to leave town. Elena erased the footage from Summer's phone, then crushed it. I had to give her money for a replacement, but, otherwise, I count the night a success."

Bridger frowned and gestured toward his side. "Claws."

"Well, yes, other than that." Pavel put his hands on his hips. "Anything else you need before I send in Nia and Bran?"

Bridger scrubbed a hand through his hair, then over his face, knuckling the sleep from his eyes. He envied Marv, who had found a patch of sunlight, curled into a fluffy ball, and was purring herself back to sleep. "Yeah. Just one. Can you come to my graduation next weekend?"

Pavel stopped short. "You want me to attend your graduation?"

"Yeah. This is me. Inviting you. And Elena. And Mindy if she wants. She probably doesn't want. But you. Definitely. Like, it'd be awesome. And it's not just my graduation, but Astrid's and Leo's too. It'd be great. You could be like the weird uncle that shows up that everyone calls uncle but may or may not be actually related." Bridger snapped his mouth shut and grimaced at the ramble, but Pavel didn't appear to mind. In fact, he beamed.

For someone who rarely emoted happiness beyond small smirks, he looked a little creepy with his face stretched into a huge smile, but Bridger went with it.

"I'd be honored, Bridger. I'll bring Elena."

"Awesome. I think I have an invitation in my bag with all the information. Which is in here somewhere."

"I think it's in the kitchen. I'll bring it to you." Pavel turned to leave but stuttered to a stop. "Should I bring a gift?"

"No, no. You have already given me a magic cat and a paycheck. That's plenty."

He nodded. "All right, then. I'm sending in the pixies. Be ready."

Bridger was never ready for the pixies. Nia and Bran were too unpredictable and too swift for Bridger to calculate their moves. He endured their poking and prodding and another round of salve after he emerged from the shower.

That's how Astrid found him, towel tucked around his waist, standing in a bathroom clouded with steam while two flittering magical creatures wrapped bandages around his torso.

"I can't even," she said, hand over her mouth. "I'd take a picture but, even then, no one would believe me."

"Hey, it's happening to me, and I hardly believe it."

"Ingrate," Nia muttered, tying off a bandage with more force than necessary.

Bridger winced. "Hey. Careful. I'm damaged goods."

Bran flew in Bridger's face. "Yes, we know. And if you think Larry is going to get his customary solstice gift this year, then you are very wrong."

"No gift," Nia agreed.

Bridger grunted as he slipped on the shirt Astrid handed him. "Is that what you two do with all that cosmetic money?"

Nia narrowed her eyes. "Don't you worry about that. Now shoo. Go to school."

Bran dropped a jar of the salve into Bridger's bag, then zipped it up. "There. For when you're at home. Take care of yourself and mirror us if you're still sore in two days."

"Great. Thanks. Now, can everyone leave while I put on my pants?"

*   *   *

BRIDGER MADE IT THROUGH HIS last day of high school. Technically, it wasn't the last day, but due to a combination of A's and B's and good attendance and being a senior, Bridger didn't have to take any of his final exams, which meant he was officially done.

He didn't all-out weep when he walked out of the front doors of Midden High the way a few of the seniors did, but he did tear up. And he did take the obligatory selfies with Astrid and Leo and then with Zeke and Luke in front of the school. His phone loaded with pictures, and his backpack empty save for the compact mirror, a jar of pixie medicine, and the myth field book, Bridger regarded the high school with a mixture of fondness, gratitude, and relief.

He'd made it out alive and mostly intact, which is really all he ever wanted to begin with. The best friend and the boyfriend were bonuses.

Leo draped his arm around Bridger's shoulders. "You okay?"

"Yeah. It's just weird," Bridger said for lack of a better term. He shrugged. "Like it's over."

"Nah," Leo said, giving Bridger a squeeze. "It's just beginning."

"Did you read that on a Hallmark card?"

"My abuela maybe said it over the phone to me last night. By the way, she's flying in from Puerto Rico on Thursday and is super-excited to meet you."

"Really?"

"Oh, yeah."

"Wow. That's different."

"She is fiercely open-minded. It's my meemaw on the other side who, well, she's not coming so you don't have to worry about her."

"You have an abuela and a meemaw?"

Leo shrugged. "My mom is from Virginia. My dad is Puerto Rican. It would be weird if I didn't have an abuela and a meemaw."

"Huh. Point taken."

"Hey!" Astrid yelled. "Turn around and smile, losers. One last picture before we're out of here!"

"We better do what she says," Bridger said, turning.

"Or we could do this."

Bridger squawked in surprise when Leo grabbed him, dipped him, and kissed him in front of the school, but he couldn't argue with the results, especially when the picture became the most liked ever on Astrid's social media.

*   *   *

THE WEEKEND AND THE FOLLOWING school week found Bridger, Astrid, and Leo camped out on the couch, eating junk food, and catching up on all the cool movies and TV shows they'd missed due to school, jobs, and baseball games. Sometimes Luke would come over as well, and on those days Astrid and Luke would snuggle on one side of the couch, while Leo and Bridger tried to out-cute them on the other. Sometimes it was just Leo and Bridger, and on those days they didn't watch much television. With baseball officially over, Midden having won the state championship, Leo had more free time than he'd had since senior year began. They made the most of it.

Bridger's wound healed within a few days thanks to the pixies' magic, and Bridger kept in touch with Pavel through the mirror. True to her word, Summer and Matt had left Midden, and Bridger could finally relax.

The general lack of structure to Bridger's days allowed graduation to sneak up on him. All too soon, it was Saturday morning, and his mom ran around the house cleaning because there would be people coming over and she had it in her head that they would judge her based on the dust on the picture frames.

But that also meant Bridger's first interaction with his dad since the night of the newspaper reveal, and if Bridger wasn't already nervous over having to walk across a stage and accept his diploma, then having to face his dad would've done it. As it was, he didn't think he could get more anxious, so his dad's arrival was merely icing on the anxiety cake.

Bridger slipped his graduation robe over his shoulders and zipped it. Underneath he wore slacks and a collared shirt and a tie. His dress shoes pinched his feet, and his hair wouldn't stay down no matter what he did to it. Oh well, at least he had a hat to wear.

"Bridger! You're going to be late for your own graduation!"

He checked his phone as he descended the stairs. "Mom, I have an hour before I have to be there. I'm fine."

She smoothed the robe along his shoulders. "Well, I'm not. So give me a minute to look at you and be proud before I ruin my makeup."

Bridger held out his arms and twirled. "Do I look okay?"

"You look so grown up."

"Oh no, don't start that. I'm just as grown up as I was at my birthday and at prom."

She yanked a tissue from a nearby box and dabbed at her eyes. "I know. Okay? But this is a big milestone for you, my baby, my darling son, my love nugget."

"You have literally never called me your love nugget and please do not do it again. Not in front of anyone. *Ever.*"

"Drama king."

"Okay, please get this out of your system before everyone shows up."

She narrowed her eyes but sighed. "Fine. I'll weep later."

"Thank you."

Bridger opened the door and stepped out onto the front lawn. It was a bright, warm day in Midden, and he enjoyed it until his dad pulled up in front of the house. A moment later, Elena swung into their driveway, and he thanked a deity that she had decided to drive and not Pavel. And across the street, Leo's front door opened, and the Riveras tumbled out, abuela and aunties and uncles and cousins in a massive group heading for a rented van.

All at once, Bridger had his boss and his werewolf friend and his dad and his boyfriend and his boyfriend's extended family bearing down on him. It was the perfect fucking storm.

"This was a bad idea," Bridger whispered to his mom, who gripped his shoulder. "Why did I think this was a good idea?"

"They all love you," his mom said. "They're all here to celebrate you, so chill out, my love nugget, and let the adults be responsible for their own behavior." She plastered on a smile as his dad approached. "Braxton, glad to see you could make it."

"Of course. I wouldn't miss Bud's graduation."

Her expression darkened. "Like you missed every other milestone in his life thus far?"

Yeah, this was starting out great.

Elena's car door opened, and Pavel stepped out, and, and, what the hell? Pavel was dressed normally, well, normally for a graduation. He wore a suit that matched and shoes that also matched. His hair was tamed, and his tie was straight, and his suit fit him the way suits are meant to fit.

Elena caught Bridger's wide eyes and winked. She was also dressed appropriately. She wore a cute sundress that flounced when she walked and strappy sandals. And her long hair was pulled back in a simple ponytail, and her makeup was understated but gorgeous. Did this mean they both knew how to dress for an occasion, and they regularly chose not to?

Mind blown.

And together, Elena's arm looped through Pavel's, they were breathtaking as they strode down the little walkway to where Bridger and his parents stood in terse silence.

Oh wow. Yeah. Definitely bi. And now to never admit to thinking thoughts like that about his boss and his boss's best friend ever, ever, ever. "You made it," Bridger said, breaking into a smile.

"Of course." Pavel reeled Bridger in for a quick, sloppy hug. "We wouldn't miss it."

When Pavel released Bridger, his dad shouldered forward. He stuck out his hand. "Paul, was it?"

"Pavel." Pavel corrected, politely, giving the offered hand a firm shake.

"What is that? German?"

"Not quite." He gestured to his side. "This is my friend, Elena."

His dad's gaze raked over Elena, and there was no way Elena missed the appraisal. No one did. All he needed was a leer and a mustache to twirl. Bridger doubted he'd be so blatant if he— one—respected Pavel at all and—two—knew that Elena was the Beast of Bray Road and could eviscerate him if she wanted. Since neither was the case, he came off as gross, and, *yep,* everything was going super-well judging by his mom's epic scowl.

This was a powder keg. All that was missing was a match. And lo, the match bounded across the yard in his own gown, grinning widely. Leo greeted the group of adults that he knew then turned to Bridger's dad, hand out.

"Hi, I'm Leo."

"Dad, this is my boyfriend," Bridger said. "From the paper."

His dad didn't smile, but he at least he shook Leo's hand. "Congratulations on graduating high school today."

"Thank you, Mr. Whitt."

"Dad, Leo is going to attend State on a baseball scholarship. He, uh, he's really good. He's the reason Midden High won the state championship this year."

Leo blushed and clutched his mortarboard in both hands. "It's a team sport, Bridge. It wasn't just me."

"He's modest too."

His dad didn't say anything, merely put his hands in his pockets. There was a moment of silence, and Leo's smile wavered. Bridger wouldn't have that, so he knocked the back of his fingers into Leo's arm.

"Hey, uh, my dad has the camera equipment out and ready if you want to cross the street and have some pictures done before we go."

"Yeah, sure. Sounds good. But maybe tell abuela to, um, not kiss me so much this time. I still have lip prints from the other night." Meeting Leo's abuela had gone far better than Bridger could've imagined, much better than whatever this travesty was turning out to be.

"I make no promises."

They stared at each other, and Bridger really wanted to leave his own lip prints on Leo, but his dad was right there. Leo bent and glanced to the side, and they settled for a weird, awkward hug thing.

"I'll be right over."

"Okay. See you in a minute." Leo nodded at the adults. "Bye Ms. Whitt, Mr. Whitt, Pavel, Elena." And then he was off like a rocket.

"He's a sweet kid," Elena said, demurely. "I see why you like him, Bridger."

Pavel put his hands in his pockets. "Yes, a very likeable young man."

Bridger's dad tensed. "I guess you encouraged the relationship."

"I didn't discourage it?" Pavel said, the end of the sentence tilting up in a question. He squirmed, and his long fingers tugged at the knot in his tie. "But I don't meddle in Bridger's life outside of work. He is very capable of making his own decisions, which is why he's an excellent assistant."

"Who are you again?" Bridger's dad asked, gaze sweeping over Pavel's frame.

"I'm Bridger's boss."

"Yeah, his boss. Not his dad."

Uh, what is happening?

Pavel straightened from his slouch and met Braxton's gaze with an even stare. "No, I'm not. I apologize if I overstepped. I'm well aware Bridger has a positive adult influence in his life since his mother has done such a fine job on her own."

Oh. Burn.

"*Excuse me?*" His dad took a step forward. Elena inserted herself between them, lip curling in a close approximation of a snarl.

"Hey, could we stop with the dick measuring contest for a minute." Bridger grabbed his dad's arm. "First, Elena would win. Easily. Hands down." Her red lips pulled into a feral grin. "And second, this is my graduation day, and I'd prefer it if we all calmed the fuck down."

His dad bristled. "Bridger! Watch your mouth!"

"Hey," his mom yelled. "Don't yell at him. He's anxious about graduating. You're not helping."

"You let our son talk this way? In front of you and guests?"

"Oh, so now you want to parent?"

Pavel paled. "Maybe, we should all take a breath. Bridger, would you like us to—"

"Oh, I don't get to parent, but you let this guy do it? Christ, Susan. You've lost control of him. No wonder our kid is gay."

Everyone froze.

The words punched Bridger right in the stomach. He couldn't move. He couldn't *think*. He couldn't *breathe*. He clenched his fingers in his robe, right over his heart. The fabric was rough between his fingers. Beneath his shirt, he touched the hard oval of Saint Dymphna.

His mom exploded. "What the hell did you just say?"

"You heard me."

They erupted into a screaming match, hurling a decade of pent-up insults, quips, and witty rejoinders at each other in front of God and the entire neighborhood.

Heat crept into Bridger's face as the Riveras watched from their driveway. Pavel tugged on his collar, and Elena's plush mouth dropped open at a particularly vicious turn of phrase.

Yeah, not embarrassing at all. Okay. Time to be an adult. Time to step in. Time to take my own advice.

Bridger cleared his throat and wedged between them. "Hey, can you guys not? It's my graduation, and you're embarrassing me."

His mom snapped her mouth shut and put her hands on her cheeks. "Oh, Bridger. I'm so sorry. I didn't mean—"

"It's okay, Mom. Why don't you all head for the cars. I'm going to talk to Dad here and join you in a minute."

His mom cast him a glance, but he nodded in reassurance. Bridger waited until they all were out of earshot, even Elena. It was the longest minute of Bridger's life, even after all the things he'd been through, but it allowed him to gather his wits and his strength.

He faced his dad. "I think we need to talk. Seriously. Adult to adult."

His father looked contrite, shoulders hunched, hands in his pockets. "Hey, Bud, I'm sorry. I shouldn't have said—"

"I think you should leave." Bridger's heart pounded in his ears. His skin went clammy. His vision darkened at the edges. He might pass out, but not until after he said what he needed. "Today I want to celebrate the people who have helped me grow and get this far and graduate high school. And that means Mom. And that means Pavel and Elena and Astrid and Leo and the Riveras. That doesn't mean you."

He frowned. "I'm your dad. I came all this way to see you. I've been here for weeks, and you haven't bothered to try and spend time with me."

"Yeah, you are my father. And I'm sorry you came all this way. I'm sorry I can't be what you wanted. I wasn't when I was eight and I'm not at eighteen. And that sucks, for both of us. But I am not going to let you ruin this for me. And I'm not going to let you ruin this for them."

Bridger looked over at the group milling around the cars: Pavel next to Elena's sportscar, his mom and her beater they'd been keeping alive, the Riveras and their minivan, all of them waiting for him.

"Bridger. I can't believe this." He licked his lips. "Fine. Is this what you want? You want to lose me over your weird boss guy and your friend?"

"Boyfriend," Bridger corrected. "Leo is my boyfriend."

"Christ." He scrubbed his hand through his hair. "I can't believe this," he said again. "Look, I'll leave, but if I walk away, we're done, Bud."

That hurt. It hurt more than Bridger cared to admit. And maybe this was the wrong decision, maybe Bridger would look back on this moment in a decade and think he should've been more forgiving, maybe he'd miss his dad on other important days of his life—like his graduation from college, his wedding, his first kid. But then again, maybe he wouldn't. In the ten years of his absence, the pain of only having the one parent at his school play and taking pictures for his prom and coming to his soccer games had dulled to an infinitesimal ache, a barely-there twinge, because his mom had filled both roles. And now he did have Pavel, and he did have Astrid, and he did have Leo, and Mindy and the pixies and, God forbid, Elena. They loved him. They wanted him.

And that was it, wasn't it? Why should he want someone who didn't want him, someone who found it so easy to walk away a second time?

"My name is Bridger. And I understand this is it. I'm good with that."

"Fuck," his dad said, looking at the ground. He shifted on his feet. "Okay. Okay then." He snapped his head up and looked at Bridger, met his gaze with a hard one of his own. He pointed a finger at Bridger's chest. "Don't call me when you need something."

"I won't need anything from you. I did when I was a kid, but I haven't in a while and I certainly don't now." It was a little mean, like turning a knife in a wound, but Bridger wasn't going to take it back.

His dad gave him one last, long look, then turned on his heel and walked across the tiny yard to his car. He got in, slammed the door, and pulled away.

Bridger stayed where he was, still as stone. A myriad of emotions lanced through him, but the one that was the strongest was *relief*. He should've taken his own advice, the advice he'd given Leo after the baseball game, sooner. Fuck anyone who couldn't handle him as himself.

"Bridge? You okay?" He hadn't realized how long he'd stood there, staring at the curb where his dad's car had been parked.

"Yeah, Mom. I'm fine."

"I'm so sorry, Bridger. I am so sorry. He doesn't deserve you."

"It's okay," he said. "It's okay." He smiled, and it wasn't as forced as he thought it might be. "Come on. I don't want to be late for graduation."

CHAPTER 16

MIDDEN HIGH HELD GRADUATION OUTSIDE on the large lawn on the side of the school. A stage was erected in front of several rows of seats that were roped off for the graduates, then surrounded by even more rows of seats for all the family members. Bridger's mom sat with the Riveras while Pavel and Elena sat in the back row, near the parking lot, and on the aisle.

Bridger was fifth from last to be called. He didn't trip across the stage. He didn't drop his diploma. He didn't try to hug the teacher while they went for a handshake. He didn't screw anything up and, when he returned to his seat, he held his freshly printed high school diploma. He turned his tassel but didn't throw his cap because those things were expensive and hurt coming back down.

Afterward, he posed for more pictures with Leo and Astrid. Mr. Rivera grabbed him in a massive hug, and Leo's abuela kissed him all over his face, and his mom had mascara smears down her cheeks.

The two acting the most normal were Pavel and Elena, who clapped politely and congratulated him with soft, proud smiles. "I know you said no presents," Pavel said, "but the pixies have something for you back at the house."

"If it's makeup, I'm not interested."

Elena snorted. "You should come by anyway. Mindy will want to see you."

"Mindy? It's Saturday. Why is she at the office?"

Pavel sent Elena a glare, and she shrugged innocently. "Mindy is, well, she has decided—"

A squeal of tires and a blare of horns cut Pavel off, and Bridger squinted over Pavel's shoulder to the street. A large white van ran a red light and almost caused an accident. A large white van with Georgia plates.

"Pavel," Bridger said slowly. "I thought you said Summer left."

"She did. Why?"

"Are you sure? Because I think I just saw her van."

Pavel turned and peered toward the street. The van was long gone, and really, Bridger had only seen a flash, just enough to catch the peach on the plate, so maybe he was wrong. He could be wrong. *Please be wrong.*

He scratched the back of his head, knocking his hat askew. "When Summer left that night after the Dogman incident, did you take her home through the portal?"

"No, I drove her home."

"She went out of the front door?"

"Yes."

"Does that mean she can go back in the front door?"

All the color drained from Pavel's face. "We need to go."

They moved like a well-oiled machine, like a seasoned trio of detectives in an HBO show, as if they'd done this kind of thing before. They hadn't. But Bridger shucked his gown while Elena kicked off her sandals, then tossed her purse to him.

"I'll run. With this traffic, it might take more time than we have to get there."

"I'll call the pixies, get them to send the portal, if they can."

"I'll drive," Bridger said, fishing out Elena's keys. "I might know a way around the traffic."

"Don't break my car, understand?"

"I'll do my best."

She took off in a sprint, drawing a few stares, but she quickly disappeared around a corner on the sidewalk; her hair was a brown comet behind her.

Pavel flipped open his mirror while they strode to the parking lot. He was trying to reach the pixies and cursing in a language Bridger had never heard before when they didn't pick up their end. Bridger gripped Elena's purse as well as his diploma; his tassel swatted against his temple.

"Bridger! Where are you going, honey?"

"Crap, my mom."

Pavel took the purse and didn't break his stride. "Deflect," he said, tone clipped, accent thick.

Nodding, Bridger jogged to his mom. He thrust the diploma and his gown into her hands. "Hey, I'll meet you back at the house. Pavel and Elena need me for a minute at work."

She huffed. "It's your graduation. Can't it wait?"

"No. It's important."

"Bridger," she shook her head. "No. We're supposed to go to dinner. We have a whole celebration planned."

"It's okay. I'll meet you."

"Bridger," she said frowning. "You know I don't agree with your dad, but he wasn't wrong about Pavel. He's not your—"

"Yeah, and Dad left. So, maybe agreeing with him right now isn't the best idea." *Yikes.* That came out heated and cutting and was a low blow. Stricken, his mom clutched the diploma tighter. "Sorry, that was bitter and mean. But I won't be long. I promise. I'll call you when I'm done."

He didn't wait for a response. And he'd be apologizing for all of it later, when they were home and he wasn't in crisis mode. Dodging cars, Bridger crossed the parking lot and threw himself into the driver's seat of Elena's sports car. He tossed his graduation cap behind him.

"Did you reach the pixies?"

"No."

"Try Mindy."

"She doesn't carry a mirror any longer."

Easing out of the parking space took finesse, since everyone who attended the graduation decided to leave at the same time. Sweating through his shirt, Bridger winced each time another car came too close to Elena's, but while everyone headed for the main exit, Bridger looped around to the back of the school. He drove through the one-way bus ramp in the opposite direction, but this was an emergency.

"Try Nia and Bran again, please," Pavel said, speaking to the mirror.

Glancing over, Bridger caught the waver of the glass, but the reflection stubbornly remained that of Pavel's concerned face.

"If she's there, they probably can't answer." He kept his foot on the gas as he went through a yellow light. "Try Elena. See if she's made it."

Pavel's grip tightened around the compact. "I can't believe I was so stupid," he said. "She promised she'd leave. I should've made sure. I should've known better."

"Hey, no, you're like the smartest guy I know. Maybe a little naïve, but you didn't know. And hey, maybe it's not her. Maybe the pixies are just getting a little rowdy without you there and can't answer the mirror. Maybe Nia can't hear it over the bubbling of her cauldron. You know how I am. I overreact all the time. Maybe this is just me overreacting again, and I imagined seeing her van."

Pavel cast him a withering glare.

"Right. Okay. Summer is there. But you couldn't know what she'd do. You only see the good in people. It's one of your great character traits. Take me for example; you could've fired me after I made a few mistakes. But you didn't. Because you saw the good things too. And you did that with her. You looked for the good and took her at face value."

"It's my job to protect the myth world. I let her *go*."

"Okay, so you made an error in judgment. I make those all the time."

"You're eighteen. I'm—"

"Really old. I know, but does that mean you have to be perfect? That would suck. Living for a long time but with the expectation that you can't continue to learn."

Pavel looked down to the mirror. "You're distracting me."

"Yes. Keeping you focused on my dialogue rather than on what could be happening at the house. It's a coping mechanism for anxiety, keeping you in the moment rather than in your head."

"I'm not anxious. I'm, I'm angry."

"Well, I am anxious." Bridger took a sharp turn onto Pavel's street. "They're my family too."

He hit the gas, and suddenly Summer's van loomed in front of them, parked half onto Pavel's lawn and half in the street. Mindy's car was absent; only Pavel's death trap sat in the small gravel driveway.

Bridger slid to a stop, tires squealing, and parked haphazardly at the curb. Before he managed to throw it into park, Pavel was out of the car striding to the front door, which hung wide open. Yanking the keys from the ignition, Bridger shoved them into his pocket as he followed, ran through the front door, and slammed it behind him.

It had only been fifteen minutes since Bridger spied the van, but the house was already a mess. Papers lay strewn all over the floor. The door to the library hung on one hinge. Scrolls littered a path to the stairs and upward. The heavy curtains were thrown open, bathing the house in natural light. Dust swirled in the air from items long untouched that had been rifled through or knocked over.

Elena had got there before them. Her sundress was soaked with sweat. The pads of her feet bled. She stalked in an imaginary line at the base of the stairs; a low, rumbling growl emanated from her as her hair swished behind her. "I can't get closer," she snarled, eyes burning amber.

Summer peered down at them from the landing above and laughed, somewhat maniacally. "Wolfsbane," Summer said, tugging on a rope of the plant draped across her shoulders. Another lay along the first few stairs, blocking Elena's path. "I figured out she was the Beast of Bray Road, a werewolf, and I watched *Teen Wolf*. She can't get near me."

"Hey, guess what, we can," Bridger yelled to her. He stepped onto the lowest stair.

"Can you?" She raised a bird cage. "Forest pixies," she said, shaking it. Nia and Bran tumbling over each other. "Lured with sugar and bound with iron. I wouldn't come any closer unless you want them to take a fall." She held the cage over the banister. "Surprised? I warned you that I knew how to research."

Pavel sparkled with incandescent rage; magic flowed from him in angry tendrils, glowing from beneath his skin. His jaw clenched, and his eyes glittered. He exuded anger and power, but Summer merely chuckled, swinging the pixies around in the iron cage.

"Don't," he warned, his voice rumbling with magic.

"Turn off the magic then, and they won't be harmed." She set them on the edge of the railing. "They are your family, aren't they?"

"What's your endgame?" Bridger asked, retreating. "What's your plan?"

"Oh, clever Bridger Whitt. Beloved of witches and unicorns and pixies. Do you think I'm going to monologue my whole plan? That I'm a Bond villain? No. Just know that soon the world will know what I know, what you know, what Mr. Chudinov knows. And I will be the reporter who broke the story."

Bridger quickly looked to Elena. "She's filming," he said, voice low. "Find it. Use the blue door."

"On it."

"That's what this is about then? Breaking through the industry that typecast you?"

She tapped her chin. "Your friend, Astrid, said to me the other night that I should seek the truth in the case of politics." She shrugged. "But I can't get near politics. Or wars. Or natural disasters. Or even local nightly news. I can't do anything important while stuck chasing monsters through the woods in tight dresses and high heels. This," she said, holding up one of Pavel's books, "*this* will be my big story. A whole organization that hides the fact that a Dogman exists. That mermaids play in Lake Michigan. That omens of death take the shapes of dogs and prowl the Ozarks. That blood-sucking beasts attack goats and children."

"You obviously didn't learn the lesson we tried to teach you the other night," Bridger said. "We're trying to protect both sides."

She scoffed. "You're obscuring the truth."

"Okay, say you reveal everything. Say this is your big break. What then? Money? Fame? I mean, we can give you money. The pixies have a profitable cosmetic line, and I'm sure—"

"Respect," she shot back. "I break this story, I show the world that werewolves are real, that vampires exist in more than stories, and I will finally have the respect I deserve."

"Maybe," Bridger agreed. "But you'll be the monster then. You'll kill them. You understand that, right? You'll be responsible when dumbasses arm themselves with guns and hunt them down. That'll be on you."

"Pavel will protect them. Won't you, Intermediary Chudinov?" She smiled sweetly and batted her eyelashes. "It's your job, isn't it?"

A low growl from the landing kept Pavel from answering. Elena was furred out as she approached, eyes glowing, the scraps of her dress hanging from her massive frame. She held the remnants of a television camera in her claws.

"My footage!" Summer tossed her hair. "It doesn't matter. I've been live streaming since I walked in here. Everything is being uploaded to my cloud right now."

Bridger smirked. "Actually, the house has some great magical protections. It blocks cell phone signals. That video isn't going anywhere." He took a step onto the stairs. "Okay, time to admit defeat, Summer. You're surrounded, and your plan didn't work. Let the pixies go."

"I still know. I still have evidence. I won't stop until someone believes me." She skittered backward, holding the cage of the pixies in front of her. "Don't come any closer. You can't come closer."

"Pavel," Bridger whispered, "be ready to catch them." At Pavel's nod, Bridger ran up the stairs.

Shrieking with threats, Summer brandished the cage in front of her, while Nia and Bran chittered in high-pitched voices.

Summer dropped the pixies over the banister as Bridger charged. Pavel caught them and ripped the cage apart with his bare hands and a surge of magic. Nia and Bran flew free and darted for the wolfsbane. Bran ripped the wolfsbane from Summer's shoulders while Nia grabbed the rope from the stairs. Elena leapt forward, and Summer ducked and bolted, knocking her shoulder into Bridger's on the stairs.

Stumbling, Bridger grabbed the banister to keep from falling ass over elbow to the ground floor. He couldn't stop Summer as she sprinted. Neither could Pavel, curled over in pain, hands smoking from the use of magic against iron.

The front door opened, then closed, and Mindy walked in and blocked the exit when she paused to survey the chaos. Hands on her hips, hair coiffed into a tower, draped in an electric floral print from head to toe, she tapped her shoe on the hardwood. "What the hell is going on?" she bellowed. It was the loudest and most expressive Mindy had ever been, and Bridger welcomed every grating syllable of it.

For some reason, Summer saw safety and sanity in Mindy's presence and darted toward her. "Help me! Help me! They're trying to kill me." She latched onto Mindy's arms and pleaded, hysterical and crying, acting the quintessential damsel in distress.

Pavel approached and held up his hands. "Mindy," he said, crisscrossed burns on his palms. "This is Summer. The individual I told you about."

Bridger released the banister and slid down the stairs, bruising himself the whole way down, until he landed on the floor. He brushed off his pants and stood. His graceful descent hadn't broken the tension at all, and no one moved or glanced his direction.

"Whatever he told you was a lie," Summer said. "Do you see that?" She pointed to Elena on the landing. "That's a werewolf. A *werewolf*. It's going to kill me. And you."

Mindy blinked, face utterly placid. "Bridger," she said, finally, "congrats on your graduation."

"Oh, oh, thanks, Mindy."

"And Pavel," she said with as much emotion as Bridger had ever heard from her, "thank you for the reference."

"You're very welcome. You will be missed."

Summer stomped her foot. "Are you listening to me? There are werewolves and pixies and things in this house that are supernatural and will kill you. There's a decapitated mannequin in the attic that was once a human." *Well, that was a lie.* "There's a book about different ways to summon a goblin. There are portraits that follow you with their eyes."

Okay, both of those were true.

"Lady," Mindy said, clamping one meaty hand around Summer's forearm. "I'm well aware."

From his angle, Bridger couldn't see Summer's face, but he could see Mindy's and her frosted orange lips pulled into the same self-satisfied smirk she wore when she won a level in the games on her phone.

"I *quit*."

The entire house shook.

The pictures wobbled. Trinkets and toasters fell to the floor. Dust and plaster rained down. Pavel darted across the room as the floor quaked, and Bridger was caught up in Pavel's embrace as the house groaned and trembled. Bridger clutched back as magic gathered in the corners of the room as a storm gathers in the sky, thick with energy and potential. The side door flew open.

Bridger had never seen the side door. It was covered in vines on the outside and had no handle on the inside. It blended perfectly with the plaster and the wainscot, and even now, as it stood open with the blooming side yard beyond, Bridger could barely discern the seams in the wall.

A stiff wind blew. The floor rippled like waves meeting the shore. And between one blink and the next, Mindy and Summer went from standing in the foyer, to pitched out of the house. Summer's scream echoed down the hall. The side door swung shut.

"What the fuck just happened?" Bridger asked.

"Mindy quit."

"Why? Why did she quit?"

Pavel tilted his head. "You seem surprised."

"I am surprised! This was like the easiest job ever."

"Did you not notice the slow decline in bobbleheads?"

"I did, but she said she wanted a change. I thought that meant porcelain babies."

"Hey," Elena yelled from the landing, "do you think you two can stop bantering for a moment and actually check on the two people who were literally thrown from the magic house?"

They released each other and ran out of the front door to the side yard.

Mindy lay in a heap in the grass while Summer stood in a patch of flowers, brow furrowed, utter confusion clearly written across her features. She blinked, then spied Pavel, picked her way to the sidewalk, and slapped him.

"How dare you waste my time!" she screeched. "You lure me here and for what? A hoax. All of it a hoax. I've had some crappy dates in my time, but this one, Mr. Chudinov, takes the ever-loving cake. Next time you want to get in a woman's bed, don't bait them with promises of pixie dust." She zeroed in on Bridger and pushed her finger into his chest. "Messages in the flour? Your voice on the EVP? Pretending to drown in a lake and scare all your friends? You're a jerk, Bridger Whitt. An absolute jerk. Senior prank or not, there is no reason to terrorize your town, your family, and your friends. I hope you grow up, but if this guy is your mentor, I weep for Midden. Good bye to both of you, and I hope you rot." She stomped off.

Pavel held the side of his face. A livid hand print bloomed on his cheek. He grinned. "It worked!"

"It bothers me that you sound so surprised that it did work. Is your track record with this that bad?"

Pavel waved his hand. "Mistakes have been made."

Bridger grimaced. He didn't want to know.

Mindy sat up from her sprawl and adjusted her glasses, which had been knocked askew. Bridger rushed to assist her to her feet. "Mindy! Are you okay?"

"I'm fine," she grumbled. "I just can't believe that after a job as boring as this one all of this excitement happened on my last day."

Pavel swallowed. "All of what?"

She pointed to where Summer had stormed. "That woman! Ranting about werewolves and goblins! Like she thought she was in a movie."

"Yes. Well. I can't believe she was able to break into the house in the first place."

Mindy brushed flower petals from her outfit, then patted her hair, feeling the shape of it. "You need to change the locks."

"I will."

"Good. Well then. I wish you luck in finding a new office manager."

"Thank you." Pavel awkwardly patted her shoulder. "Good luck in your new job. I hope it is not as boring as this one."

She huffed a laugh. "This one will be difficult to beat." Waving, she toddled down the sidewalk; her clunky heels smacked on the concrete. Bridger stood there until she got into her car and drove away.

"It's sad, isn't it?" Bridger asked as he and Pavel entered the house. The door swung shut behind them.

"What is?"

"Summer and Mindy. Summer wanted so badly to find a way out of the pigeonhole created for her that she was willing to destroy lives to do it. I know what it's like to feel trapped, and I, I hate that anyone feels like that. And Mindy! Mindy worked here for years in the presence of pixies and all the other creatures that came and went through your door and she won't remember a single thing about it."

Pavel hummed. "They both made choices. But I have a feeling Summer will be fine. She seems the type to land on her feet."

"And Mindy?"

"She could've stayed, but, in the end, she wanted to live a more normal life. And that's fine. Besides, it wasn't like she was much interested in anything that went on upstairs. She preferred to stay out of it all."

"Do you ever think about it?" Bridger asked, leaning on Mindy's old desk. "Leaving?"

"Some days." Pavel put his hands in his pockets and rocked back on his heels. "But I'd miss it too much. And regular life seems so dull. I don't know what I would do with myself if I wasn't chasing after unicorns."

"Yeah. I guess it would seem dull after a life like this."

Gripping his shoulder, Pavel gave Bridger a small shake. "Will you be all right?"

"Sure. What about you?"

"Me?"

"Well, yeah, this is the second time in a year that your whole life has been threatened by something out of your control. It's a wonder you're not jumping at anything out of the ordinary."

Pavel cocked his head. "I'll be fine. I have Elena and the pixies. And I have a wonderful assistant."

Bridger smiled. "Yeah. You do."

"Don't you have graduation festivities to get to? Your mother will be waiting for your call."

Bridger smacked his forehead. "Oh, crap. Good thing I'm an adult or she'd ground me forever." He crossed the room. "You want to come? I know it was awkward with my dad, but my mom really likes you, and it'd be nice."

Pavel's lips twitched. He looked around the room and sighed. "I should stay here. Check on Elena and Nia and Bran and have this…" He gestured at his hands and his face. "…looked to. But have fun."

"Yeah. Okay." Bridger paused at the doorway. He didn't really know why he did it, but in the moment, with all the changes they'd been through, with Mindy leaving, and Bridger preparing for the next chapter of his life, graduating and losing his dad in the same day, maybe they both needed a little reassurance. "Hey, I'll see you Monday."

Pavel brightened. "Yes. I'll see you Monday."

Bridger waved, and bounced through the front door, phone in his hand.

CHAPTER 17

Six Weeks Later

"I guess that whole virgin purity schtick really was an antiquated notion used to oppress women," Bridger said as he stroked the unicorn's muzzle. "Who knew, huh?"

The unicorn rolled its eyes. Apparently, it knew, and didn't deign to tell him. *Jerk.* That would've cut down by at least fifty percent his anxiousness over whether he was going to be gored when he entered the woods. The unicorn nudged his shoulder and snuffled at the bag on Bridger's back.

"Yeah, yeah. I know." He unzipped his backpack and pulled out the burrito. "Just so you know, this is the last one. Pavel is worried for your health and says burritos aren't a unicorn's natural diet. Don't get pissed at me. Take it up with him."

Bridger peeled off the tinfoil and dropped the log-shaped tortilla on a paper plate, then set it next to the rock.

"Enjoy." He hefted the bag back on his shoulder. "I have to head out. Beach trip today with Leo and a few friends." Bridger patted the unicorn's bent neck. "I'll make sure to come by before I leave for college in a few weeks. Until then, be a good unicorn and don't try to murder anyone."

The unicorn whickered in goodbye, and Bridger left the woods, heading toward the nearest Commons parking lot.

Despite all the major changes Bridger had experienced during his last semester in high school, several things had stayed the same. He still had a boyfriend. He still had a best friend. He still had a job. He still had one parent who loved him. He had gained a magical cat that appeared when he was in imminent peril, but only if she was paying attention.

Yet, there was no doubt that *he* had changed. Yes, him. Bridger Whitt. No longer a high school senior, and one year older, and maybe not as much of an awkward dumpster fire as when the semester began. He hoped to approach situations with a little more maturity and he began to understand what it meant to be an adult and how actions and decisions had repercussions and consequences and could affect others in ways he didn't intend. It was a scary prospect, but at least he had a few great role models.

In addition, Bridger was secure in himself in a way he hadn't thought he'd ever achieve. And he didn't care who saw or what they thought when he bounded into Leo's car and leaned over and kissed him square on the mouth.

"Hey," he said.

Leo grinned, brown eyes crinkling. "Hey, yourself. How's Pointy?"

"That's not its name, and the unicorn is great. Eating a burrito as we speak."

"Good, because Astrid has texted me ten times. I think she really wants to get to the beach."

"I think she really wants to get to Luke, but, hey, I'm not judging." Leo laughed and turned the ignition of his new-to-him vehicle. "I can't believe your uncle Roberto bought you a car," Bridger said, running his fingers over the interior and inhaling the new-car smell. "This is amazing."

"I know, right?" Leo said, pulling out of the parking spot. "He said it was to be able to drive back and forth and visit my mom from college. But knowing Roberto, it's definitely to be the cool freshman who can make beer runs."

Bridger snorted. "You're already the cool freshman, and we're not even there yet. I'm certain there will be a parade and a welcoming committee on the first day of orientation."

Blushing, Leo rolled his eyes. "You're going to give me a big ego."

"Well, you know what they say about flattery? That it will get you everywhere."

Leo placed a kiss on Bridger's cheek while they waited at a stoplight. "Everywhere, huh? Like the back seat of a used car."

Squirming, Bridger flushed. "Hey, we have to pick up Astrid, then Luke. So maybe tone that down until we're alone later."

Leo gave him a wink. "Later then."

In the six weeks since graduation, Bridger had spent as much time with Leo and Astrid as possible, planning for college, hanging out around Midden, helping Pavel when needed, though Pavel was giving Bridger freer rein than regular employment would allow to enjoy his summer.

Leo eased the car into Astrid's driveway, where she waited.

"Hey, did you see the google alert?" Astrid asked, sliding into the back.

Bridger swiped his hair from his forehead. "No. About what?"

"About *Monster of the Week*. The season premiere has been postponed."

"What?" Bridger turned in his seat and peered around the headrest. "Why?"

Astrid held up her phone. "Apparently Summer Lore walked off set and quit."

Squinting, Bridger read the first line of the article. "Citing a contract breach and dissatisfaction with production, Summer Lore has left her defining role as host of the show in pursuit of other opportunities." *Huh*. "Good for her."

"Good for her? She made your life hell." Astrid fell back to her seat.

Shrugging, Bridger turned around as Leo backed out of Astrid's driveway. "I hope she finds happiness."

"How very mature of you," Leo said, patting Bridger's knee. "It's like you're an adult or something."

Bridger snorted.

"Nice car, by the way," Astrid said, snuggling into the seat. "Tell Uncle Roberto he has great taste."

"I'll let him know Mercutio approves."

Bridger groaned. "Can you two please come up with better nicknames for each other? Not that I mind that it makes me Juliet in the scenario, but that play is so dark. All three of those characters die. I'd like to be in a romance for once, not a tragedy."

"You are in a romance," Leo said, shooting Bridger a side-eye. "Right? Or did we switch genres when I wasn't paying attention?"

Bridger twined their fingers. "Definitely romance."

"Okay, if you two are done being sappy. And if you're going to whine about it. We'll come up with a better trio. What do you think of Kirk, Spock, and McCoy?"

"No," Bridger said as Leo shook his head. "Not even close."

"Um, Luke, Han, and Leia?"

"Rey, Finn, and Poe," Leo countered.

"Not sci-fi, please. I get enough of that at work. How about Athos, Porthos, and Aramis?"

Astrid considered it. "Would that make Luke d'Artagnan?"

"Good question—"

The sound of clanging bells rang from Bridger's bag, interrupting the smooth flow of conversation. He fished the glowing and vibrating compact from the bottom and flipped it open to find Nia peering at him. Her pinched face filled the entire mirror; pink fizzles of light popped behind her.

"Bridger, I need you to come to the house right away. It's an emergency."

"A real emergency?" Bridger asked, holding the mirror in his palm. "Or a pixie emergency. I have learned the difference."

"A real—hey! Pixie emergencies are real emergencies."

Bridger sighed. "Hey, do you two mind if we run by the house quick before we pick up Luke?"

"Fine by me," Astrid said. "I'm up for a visit. As long as it's quick. Luke is expecting us."

A few minutes later, Leo pulled up to the house. "I'll be back in a flash. You guys continue naming trios that are nothing like us."

"Parker, Hardison, and Eliot," Astrid yelled as Bridger closed the door. Okay, he had to admit. That one wasn't bad.

He skipped up the sidewalk to the house. The door swung open, and, as he stepped across the threshold, the familiar tingle of the magic ward scrubbed down his spine.

A young woman with ashy blonde hair and big blue eyes straightened from her slump at the mammoth desk in the foyer. She had circular glasses and pink lips and smiled wide when Bridger waved.

"Bridger!" she said, with enough enthusiasm to power the block. "I wasn't expecting you today!"

"Hi, Christine." He held up the compact. "Pixie emergency."

"Oh, I hope everything is okay." She clasped her hands.

"I'm sure it's about unicorn poop or black blister beetles. Nothing I can't handle."

She giggled.

Bridger was still getting accustomed to Mindy's replacement, but Elena's girlfriend was nice, and she kept the sasquatch bobblehead Bridger gave her right next to her keyboard.

Nia flew down the stairs, tugging a tote and with Bran fluttering close by.

"Human," she muttered, dropping the satchel at Bridger's feet, "it is not an ingredient emergency. I have closed the cosmetic line and sent out the last of my orders."

Bridger stopped short. "What? You closed your wildly successful business? Why?"

She didn't answer him. "Here are my profits," she said, pointing to the bag. "For you."

Bridger stared at the bag. "Come again?"

"The profits," Bran said. "What? Do you think we have need of human money?"

Stunned, Bridger stared into the bag at the rolls of bills, each worth more than anything he had in his wallet.

"Pavel!" he yelled. "Pavel!"

Pavel appeared on the landing and dashed down the stairs, skidding the last few steps in his bunny slippers. "What? What's happening? Are you okay?"

"What? I'm fine. I think. I… The pixies are trying to give me thousands of dollars in cash!"

"Oh!" He clutched a hand over his heart; his polka-dot robe fluttered behind him. "Oh, yes, is that all? I know. It's been their plan all along." He peered into the bag. "That should pay for four years, correct?"

"I, I don't know what's happening."

"Right. Cash probably wasn't a good option," Pavel said. "Oh, I know. I'll keep this, put it in the bank, and pay your tuition from it until you graduate. Is that a good plan?"

"Are you serious?"

"You're right; you need spending money and books. Books are expensive."

"No, I mean, are you *serious?*"

Pavel's brow furrowed. "Why wouldn't we be?"

"That's a lot of money. That's… I don't understand."

Nia fluttered near Bridger's face and pressed her tiny hand to his cheek. "We did it for you. You're one of *our* humans."

Bran sat on his shoulder. "You're our family."

Bridger's mouth flapped open, and he did the only thing he could think of. He grabbed Pavel into a tight hug.

"Oh, are you all right? Do you need tea?" Pavel asked as he tentatively patted Bridger's back. "We still have a bit of the fortifying blend from Grandma Alice."

"No, no. I'm good." He squeezed Pavel tighter than he probably should have. "I'm really good. Thank you."

"You're welcome, Bridger."

And yeah, things were going to change. That was the nature of life. It was inevitable. Bridger would leave town and go to college, and maybe he wouldn't come back. Maybe he would. Maybe he and Leo would break up, or maybe they'd stay together. Maybe he'd lose touch with Astrid, or maybe they'd be best friends for the rest of their lives.

Whatever happened, Bridger had a family, a family who loved him, and he was going to hold on to them as long as he could, as long as life would allow—terrifying portals, beautiful werewolves, unicorn poop, and all.

THE END

ACKNOWLEDGMENTS

Unicorn Poop.

I never thought I'd get to begin a book with those words. I think it's a special privilege afforded an author that at the five-book milestone, you get to start a novel with pure ridiculousness. I took full advantage of that privilege. If you've made it this far into the pages of this book, you should know by now that I love ridiculousness. Surely you appreciate it as well, though the only person I know who actually reads acknowledgments is my brother (Hi, Rob!). He appreciates ridiculousness as much as I do—perhaps more so. We all need a little absurdity in our lives.

So, dear reader, to answer a few of the questions I know you have after finishing the novel, yes, the Pope Lick Monster/ Goatman is a thing that exists. It has its own Wikipedia entry. Please approach all train trestles with caution. Goatmen aside, this is probably a good piece of advice to adhere to in all life situations that involve trains, or goatmen, or both.

Also, dear reader, the Michigan Dogman is not really named Larry. I made that up. I don't know the Dogman's real name. As far as I know, the Dogman has not given an interview in which he reveals that bit of information. So I had to take some creative liberty—unless the Dogman's name really is Larry, and, if that is the case, I totally knew that.

And last thing, dear reader, I do not own a magical, shapeshifting cat named Marv. I know that was on everyone's mind. First, could anyone truly own a magical, shapeshifting cat? I think the relationship would be a bit different. I mean, I have two cats now that I think I don't "own," but rather we have a tenuous agreement: I feed them, and they don't kill me. Second, if I had a magical shapeshifting cat, I wouldn't be writing books. I'd be touring morning chat shows and selling merchandise. That would be way easier and probably more lucrative.

Anyway, back to the task at hand, I would like to thank a whole group of people who have helped me make it to my fifth published book. First, I'd like to thank my family, especially my husband and children who are supportive and patient. My husband keeps the household running while I write or run away to exotic convention locations like Newark. He also drives five hours round trip to pick me up after I get stranded in the airport for approximately twenty hours. I also would like to thank my niece, Emma, who is always willing to be my assistant at conventions. And I would like to thank my other nieces and nephews (see the dedication for their names) who tell their school librarians about their aunt's books and talk them up to their teachers and friends. I would like to thank my brother, Rob, who wrote "famous author and super genius" on my website and didn't tell me how to change it.

I'd like to thank a group of authors who are not only friends, but amazing colleagues, and who are my cheerleaders, beta readers, support group, and confidants—Carrie Pack, Julian Winters, CB Lee, Jude Sierra, Killian Brewer, Lauren Devora, Michelle Osgood,

Taylor Brooke-Barton, Laura Stone, DL Wainright, SJ Martin, and Jenn Fitzpatrick. Buy their books, folks, and support authors who support others.

I'd also like to thank the authors who run the Asheville/WNC Writer's Coffeehouse: Beth Revis, Jamie Mason, Brian Rathbone, and Jake Bible, for all their amazing advice and encouragement. I'd like to thank the folks at Malaprop's Bookstore/Cafe in Asheville, my local, amazing indie store, who have been so kind to me the past few years.

It wouldn't be my acknowledgment section if I didn't thank my fandom lifemate Kristinn and my fandom twitter pals who are the greatest when I need a name suggestion or help deciding on a detail. I'd also like to specifically mention my patrons Kim and M.

Lastly, this book wouldn't be a book without the team at Interlude Press—Choi, Annie, and Candy.

Readers, I hope you enjoyed reading this book as much as I enjoyed writing it. I hope that you all find happiness and love like Bridger. And I hope you get to pet a unicorn at least once in your life. Also, don't walk on train trestles.

Much love,

F.T.

ABOUT THE AUTHOR

F.T. LUKENS IS AN AWARD-WINNING author of young adult fiction who holds degrees in Psychology and English Literature. A cryptid enthusiast, F.T. loves folklore and myths, specifically the weird and wonderful creatures of North America. She also enjoys sci-fi and fantasy television shows, superhero movies, and writing. F.T. lives in the mountains of North Carolina, a perfect area for sasquatch sightings, with her husband, three kids, and three cats.

Her novel, *The Rules and Regulations for Mediating Myths & Magic*, won several awards, including the 2017 Foreword INDIES Gold Award for Young Adult Fiction and the 2017 IPBA Benjamin Franklin Gold Award for Best Teen Fiction.

CONNECT 🌐 ftlukens.com
WITH F.T. 🐦 @ftlukens
ONLINE 📘 FTLukens

For a reader's guide to **Monster of the Week**
and book club prompts, please visit duetbooks.com.

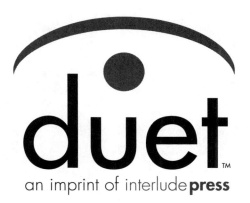

an imprint of interlude**press**

🌐 duetbooks.com
🐦 @duetbooks
📘 duetbooks
🛒 store.interludepress.com

also from  duet.

The Rules and Regulations for Mediating Myths & Magic by F.T. Lukens

The Rules, Book One
IBPA Benjamin Franklin Gold Award Winner

When Bridger Whitt learns his eccentric employer is actually an intermediary between the human world and its myths, he finds himself in the center of chaos: The myth realm is growing unstable, and now he's responsible for helping his boss keep the real world from ever finding out.

ISBN (print) 978-1-945053-24-5 | (eBook) 978-1-945053-38-2

The Star Host by F.T. Lukens

Broken Moon series, Book One

Ren grew up listening to his mother tell stories about the Star Hosts— mythical people possessed by the power of the stars. Captured by a nefarious Baron, Ren discovers he may be something out of his mother's stories. He befriends Asher, a member of the Phoenix Corps. Together, they must master Ren's growing power, and try to save their friends while navigating the growing attraction between them.

ISBN (print) 978-1-941530-72-6 | (eBook) 978-1-941530-73-3

Ghosts & Ashes by F.T. Lukens

Broken Moon series, Book Two

Three months after the events of *The Star Host*, Ren is living under the watchful eyes of the Phoenix Corps, fearing he's traded one captor for another. His relationship with Asher fractures, and Ren must return to his home planet if he has any hope of regaining humanity. There, he discovers knowledge that puts everyone's allegiance to the test.

ISBN (print) 978-1-945053-18-4 | (eBook) 978-1-945053-31-3

Zenith Dream by F.T. Lukens

Broken Moon series, Book Three

In the Broken Moon series finale, Ren embarks on one final mission: find Asher, free Liam, and escape the Corps' reach. But a war is brewing, and Ren is drawn into the conflict. With his friends by his side, he must make a choice that will affect the future of his found family and cluster forever.

ISBN (print) 978-1-945053-76-4 | (eBook) 978-1-945053-77-1